William Shakespeare, Frank F. Taylor

Gems from the Loves of the Heroes and Heroines of Wm. Shakespeare

William Shakespeare, Frank F. Taylor

Gems from the Loves of the Heroes and Heroines of Wm. Shakespeare

ISBN/EAN: 9783337214142

Printed in Europe, USA, Canada, Australia, Japan

Cover: Foto ©Andreas Hilbeck / pixelio.de

More available books at **www.hansebooks.com**

GEMS

FROM THE

LOVES

OF THE

HEROES and HEROINES

— OF —

Wm. Shakespeare.

ARRANGED FOR SOCIAL READING

SAN FRANCISCO:

JOS. WINTERBURN & CO., PRINTERS AND ELECTROTYPERS, 417 CLAY STREET.

1884.

PREFACE.

For those who are familiar with the Shakesperian plays this preface is not intended; but rather for them who, "by the shot of accident," or "dart of chance," or the environments of a not kind fortune, lacked the leisure to read them, and therefore it will not be considered "wasteful and ridiculous excess."

It is, perhaps, needless to say, that throughout the civilized world, wherever culture and intelligence is found,—among all classes of people--the young, the middle-aged and aged, a profound admiration exists for the splendid creations of that great genius—that Emperor of the domain of poesy, William Shakespeare.

His admirers fondly believe, that the advent of no other planet in the realms of poetic literature can obscure with the shadow of eclipse the light of his unquenchable glory, but, that it will, like an enormous gem of purest ray, "set on the outstretched forefinger of all time, there to sparkle forever."

The writer believes that a large portion of the reading people of the country, desire something of the kind, which this little unpretentious book purports to be—a cheap pocket edition; for the reason, that many, especially travelers on cars, steamers, or in hotels, have not the time to indulge in reading the full text of the various plays, while they would gladly seize the opportunity of improving time on what many think to be the most charming of the many charming things uttered by the great bard.

The book is so arranged as to show the numbers of the

different acts and scenes in which the selections may, if desired, be readily found in the originals. Again, it is well known that in Shakespeare's time, much of what was deemed wit was, and is, so broad that its use would not now be tolerated on the stage of any respectable theater; in fact, now, his plays as prepared for *acting* are carefully eliminated of all expressions not in unison with the public taste; therefore, it has been the aim of the publishers to **omit any and all words which might seem to border on coarseness, so that any part of the contents of the book may freely and fearlessly be opened and read by the most refined of either sex, in the presence of each other and their friends, without the slightest fear of their brows mantling with a crimson flush therefrom.**

From the comments made by various Shakesperian editors, I am of the opinion that much of what is ascribed to Shakespeare—especially that which is not agreeable to the modern ear—*was not written by himself;* nor is it surprising that such might be so, when it is known that a number of his plays were edited some eight years after his decease. He seemed to be singularly indifferent to posthumous fame, if not to any other.

A gentleman, whose name is familiar to both continents, recently said to the writer, " that, (concerning Shakespeare) he believed no man had ever fully comprehended him; that the summit of that colossal mental monument was wrapped in mystery."

While the writer knows that such a work cannot meet with the approbation of all, and must necessarily be incomplete, yet as tastes essentially differ, and as there is no fixed standard for its construction and style, he earnestly hopes that its readers will at least find more in its pages to give them pleasure than disappointment. He hopes it will meet with cordial welcome by the youthful as well as by the adults who may not have time for **general reading.**

Truly has Shakespeare been called "the great **poet of humanity.**" The people never **tire of seeing his plays rendered, or** of reading them; his comprehensive **mind** seems to scan the whole domain of human thought and **habitations.**

In thrilling melody it sweeps with the master hand of unrivalled genius the diapason of the chords of feeling, thought and emotions common to the human heart, and in response, crystal tears and joyous laughter are the spontaneous tributes of homage which his readers pay to him.

Love and hate, joy **and sorrow, hope and** despair, affection and anger, avarice and prodigality, are painted in glowing colors, and in a brilliance of imagery, resembling at times, flashes of meteoric showers, and again blazing like the noon-day sun in the literary firmament.

Many other poets are great; many **are famed for the** silvery sweetness of their songs, and charming, startling **in a high degree in many things; but, it is** the prerogative of Shakespeare "to unite them all in one glow of associated **beauty,"** which renders his works as **a** whole *unapproached* and *unapproachable.*

In the May and June numbers of the *Atlantic Monthly,* of 1884, Richard Grant White very properly says:

"**If Shakespeare had but** known what **he was doing!** Not the greatness of his work; **which, even if he had** suspected it, would not **have pleased him** much, and would have troubled him little. But had he been able to foresee the load of labor which he was lying upon the shoulders of many worthy men, poets, scholars, and critics, and of **more** who, not poets, are neither scholars nor critics; and could **he, with** all his imagination, have imagined the sort of lit-

erature and the quantity with which he would cause the
world to be afflicted, in the one case his easy good nature
when his interests were not at stake, and in the other his
supreme and ever-present sense of humor, would have led
him to leave his plays unwritten,—*if* he could have got the
money he wanted by any other writing or doing. The
shadow never falls toward the light, and Shakespeare only
knew that he was shining,—how brightly and how warmly
he was as careless and ignorant as the sun in the heavens,—
and could not see what lay beyond those who rejoiced in the
beams of his intellect. More inflated nonsense, more
pompous platitude, more misleading speculation, has been
uttered upon Shakespeare and his plays than upon any other subject but music and religion. The occasion of which
calamity is that of all subjects which are of general interest,
these are the most remote from reason, the most incompre-
hensible."

And speaking of his critics, he says:

"They attained their end, and were able to do so the
more readily because this Shakespeare *was* the most potent
spirit that ever cast a spell upon the minds of men. More-
over, he *was* a miraculous manifestation of the power of
the human mind. He did not work according to any
known law: nor did he reveal the law of his action, or
leave behind him the evidence by which that law could be
discovered. In Shakespeare, nature produced as nearly
as possible the supernatural. Springing from nearly the
lowest social level, without education, without instruction,
without discipline of any kind, and limited means of ob-
taining knowledge, at twenty-two years of age a poverty-
stricken vagabond, by the time he was forty years old he
had done that which places him at the intellectual summit
of the human race. This he had done with no strong im-
pulse to literary art, no social aim, religious or political,

no motive of intellectual ambition, but merely **at first to** earn his bread, **and** afterward in the furtherance of an almost sordid desire for money, and for the poor sort **of** consideration which is awarded to the possessors of money. In all he had his heart's desire. The outcast of the dirty little village returned to live in its largest and handsomest mansion; **to** have **the** profitable investment of **his money** in parish 'securities' accepted, and **even solicited, as if it** were a favor; to take his place among the notables of the neighborhood, **where the** meagre annals of his life give us our last glimpse of him standing against the interests of the poor, and on the side of grasping privilege. **The** world's history has no record of a similar achievement."

Again:

"Of all his dramas, that which shows the peculiar traits of his genius in their highest manifestation, their most unapproachable splendor and beauty **of strength,** is Antony **and Cleopatra.** It is not the greatest of his works in dramatic interest, although it is dramatically great; and although **wise and profound,** it is not the wisest of them nor the profoundest. * * * Plutarch filtered drop **by drop** through Shakespeare's **brain, and not** only purging **thus of prose and** dross, but taking tint and quality and **force and fire** from the medium through which it passed, issued in that dazzling, flaming flood of gold and jewels."

But why attempt "to gild refined gold, or **paint the** lily, or add perfume unto the violet?"

Born **of humble parentage,** raised without sufficient means for an illiberal education, with **no one to** direct his energies and tastes, and **at one time** a law-breaker, compelled for a trival offence to fly from legal prosecution, without money, means or friends, or any introduction to parties of wealth **or** power, he boldly entered England's great metropolis in **his youth;** and thenceforth by the force of his own prodigious mentality, steadily rose until he attained the zenith of his ambition, and with Heaven's signet on his lofty brow—that "dome of thought, the palace of the soul"—filled the niche which Fame assigned to him in her temple, and gave eternal grandeur to the crowned heads of royal lineage, and glory to the titled nobility of England's proud and mighty realm.

Thus was this strange course—from the humble peasant cot to halls of grandeur—from the mists of rural obscurity to the expanse of the blue empyrean above him.

On his head "it seemed as if every God did set his seal, that nature might say to the world: *here is a man*," the object of admiration for countless millions of advancing generations.

For more than three hundred years his mortal remains have been protected from rude sacrilege by his awful imprecation inscribed on the marble of his tomb, around which glows the intense increasing splendor of his mighty genius, as bright as the fires of Heaven, which by day and by night maintain a perpetual guard above him.

Truly, "take him all in all, we shall never look upon his like again."

Like most of all other great things in nature, while contemplating his majestic conceptions they grow on the mind, increasing its profound wonder and enjoyment, so, with increasing facilities for the spread of literature will constantly increase the thirst for full knowledge of all the intelligence he has given to man.

Annually, like the procession of devoted Moslems in their pilgrimage to Mecca, will the worshippers at the shrine of that great poet and actor, repair to the spot of consecrated earth, made famous by its possession of the remains of William Shakespeare. Well we may say, "his fame is folded in this orb o' the earth." EDITOR.

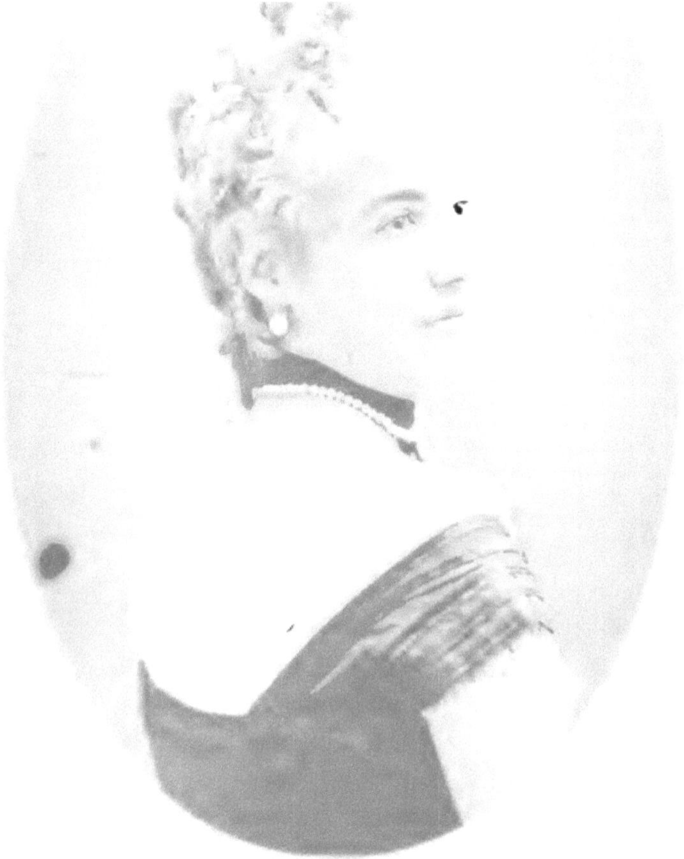

MISS NEILSON.

Bradley & Rulofson SAN FRANCISCO, CAL.

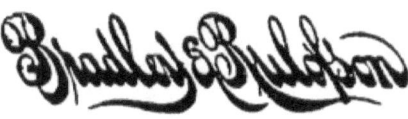

ANTONY AND CLEOPATRA.

—•—

ACT I.

Scene I.—*Alexandria. A Room in Cleopatra's Palace.*

Description of Antony's weakness.

Enter Demetrius *and* Philo.

Phi. Nay, but this dotage of our general's
O'erflows the measure: those his goodly eyes
That o'er the files and musters of the war
Have glow'd like plated Mars, now bend, now
     turn,
The office and devotion of their view
Upon a tawny front: his captain's heart,
Which in the scuffles of great fights hath burst
The buckles on his breast, reneges all temper.
Take but good note, and you shall see in him
The triple pillar of the world transform'd.

Cleo. If it be love indeed, tell me how much.

Ant. There's beggary in the love that can be
    reckon'd.

Cleo. I'll set a bourn how far to be beloved.

Ant. Then must thou needs find out new heaven,
    new earth.

2

ANTONY'S DEVOTION.

Ant. Let Rome in Tyber melt! and the wide arch
Of the ranged empire fall! here is my space;
Kingdoms are clay: earth alike
Feeds beast as man.

SCENE III.

CLEOPATRA'S APPEAL TO ANTONY.

Cleo. Your honour calls you hence;
Therefore be deaf to my unpitied folly,
And all the gods go with you! upon your sword
Sit laurel'd victory! and smooth success
Be strew'd before your feet!

SCENE IV.

CÆSAR'S DESCRIPTION OF ANTONY.

                                        You shall
        find there
A man, who is the abstract of all faults
That all men follow.
    Lep. I must not think there are
Evils enough to darken all his goodness:
His faults, in him, seem as the spots of heaven
More fiery by night's blackness.

CÆSAR'S APPEAL TO ANTONY.

Cæs. Antony,
Leave thy lascivious wassels. When thou once
Wast beaten from Modena, where thou slews't
Hirtius and Pansa, consuls, at thy heel
Did famine follow; whom thou fought'st against,
Though daintily brought up, with patience more

Than savages could suffer; Thou didst drink
The stale of horses, and the gilded puddle
Which beasts would cough at: thy palate then did
      deign
The roughest berry on the rudest hedge;
Yea, like the stag, when snow the pasture sheets,
The barks of trees thou browsed'st; on the Alps,
It is reported, thou didst eat strange flesh,
Which some did die to look on: And all this
(It wounds thy honour that I speak it now)
Was borne so like a soldier, that thy cheek
So much as lank'd not.

Scene V.

Cleopatra's soliloquy.

Cleo. O Charmian,
Where think'st thou he is now?   Stands he, or sits
      he?
Or does he walk? or is he on his horse?
O happy horse, to bear the weight of Antony!
Do bravely horse! for wot'st thou whom thou
      mov'st?
The demi-Atlas of this earth, the arm
And burgonet of men.—He's speaking now,
Or murmuring, *Where's my serpent of old Nile?*
For so he calls me; Now I feed myself
With most delicious poison.

Cleopatra's delight to hear Antony.

Alex. Sovereign of Egypt, hail!
Cleo. How much unlike art thou Mark Antony!
Yet, coming from him, that great medicine hath

With his tinct gilded thee.—

How goes it with my brave Mark Antony?

 Alex. Last thing he did, dear queen,

He kiss'd,—the last of many doubled kisses,—

This orient pearl;—His speech sticks in my heart.

 Cleo. Mine ear must pluck it thence.

 Alex. Good friend, quoth he,

Say, *the firm Roman to great Egypt sends*

This treasure of an oyster; at whose foot,

To mend the petty present, I will piece

Her opulent throne with kingdoms: All the east,

Say thou, *shall call her mistress.* So he nodded,

And soberly did mount a termagant steed,

Who neigh'd so high, that what I would have spoke

Was beastly dumb'd by him.

 Cleo. What, was he sad or merry?

 Alex. Like to the time o' the year between the
   extremes

Of hot and cold; he was nor sad nor merry.

 Cleo. O well-divided disposition!—Note him,

Note him, good Charmian, 'tis the man; but note
   him;

He was not sad; for he would shine on those

That make their looks by his: he was not merry;

Which seem'd to tell them his remembrance lay

In Egypt with his joy: but between both:

O heavenly mingle!—Be'st thou sad or merry,

The violence of either thee becomes;

So does it no man else.—Met'st thou my posts?

 Alex. Ay, madam, twenty several messengers:

Why do you send so thick?

 Cleo. Who's born that day

When I forget to send to Antony,

Shall die a beggar.—Ink and paper, Charmian.—
Welcome, my good Alexas.—Did I, Charmian,
Ever love Cæsar so?

   Char. O that brave Cæsar!

   Cleo. Be choked with such another emphasis!
Say, the brave Antony.

   Char. The valiant Cæsar!

   Cleo. By Isis, I will give thee bloody teeth,
If thou with Cæsar paragon again
My man of men.

   Char. By your most gracious pardon,
I sing but after you.

   Cleo. My salad days;
When I was green in judgment:—Cold in blood,
To say, as I said then!—But, come, away:
Get me ink and paper: he shall have every day
A several greeting, or I'll unpeople Egypt.

ACT II.—Scene I.

Description of Cleopatra's barge.

   Eno. When she first met Mark Antony, she pursed
up his heart, upon the river of Cydnus.

   Agr. There she appeared indeed; or my reporter
devised well for her.

   Eno. I will tell you:
The barge she sat in, like a burnish'd throne,
Burn'd on the water: the poop was beaten gold:
Purple the sails, and so perfumed, that
The winds were love-sick with them; the oars were
     silver;

Which to the tune of flutes kept stroke, and
      made
The water, which they beat, to follow faster,
As amorous of their strokes.   For her own person,
It beggar'd all description: she did lie
In her pavilion, (cloth of gold, of tissue,)
O'erpicturing that Venus, where we see,
The fancy out-work nature; on each side her,
Stood pretty dimpled boys, like smiling Cupids,
With divers coloured fans, whose wind did seem
To glow the delicate cheeks which they did cool,
And what they undid, did.

   Agr. O, rare for Antony!

   Eno. Her gentlewomen, like the Nereides,
So many mermaids, tendered her i' the eyes,
And made their bends adornings: at the helm
A seeming mermaid steers; the silken tackle
Swell with the touches of those flower-soft
      hands,
That yarely frame the office.   From the barge
A strange invisible perfume hits the sense
Of the adjacent wharfs.   The city cast
Her people out upon her; and Antony,
Enthroned in the market-place, did sit alone,
Whistling to the air, which, but for vacancy
Had gone to gaze on Cleopatra too,
And made a gap in nature.

   Agr. Rare Egyptian!

   Eno. Upon her landing, Antony sent to her,
Invited her to supper: she replied,
It should be better, he became her guest;
Which she entreated: Our courteous Antony,
Whom ne'er the word of *No* woman heard speak,

Being barber'd ten times o'er, goes to the feast;
And, for his ordinary, pays his heart,
For what his eyes eat only.

POMPEY'S EXPLANATION.

Pom. To you all three,
The senators alone of this great world,
Chief factors for the gods,—I do not know,
Wherefore my father should revengers want,
Having a son, and friends: since Julius Cæsar,
Who at Phillippi the good Brutus ghosted,
There saw you labouring for him. What was it,
That moved pale Cassius to conspire? And what
Made the all-honour'd honest Roman, Brutus,
With the arm'd rest, courtiers of beauteous free-
  dom,
To drench the Capitol; but that they would
Have one man but a man? And that is it,
Hath made me rig my navy; at whose burden
The anger'd ocean foams; with which I meant
To scourge the ingratitude that despiteful Rome
Cast on my noble father.

DESCRIPTION OF A CROCODILE.

Lep. What manner o' thing is your crocodile?

Ant. It is shaped, sir, like itself; and it is as broad as it
hath breadth; it is just so high as it is, and moves with its
own organs; it lives by that which nourisheth it; and the
elements once out of it, it transmigrates.

Lep. What colour is it of?

Ant. Of its own colour too.

Lep. 'Tis a strange serpent.

Ant. 'Tis so. And the tears of it are wet.

ACT III.—Scene VI.

Cæsar to Octavia, his sister.

Cæs. Why have you stol'n upon us thus? You
  come not
Like Cæsar's sister: The wife of Antony
Should have an army for an usher, and
The neighs of horse to tell of her approach,
Long ere she did appear; the trees by the way
Should have borne men; and expectation fainted,
Longing for what it had not: nay, the dust
Should have ascended to the roof of heaven,
Raised by your populous troops: But you are come
A market-maid to Rome; and have prevented
The ostent of our love, which, left unshewn,
Is often left unloved: we should have met you
By sea and land; supplying every stage
With an augmented greeting.

Scene IX.

Antony's lament over his defeat and lost reputation.

Ant. I have offended reputation;
A most unnoble swerving.
  Eros. Sir, the queen.
  Ant. O, whither hast thou led me, Egypt? See,
How I convey my shame out of thine eyes
By looking back on what I have left behind
'Stroyed in dishonour.
  Cleo. O my lord, my lord!
Forgive my fearful sails! I little thought,
You would have follow'd.

Ant. Egypt, thou knew'st too well,
My heart was to thy rudder tied by the strings,
And thou shouldst tow me after: O'er my spirit
Thy full supremacy thou knew'st; and that
Thy beck might from the bidding of the gods
Command me.

   Cleo. O, my pardon.

   Ant. Now I must,
To the young man send humble treaties, dodge
And palter in the shifts of lowness; who
With half the bulk o' the world play'd as I pleased,
Making and marring fortunes. You did know,
How much you were my conqueror; and that
My sword, made weak by my affection, would
Obey it on all cause.

   Cleo. O, pardon, pardon.

   Ant. Fall not a tear, I say; one of them rates
All that is won and lost: Give me a kiss;
Even this repays me.—We sent our schoolmaster,
Is he come back?—Love, I am full of lead:—
Some wine within there, and our viands:—Fortune
      knows,
We scorn her most, when most she offers blows.

Scene II.

Cleopatra's message to Cæsar.

   Cleo. Most kind messenger,
Say to great Cæsar this: In deputation
I kiss his conqu'ring hand; tell him, I am prompt
To lay my crown at his feet, and there to kneel:

   Eno. Yes, like enough, high-battled Cæsar will
Unstate his happiness, and be staged to the shew

Against a sworder.—I see men's judgments are
A parcel of their fortunes; and things outward
Do draw the inward quality after them,
To suffer all alike   That he should dream,
Knowing all measures, the full Cæsar will
Answer his emptiness!—Cæsar, thou hast subdued
His judgment too.

ACT IV—Scene VIII.

Antony's triumph.

Enter CLEOPATRA, *attended.*

To this great fairy I'll commend thy acts,
Make her thanks bless thee —O thou day o' the
              world,
Chain mine arm'd neck; leap thou, attire and all,
Through proof of harness to my heart, and there
Ride on the pants triumphing.
    Cleo. Lord of lords!
O infinite virtue! com'st thou smiling from
The world's great snare uncaught ?
    Ant. My nightingale,
We have beat them to their beds.   What, girl,
              though grey
Do something mingle with our brown; yet have we
A brain that nourishes our nerves, and can
Get goal for goal of youth.   Behold this man;
Commend unto his lips thy favouring hand;—
Kiss it, my warrior;—He hath fought to-day,
As if a god, in hate of mankind, had
Destroy'd in such a shape.
    Cleo. I'll give thee, friend,
An armour all of gold; it was a king's.

Ant. He has deserved it, were it carbuncled
Like holy Phœbus' car.—Give me thy hand;
Through Alexandria make a jolly march;
Bear our hack'd targets like the men that owe them:
Had our great palace the capacity
To camp this host, we all would sup together;
And drink carouses to the next day's fate,
Which promises royal peril.—Trumpeters,
With brazen din blast you the city's ear;
Make mingle with our rattling tabourines;
That heaven and earth may make their sounds
       together,
Applauding our approach.   [*Exeunt.*

Scene XII.

Antony's visions.

Ant. Sometime, we see a cloud that's dragonish;
A vapour, sometime, like a bear, or lion,
A tower'd citadel, a pendent rock,
A forked mountain, or blue promontory
With trees upon 't, that nod unto the world,
And mock our eyes with air: Thou hast seen these
       signs;
They are black vesper's pageants.

Antony's complaint of Cleopatra.

She has robb'd me of my sword.
  Mar. No, Antony,
My mistress loved thee, and her fortunes mingled
With thine entirely.
  Ant. Hence, saucy eunuch; peace!
She hath betray'd me, and shall die the death.

Mar. Death of one person can be paid but once,
And that she has discharged: what thou wouldst do,
Is done unto thy hand: the last she spake
Was, " Antony! most noble Antony!"
Then in the midst a tearing groan did break
The name of Antony; it was divided
Between her heart and lips: she render'd life,
Thy name so buried in her.

    Ant. Dead then?

    Mar. Dead.

    Ant. Eros, unarm; the long day's task is done,
And we must sleep.—That thou depart'st hence safe
Does pay thy labour richly; go.—Off, pluck off:—

                            [*Exit* MARDIAN.

The seven-fold shield of Ajax cannot keep
The battery from my heart.   O, cleave, my sides!
Heart, once be stronger than thy continent,
Crack thy frail case!—Apace, Eros, apace.—
No more a soldier:—bruised pieces, go;
You have been nobly borne.—From me a while.—

                            [*Exit* EROS.

I will o'ertake thee, Cleopatra, and
Weep for my pardon.   So it must be, for now
All length is torture:—since the torch is out,
Lie down and stray no further: now all labour
Mars what it does; yea, very force entangles
Itself with strength: seal then, and all is done —
Eros!—I come, my queen —Eros!—Stay for me:
Where souls do couch on flowers, we'll hand in hand,
And with our sprightly port make the ghosts gaze:

                    Re-enter EROS.

    Eros. What would my lord?

    Ant. Since Cleopatra died,

I have lived in such dishonour, that the gods
Detest my baseness. **I**, that with my sword
Quartered the world, and **o'er green** Neptune's **back**
With ships made cities condemn myself to lack
The courage **of a woman; less noble mind**
Than she, which by her death our Cæsar **tells,**
" **I am conqueror of myself.**" **Thou art sworn, Eros,**
That, when the exigent should come, (which **now**
Is come indeed.) when I should see behind me
The inevitable **prosecution** of
Disgrace and **horror, that,** on my command,
Thou **then wouldst kill me:** do't; the time is come:
Thou strik'st not me, 'tis Cæsar thou defeat'st.
Put colour in **thy cheek.**
    Eros. **The gods withhold me!**
Shall **I** do that, **which all the** Parthian darts,
Though enemy, **lost** aim, and could not ?
    Ant. Eros,
Wouldst thou be window'd **in** great Rome, and see
Thy master thus with pleach'd arms, bending **down**
His corrigible **neck,** his face subdued
To penetrative shame, whilst the wheel'd **seat**
Of **fortunate Cæsar, drawn** before him, branded
His baseness that ensued?
    Eros. **I** would **not see't**
    Ant. Come **then;** for with a wound I must be cured.
Draw that thy honest sword, which thou hast worn
Most useful **for thy** country.
    Eros O, Sir! pardon me.
    Ant. When I did make thee free, **swor'st thou not then**
To do this when I bade thee ? Do **it at once;**
Or thy precedent services **are all**
But accidents **unpurposed.** Draw, and come.

Eros. Turn from me, then, that noble countenance,
Wherein the worship of the whole world lies.

    Ant. Lo thee!   [*Turning from him.*

    Eros. My sword is drawn.

    Ant. Then let it do at once
The thing why thou hast drawn it.

    Eros. My dear master,
My captain, and my emperor! let me say,
Before I strike this bloody stroke, farewell.

    Ant. 'Tis said, man;—and farewell.

    Eros. Farewell, great chief.   Shall I strike now?

    Ant. Now, Eros

    Eros. Why, there then:—[*Falls on his sword.*] thus
     .   do I escape the sorrow
Of Antony's death.   [*Dies.*

    Ant. Thrice nobler than myself!
Thou teachest me, O valiant Eros, what
I should, and thou couldst not. My queen and Eros
Have, by their brave instruction, got upon me
A nobleness in record: but I will be
A bridegroom in my death, and run into't
As to a lover's bed. Come, then; and, Eros,
Thy master dies thy scholar; to do thus

                     [*Falling on his sword.*

I learn'd of thee.—How! not yet dead? not dead?—
The guard!—ho!—O, despatch me!

Scene XIII.

Death scene of Antony, and Cleopatra's lament.

Enter Antony, *borne by the Guards.*

  Cleo. O thou sun,
Burn the great sphere thou movest in!—darkling
       stand

The varying shore o' the world!—O Antony!
Antony, Antony!—Charmian, help; help, Iras;
Help, friends below: let's draw him hither.

    Ant. Peace:
Not Cæsar's valour hath o'erthrown Antony,
But Antony's hath triumph'd on itself.

    Cleo. So it should be, that none but Antony
Should conquer Antony; but woe 'tis so!

    Ant. I am dying, Egypt, dying; only
I here importune death awhile, until
Of many thousand kisses the poor last
I lay upon thy lips.—

    Cleo. I dare not, dear,
(Dear my lord, pardon,) I dare not,
Lest I be taken: not the imperious shew
Of the full-fortuned Cæsar ever shall
Be brooch'd with me; if knives, drugs, serpents,
        have
Edge, sting, or operation, I am safe:
Your wife Octavia, with her modest eyes,
And still conclusion, shall acquire no honour
Demuring upon me.—But come, come, Antony,—
Help me, my women,—we must draw thee up,—
Assist, good friends.

    Ant. O, quick, or I am gone.

    Cleo. Here's sport, indeed!—How heavy weighs
        my lord!
Our strength is all gone into heaviness,
That makes the weight! Had I great Juno's power,
The strong-wing'd mercury should fetch thee up,
And set thee by Jove's side. Yet, come a little,—
Wishers were ever fools;—O, come, come, come;

             (*They draw Antony up.*)

And welcome, welcome! die, where thou hast lived:
Quicken with kissing; had my lips that power,
Thus would I wear them out.

   All. A heavy sight!

   Ant. I am dying, Egypt, dying:
Give me some wine, and let me speak a little.

   Cleo. No, let me speak; and let me rail so high,
That the false housewife Fortune break her wheel,
Provoked by my offence.

   Ant. One word, sweet queen:
Of Cæsar seek your honour with your safety.—O!

   Cleo. They do not go together.

   Ant. Gentle, hear me:
None about Cæsar trust, but Proculeius.

   Cleo. My resolution, and my hands, I'll trust;
None about Cæsar.

   Ant. The miserable change now at my end,
Lament nor sorrow at: but please your thoughts,
In feeding them with those my former fortunes
Wherein I lived, the greatest prince o' the world,
The noblest: and do now not basely die,
Nor cowardly; put off my helmet to
My countryman, a Roman, by a Roman
Valiantly vanquish'd.   Now, my spirit is going:
I can no more.   *(Dies.)*

   Cleo. Noblest of men, woo't die?
Hast thou no care of me? shall I abide
In this dull world, which, in thy absence is
No better than a sty?—O, see, my women,
The crown o' the earth doth melt:—My lord!—
O, wither'd is the garland of the war,
The soldier's pole is fallen; young boys and girls

Are level now with men; the odds is gone,
And there is nothing left remarkable
Beneath the visiting moon.   (*She faints.*)

   Char. O, quietness, lady!

   Iras. She is dead too, our sovereign.

   Char. Lady!

   Iras. Madam!

   Char. O Madam, Madam, Madam!

   Iras. Royal Eyypt!
Empress!

   Char. Peace, peace, Iras!

   Cleo. No more, but e'en a woman; and commanded
By such poor passion as the maid that milks,
And does the meanest chares.—It were for me
To throw my sceptre at the injurious gods;
To tell them that this world did equal theirs,
Till they had stolen our jewel.   All's but naught;
Patience is sottish, and impatience does
Become a dog that's mad: then is it sin
To rush into the secret house of death,
Ere death dare come to us?—How do you, women?
What, what? good cheer!   Why, how now, Charmian?
My noble girls!—Ah, women, women! look,
Our lamp is spent, it's out!—Good Sirs, take heart:—
                   [*To the Guard below.*
We'll bury him; and then, what's brave, what's noble,
Let's do it after the high Roman fashion,
And make death proud to take us.   Come, away:—
This case of that huge spirit now is cold.
Ah, women, women! come, we have no friend
But resolution, and the briefest end.
      [*Exeunt; those above bearing off* ANTONY's *body.*

3

ACT V—Scene I.

Der. I say, O Cæsar, Antony is dead.

Cæs. The breaking of so great a thing should
make
A greater crack: The round world should have
shook
Lions into civil streets,
And citizens to their dens: The death of Antony
Is not a single doom; in the name lay
A moiety of the world.

Der. He is dead, Cæsar;
Not by a public minister of justice,
Nor by a hired knife; but that self hand
Which writ his honour in the acts it did,
Hath, with the courage which the heart did lend it
Splitted the heart.—This is his sword,
I robb'd his wound of it; behold it stain'd
With his most noble blood.

Cæs. Look you sad, friends?
The gods rebuke me, but it is tidings
To wash the eyes of kings.

Agr. And strange it is,
That nature must compel us to lament
Our most persisted deeds.

Mec. His taints and honours
Waged equal with him.

Agr. A rarer spirit never
Did steer humanity: but you, gods, will give us
Some faults to make us men. Cæsar is touch'd.

Mec. When such a spacious mirror's set before
him
He needs must see himself.

Cæs. O Antony!
I have follow'd thee to this;—But we do lance
Diseases in our bodies: **I must** perforce
Have shown to thee **such a** declining day,
Or look on thine; we could not stall together
In the whole world: But yet let me lament,
With tears as sovereign as the blood of hearts,
That thou, my brother, my competitor
In top of all design, my mate in empire,
Friend and companion in the front of war,
The arm of mine own body, and the heart
Where mine his thoughts did kindle,—that our
        stars,
Unreconcileable, should divide
Our equalness to this.—**Hear** me, good friends,—
But I will tell you **at some meeter** season;

Scene II.

Cleopatra's sorrowful reflections.

Cleo. **My** desolation does begin **to make**
A better life: 'Tis paltry to be Cæsar;
Not being fortune, he's but fortune's knave,
A minister of her will; and it is great
To do that thing that ends all other deeds;
Which **shackles** accidents, and bolts **up change;**
Which **sleeps,** and never palates more the dug,
The beggar's **nurse and** Cæsar's.

Cleopatra prefers death to captivity.

Iras. Royal queen!
Char. O Cleopatra! thou art taken, queen!
Cleo. Quick, quick, good hands. [*Drawing a dagger.*

Pro. Hold, worthy lady, hold!   [*Seizes and disarms her.*
Do not yourself such wrong, who are in this
Relieved, but not betray'd.

Cleo. What, of death too,
That rids our dogs of languish?

Pro. Cleopatra,
Do not abuse my master's bounty, by
The undoing of yourself: let the world see
His nobleness well acted, which your death
Will never let come forth.

Cleo. Where art thou, death?
Come hither, come! come, come and take a queen
Worth many babes and beggars!

Pro. O, temperance, lady!

Cleo. Sir, I will eat no meat, I'll not drink, Sir;
If idle talk will once be necessary,
I'll not sleep neither: this mortal house I'll ruin,
Do Cæsar what he can.   Know, Sir, that I
Will not wait pinion'd at your master's court;
Nor once be chastised with the sober eye
Of dull Octavia.   Shall they hoist me up,
And shew me to the shouting varletry
Of censuring Rome?   Rather a ditch in Egypt
Be gentle grave to me! rather on Nilus' mud
Lay me stark naked, and let the water-flies
Blow me into abhorring! rather make
My country's high pyramids my gibbet,
And hang me up in chains!

CLEOPATRA'S DREAM OF ANTONY.

Cleo. I dreamed, there was an emperor Antony; —
O, such another sleep, that I might see
But such another man! ·

Dol. If it might please you,—

Cleo. His face was as the heavens; and therein
  stuck
A sun, and moon; which kept their course, and
  lighted
The little O, the earth.

Dol. Most sovereign creature,—

Cleo. His legs bestrid the ocean; his rear'd arm
Crested the world: his voice was propertied
As all the tuned spheres, and that to friends;
But when he meant to quail and shake the orb,
He was as rattling thunder. For his bounty,
There was no winter in 't, an autumn 'twas,
That grew the more by reaping: His delights
Were dolphin-like; they shew'd his back above
The element they lived in: In his livery
Walk'd crowns and crownets; realms and islands
  were
As plates dropp'd from his pocket.

Dol. Cleopatra,—

Cleo. Think you, there was, or might be such a
  man
As this I dream'd of?

Dol. Gentle madam, no.

Cleo. You lie, up to the hearing of the gods.
But, if there be, or ever were one such,
It's past the size of dreaming: Nature wants stuff
To vie strange forms with fancy; yet, to imagine
An Antony, were nature's piece 'gainst fancy,
Condemning shadows quite.

CLEOPATRA CONTEMPLATING CAPTIVITY.

Cleo.   Now,
       Iras, what think'st thou?
Thou, an Egyptian puppet, shall be shewn
In Rome, as well as I: mechanic slaves,
With greasy aprons, rules, and hammers, shall
Uplift us to the view; in their thick breaths,
Rank of gross diet, shall we be enclouded,
And forced to drink their vapour.
    Iras. The gods forbid!
    Cleo. Nay, 'tis most certain, Iras; Saucy lictors
Will catch at us, and scald
          rhymers
Ballad us out o' tune: the quick comedians
Extemporily will stage us, and present
Our Alexandrian revels; Antony
Shall be brought drunken forth, and I shall see
Some squeaking Cleopatra boy my greatness.
    Iras. O the good gods!
    Cleo. Nay, that is certain.
    Iras.   I'll never see it; for, I am sure, my nails
Are stronger than mine eyes.
    Cleo.   Why, that's the way
To fool their preparation, and to conquer
Their most absurd intents:—Now, Charmian?
Shew me, my women, like a queen;—Go fetch
My best attires;—I am again for Cydnus,

CLEOPATRA PREPARING FOR DEATH.

    Cleo. Give me my robe, put on my crown;
          I have
Immortal longings in me: Now no more

The juice of Egypt's grape shall moist this lip:—
Yare, yare, good Iras; quick.—Methinks I hear
Antony call; I see him rouse himself
To praise my noble act; I hear him mock
The luck of Cæsar, which the gods give men
To excuse their after wrath: Husband, I come:
Now to that name my courage prove my title!
I am fire and air; my other elements
I give to baser life·—So,—have you done?
Come, then, and take the last warmth of my lips.
Farewell, kind Charmian!—Iras, long farewell!
                        (*Kisses them. Iras falls and dies.*)
Have I the aspick in my lips? Dost fall?
If thou and nature can so gently part,
The stroke of death is as a lover's pinch,
Which hurts, and is desired. Dost thou lie still?
If thus thou vanishest, thou tell'st the world
It is not worth leave-taking.
    Char. Dissolve, thick cloud and rain; that I may
        say,
The gods themselves do weep!
    Cleo. This proves me base:
If she first meet the curled Antony,
He'll make demand of her: and spend that kiss
Which is my heaven to have. Come, mortal
        wretch.
               (*To the asp, which she applies to her breast.*)
With thy sharp teeth this knot intrinsicate
Of life at once untie: poor venomous fool,
Be angry, and despatch. O, couldst thou speak!
That I might hear thee call great Cæsar, ass
Unpolicied!
    Char. O eastern star!

Cleo. Peace, peace!
Dost thou not see my baby at my breast,
That sucks the nurse asleep?

Char. O, break! O, break!

Cleo. As sweet as balm, as soft as air, as gentle,—
O Antony!—Nay, I will take thee too:—

　　　　　　　　　(Applying another asp to her arm.)
What should I stay—

　　　　　　　　　(Falls on a bed and dies.)

Char. In this wide world?—So, fare thee well.—
Now boast thee, death! in thy possession lies
A lass unparallel'd.—Downy windows, close;
And golden Phœbus never be beheld
Of eyes again so royal! Your crown's awry
I'll mend it, and then play.

ROMEO AND JULIET.

ACT 1.—Scene 1.

DESCRIPTION OF LOVE.

This love, that thou hast
shewn,
Doth add more grief to too much of mine own.
Love is a smoke, raised with the fume of sighs;
Being purged, a fire, sparkling in lovers' eyes;
Being vex'd, a sea, nourish'd with lovers's tears:
What is it else? a madness most discreet,
A choking gall, and a preserving sweet.

SCENE III.

DESCRIPTION OF PARIS.

La Cap. What say you? can you love the gentle-
man?
This night you shall behold him at our feast;
Read o'er the volume of young Paris' face,
And find delight writ there with beauty's pen;
Examine every married lineament,
And see how one another lends content;
And what obscured in this fair volume lies,
Find written in the margin of his eyes.
This precious book of love, this unbounded lover,

To beautify him, only lacks a cover:
The fish lives in the sea; and 'tis much pride,
For fair without the fair within to hide:
That book in many's eyes doth share the glory,
That in gold clasps locks in the golden story;
So shall you share all that he doth possess,
By having him, making yourself no less.

Scene IV.

Queen Mab, the Fairy.

Mer. O, then, I see, queen Mab hath been with
    you.
She is the fairies' midwife, and she comes
In shape no bigger than an agate-stone
On the fore-finger of an alderman,
Drawn with a team of little atomies
Athwart men's noses as they lie asleep:
Her waggon-spokes made of long-spinners' legs,
The cover, of the wings of grasshoppers;
The traces, of the smallest spider's web;
The collars, of the moonshine's watery beams;
Her whip, of cricket's bone; the lash, of film:
Her waggoner, a small grey-coated gnat,
Not half so big as a round little worm
Prick'd from the lazy finger of a maid:
Her chariot is an empty hazel-nut,
Made by the joiner squirrel, or old grub,
Time out of mind the fairies' coach-makers.
And in this state she gallops night by night
Through lover's brains, and then they dream o'
    love!

O'er courtier's knees, that dream on courtsies
     straight;
O'er lawyers' fingers, who straight dream on fees:
O'er ladies lips, who straight on kisses dream;
Which oft the angry Mab with blisters plagues,
Because their breaths with sweet-meats tainted
     are.
Sometimes she gallops o'er a courtier's nose,
And then dreams he of smelling out a suit:
And sometimes comes she with a tithe-pig's tail,
Tickling a parson's nose as 'a lies asleep,
Then dreams he of another benefice:
Sometimes she driveth o'er a soldier's neck,
And then dreams he of cutting foreign throats,
Of breaches, ambuscadoes, Spanish blades,
Of healths five fathom deep; and then anon
Drums in his ear; at which he starts and wakes;
And being thus frighted, swears a prayer or
     two,
And sleeps again.   This is that very Mab,
That plats the manes of horses in the night;
And bakes the elf-locks in foul sluttish hairs,
Which, once untangled, much misfortune bodes.

DREAMS.

  Mer. True, I talk of dreams;
Which are the children of an idle brain,
Begot of nothing but vain fantasy;
Which is as thin of substance as the air;
And more inconstant than the wind, who wooes
Even now the frozen bosom of the north,
And, being anger'd puffs away from thence,
Turning his face to the dew-dropping south.

Scene V.

Beauty.

Rom. O, she doth teach the torches to burn
    bright!
Her beauty hangs upon the cheek of night
Like a rich jewel in an Ethiop's ear:
Beauty too rich for use, for earth too dear:
So shews a snowy dove trooping with crows,
As yonder lady o'er her fellows shews.
The measure done, I'll watch her place of stand,
And, touching hers, make happy my rude hand.
Did my heart love till now? forswear it, sight!
For I ne'er saw true beauty till this night.

Kisses.

Rom. |*To* Juliet.| If I profane with my unworthy hand
    This holy shrine, the gentle fine is this,—
My lips, two blushing pilgrims, ready stand
    To smooth that rough touch with a tender kiss.
Jul. Good pilgrim, you do wrong your hand too much,
    Which mannerly devotion shews in this;
For saints have hands that pilgrims' hands do touch,
    And palm to palm is holy palmers' kiss.
Rom. Have not saints lips, and holy palmers too?
Jul. Ay, pilgrim, lips that they must use in prayer.
Rom. O then, dear saint, let lips do what hands do;
    They pray, grant thou, lest faith turn to despair.
Jul. Saints do not move, though grant for prayers' sake.
Rom. Then move not, while my prayer's effect I take.
Thus from my lips, by yours, my sin is purged.

                              |*Kissing her.*

Jul. Then have my lips the sin that they have took.

Rom. Sin from my lips?   O trespass sweetly urged!
Give me my sin again.

Jul. You kiss by the book.

ACT II.—Scene II.

Juliet's beauty.

Enter Romeo.

Rom. He jests at scars, that never felt a wound.—
　　　　　[Juliet *appears above, at a window.*
But, soft! what light through yonder window breaks!
It is the east, and Juliet is the sun!—
Arise, fair sun, and kill the envious moon,
Who is already sick and pale with grief,
That thou, her maid, art far more fair than she:
Be not her maid, since she is envious;
Her vestal livery is but sick and green,
And none but fools do wear it; cast it off.—
It is my lady; O, it is my love!
O, that she knew she were!—
She speaks, yet she says nothing; what of that?
Her eye discourses, I will answer it.—
I am too bold, 'tis not to me she speaks:
Two of the fairest stars in all the heaven,
Having some business, do entreat her eyes
To twinkle in their spheres till they return.
What if her eyes were there, they in her head?
The brightness of her cheek would shame those stars,
As daylight doth a lamp; her eye in heaven
Would through the airy region stream so bright,
That birds would sing, and think it were not night.
See how she leans her cheek upon her hand!

O, that I were a glove upon that hand,
That I might touch that cheek !

 Jul. Ah me !

 Rom. She speaks:—

O, speak again, bright angel ! for thou art
As glorious to this night, being o'er my head,
As is a winged messenger of heaven
Unto the white upturned wondering eyes
Of mortals, that fall back to gaze on him,
When he bestrides the lazy-pacing clouds,
And sails upon the bosom of the air.

 Jul. O Romeo, Romeo ! wherefore art thou Romeo ?
Deny thy father, and refuse thy name;
Or, if thou wilt not, be but sworn my love,
And I'll no longer be a Capulet.

 Rom. [*Aside.*] Shall I hear more, or shall I speak at this ?

 Jul. 'Tis but thy name that is my enemy:—
Thou art thyself though, not a Montague.
What's Montague ? it is nor hand nor foot,
Nor arm nor face, nor any other part
Belonging to a man. O, be some other name !
What's in a name ? that which we call a rose,
By any other name would smell as sweet;
So Romeo would, were he not Romeo call'd,
Retain that dear perfection which he owes,
Without that title:—Romeo, doff thy name;
And for that name, which is no part of thee,
Take all myself.

 Rom. I take thee at thy word:
Call me but love, and I'll be new baptised;
Henceforth I never will be Romeo.

 Jul. What man art thou, that, thus bescreen'd in night,
So stumblest on my counsel ?

Rom. By a name
I know not how to tell thee who I am:
My name, dear saint, is hateful to myself,
Because it is an enemy to thee;
Had I it written, I would tear the word.

Jul. My ears have not yet drunk a hundred words
Of that tongue's utterance, yet I know the sound:
Art thou not Romeo, and a Montague?

Rom. Neither, fair saint, if either thee dislike.

Jul. How cam'st thou hither, tell me? and wherefore?
The orchard walls are high and hard to climb;
And the place death, considering who thou art,
If any of my kinsmen find thee here.

Rom. With love's light wings did I o'erperch these walls;
For stony limits cannot hold love out:
And what love can do, that dares love attempt;
Therefore thy kinsmen are no let to me.

Jul. If they do see thee, they will murder thee.

Rom. Alack! There lies more peril in thine eye,
Than twenty of their swords; look thou but sweet,
And I am proof against their enmity.

Jul. I would not for the world they saw thee here.

Rom. I have night's cloak to hide me from their sight
And but thou love me, let them find me here;
My life were better ended by their hate,
Than death prorogued, wanting of thy love.

Jul. By whose direction found'st thou out this place?

Rom. By Love, who first did prompt me to inquire;
He lent me counsel, and I lent him eyes.
I am no pilot; yet, wert thou as far
As that vast shore wash'd with the furthest sea,
I would adventure for such merchandise.

Jul. Thou know'st the mask of night is on my face,

Else would a maiden blush bepaint my cheek,
For that which thou hast heard me speak to-night.
Fain would I dwell on form, fain, fain deny
What I have spoke; but farewell compliment!
Dost thou love me? I know thou wilt say—Ay;
And I will take thy word: yet, if thou swear'st,
Thou mayst prove false; at lovers' perjuries,
They say, Jove laughs. O gentle Romeo,
If thou dost love, pronounce it faithfully:
Or if thou think'st I am too quickly won,
I'll frown and be perverse, and say thee nay,
So thou wilt woo; but else, not for the world.
In truth, fair Montague, I am too fond;
And therefore thou mayst think my 'haviour light:
But trust me, gentleman, I'll prove more true
Than those that have more cunning to be strange.
I should have been more strange, I must confess,
But that thou over-heard'st, ere I was 'ware,
My true love's passion: therefore pardon me;
And not impute this yielding to light love,
Which the dark night hath so discovered.

Rom. Lady, by yonder blessed moon I swear,
That tips with silver all these fruit-tree tops,—

Jul. O, swear not by the moon, the inconstant moon,
That monthly changes in her circled orb,
Lest that thy love prove likewise variable.

Rom. What shall I swear by?

Jul. Do not swear at all;
Or, if thou wilt, swear by thy gracious self,
Which is the god of my idolatry,
And I'll believe thee.

Rom. If my heart's dear love—

Jul. Well, do not swear: although I joy in thee,

I have no joy of this contract to-night:
It is too rash, to unadvised, too sudden;
To like the lightning, which doth cease to be
Ere one can say—It lightens. Sweet, good night!
This bud of love, by summer's ripening breath,
May prove a beauteous flower when next we meet.
Good night, good night! as sweet repose and rest
Come to thy heart, as that within my breast!

 Rom. O, wilt thou leave me so unsatisfied?

 Jul. What satisfaction canst thou have to-night?

 Rom. The exchange of thy love's faithful vow for mine.

 Jul. I gave thee mine before thou didst request it:
And yet I would it were to give again.

 Rom. Wouldst thou withdraw it? for what purpose, love?

 Jul. But to be frank, and give it thee again.
And yet I wish but for the thing I have:
My bounty is as boundless as the sea,
My love as deep; the more I give to thee,
The more I have, for both are infinite.

         [Nurse *calls within.*
I hear some noise within; dear love, adieu!—
Anon, good nurse!—Sweet Montague, be true.
Stay but a little, I will come again.   [*Exit.*

 Rom. O blessed, blessed night! I am afeard,
Being in night, all this is but a dream,
Too flattering-sweet to be substantial.

    Re-enter JULIET, *above,*

 Jul. Three words, dear Romeo, and good night indeed.
If that thy bent of love be honourable,
Thy purpose marriage, send me word to-morrow,
By one that I'll procure to come to thee,
 4

Where and what time thou wilt perform the rite,
And all my fortunes at thy foot I'll lay,
And follow thee, my lord, throughout the world.

LOVE.

Jul. Hist, Romeo, hist!—O, for a falconer's voice,
To lure this tassel-gentle back again!
Bondage is hoarse, and may not speak aloud;
Else would I tear the cave where echo lies,
And make her airy tongue more hoarse than mine
With repetition of my Romeo's name:
  Rom. It is my soul that calls upon my name:
How silver-sweet sound lovers' tongues by night,
Like softest music to attending ears!

SCENE V.—*Capulet's Garden.*

LOVE'S IMPATIENCE.

Enter JULIET.

Jul. The clock struck nine, when did I send the nurse;
In half an hour she promised to return.
Perchance, she cannot meet him:—that's not so.—
O, she is lame! love's heralds should be thoughts,
Which ten times faster glide than the sun's beams,
Driving back shadows over lowering hills:
Therefore do nimble-pinioned doves draw love,
And therefore hath the wind-swift Cupid wings.
Now is the sun upon the highmost hill
Of this day's journey; and from nine till twelve
Is three long hours,—yet she is not come.

Scene VI.

Love moderately.

Fri. These violent delights have violent ends,
And in their triumph die; like fire and powder,
Which, as they kiss, consume: The sweetest honey
Is loathsome in his own deliciousness,
And in the taste confounds the appetite:
Therefore, love moderately; long love doth so;
Too swift arrives as tardy as too slow.

Lightness of vanity.

Here comes the lady; O, so light a foot
Will ne'er wear out the everlasting flint:
A lover may bestride the gossamers,
That idle in the wanton summer air,
And yet not fall: so light is vanity.

Countless value of love.

Rom. Ah, Juliet, if the measure of thy joy
Be heap'd like mine, and that thy skill be more
To blazon it, then sweeten with thy breath
This neighbour air, and let rich music's tongue
Unfold the imagined happiness, that both
Receive in either by this dear encounter.
Jul. Conceit, more rich in matter than in words,
Brags of his substance, not of ornament:
They are but beggars that can count their worth;
But my true love is grown to such excess,
I cannot sum up half my sum of wealth.

ACT III.

LOVE'S IMPATIENCE.

Enter JULIET.

Jul. Gallop apace, you fiery-footed steeds,
Towards Phœbus' mansion; such a waggoner
As Phaeton would whip you to the west,
And bring in cloudy night immediately.—
Spread thy close curtain, love-performing night !
That run-away's eyes may wink; and Romeo
Leap to these arms, untalk'd of, and unseen!
Lovers can see to do their amorous rites
By their own beauties, or, if love be blind,
It best agrees with night —Come, civil night,
Thou sober-suited matron, all in black,
Hood my unmann'd blood, bating in my cheeks,
With thy black mantle; till strange love, grown
          bold,
Think true love acted, simple modesty.
Come, night!—Come, Romeo !—come, thou day in
          night;
For thou wilt lie upon the wings of night
Whiter than new snow on a raven's back.—
Come, gentle night; come, loving, black-brow'd
          night,
Give me my Romeo: and, when he shall die,
Take him, and cut him out in little stars,
And he will make the face of heaven so fine,
That all the world will be in love with night,
And pay no worship to the garish sun.—
O, I have bought the mansion of a love,

But not possess'd it; and though I am sold,
Not yet enjoyed: So tedious is this day,
As is the night before some festival
To an impatient child, that hath new robes,
And may not wear them. O, here comes my
      nurse.

Scene V.—*Juliet's Chamber.*

Parting lovers.

Enter Romeo and Juliet.

Jul. Wilt thou be gone? it is not yet near day:
It was the nightingale, and not the lark,
That pierced the fearful hollow of thine ear:
Nightly she sings on you pomegranate tree:
Believe me, love, it was the nightingale.

Rom. It was the lark, the herald of the morn,
No Nightingale: look, love, what envious streaks
Do lace the severing clouds in yonder east:
Night's candles are burnt out, and jocund day
Stands tiptoe on the misty mountain tops;
I must be gone and live, or stay and die.

Jul. Yon light is not day-light, I know it, I:
It is some meteor, that the sun exhales,
To be to thee this night a torch-bearer,
And light thee on thy way to Mantua:
Therefore stay yet, thou need'st not be gone.

Rom. Let me be ta'en, let me be put to death;
I am content, so thou wilt have it so:
I'll say, yon grey is not the morning's eye,
'Tis but the pale reflex of Cynthia's brow;
Nor that is not the lark, whose notes do beat
The vaulty heaven so high above our heads:

I have more care to stay, than will to go:—
Come, death, and welcome! Juliet wills it so.—
How is't, my soul? let's talk, it is not day.

Jul. It is, it is, hie hence, be gone, away;
It is the lark that sings so out of tune,
Straining harsh discords, and unpleasing sharps.
Some say, the lark makes sweet division.
This doth not so, for she divideth us:
Some say, the lark and loathed toad change eyes;
O, now I would they had changed voices too!
Since arm from arm that voice doth us affray,
Hunting thee hence, with hunts-up to the day.
O, now be gone; more light and light it grows.

    Rom. More light and light?—more dark and dark
        our woes.

ACT IV.—Scene I.

Juliet's devotion.

Jul. O, bid me leap, rather than marry Paris,
From off the battlements of yonder tower;
Or walk in thievish ways; or bid me lurk
Where serpents are; chain me with roaring
        bears;
Or shut me nightly in a charnel-house,
O'er-covered quite with dead men's rattling bones,
With reeky shanks, and yellow chapless skulls;
Or bid me go into a new-made grave,
And hide me with a dead man in his shroud;
Things that, to hear them told, have made me
        tremble;
And I will do it without fear or doubt,
To live an unstain'd wife to my sweet love.

Scene III.

Juliet's fears.

Jul. Farewell !—God knows, when we shall meet
    again.
I have a faint cold fear thrills through my veins,
That almost freezes up the heat of life:
I'll call them back again to comfort me;—
Nurse !—What should she do here?
My dismal scene I needs must act alone.—
Come, phial.—
What if this mixture do not work at all !
Must I of force be married to the county?
No, no;—this shall forbid it:—lie thou there.—

                    [Laying down a dagger.

What if it be poison, which the friar
Subtly have minister'd to have me dead;
Lest in this marriage he should be dishonour'd,
Because he married me before to Romeo.
I fear, it is: and yet, methinks, it should not,
For he hath still been tried a holy man:
I will not entertain so bad a thought.
How if, when I am laid into the tomb,
I wake before the time that Romeo
Come to redeem me? there's a fearful point!
Shall I not then be stifled in the vault,
To whose foul mouth no healthsome air breathes
    in,
And there die strangled ere my Romeo comes?
Or, if I live, is it not very like
The horrible conceit of death and night,
Together with the terror of the place,—

As in a vault, an ancient receptacle,
Where, for these many hundred years, the bones
Of all my buried ancestors are pack'd;
Where bloody Tybalt, yet but green in earth,
Lies fest'ring in his shroud; where, as they say,
At some hours in the night spirits resort;—
Alack, alack! is it not like, that I,
So early waking,—what with loathsome smells;
And shrieks like mandrakes torn out of the earth,
That living mortals, hearing them, run mad;—
O ! if I wake, shall I not be distraught,
Environed with all these hideous fears ?
And madly play with my forefathers' joints ?
And pluck the mangled Tybalt from his shroud ?
And, in his rage, with some great kinsman's bone,
As with a club, dash out my desperate brains ?
O, look ! methinks, I see my cousin's ghost
Seeking out Romeo, that did split his body
Upon a rapier's point:—Stay, Tybalt, stay!--
Romeo, I come ! this do I drink to thee.

(She throws herself upon the bed.)

ACT V.

Scene I--*Mantua.   A street.*

Romeo's soliloquy.

Enter Romeo.

Rom. If I may trust the flattering eye of sleep,
My dreams presage some joyful news at hand:
My bosom's lord sits lightly in his throne;
And, all this day, an unaccustom'd spirit
Lifts me above the ground with cheerful thoughts.
I dreamt, my lady came and found me dead,

(Strange dream! that gives a dead man leave to
       think,)
And breathed such life with kisses in my lips,
That I revived, and was an emperor.
Ah me! how sweet is love itself possess'd,
When but love's shadows are so rich in joy!
   Rom. No matter; get thee gone,
And hire post horses, I'll be with the straight.
                    [*Exit Balthazar.*
Well, Juliet, I will lie with thee to-night.
Let's see for means:—O, mischief, thou art swift
To enter in the thoughts of desperate men!
I do remember an apothecary,—
And hereabouts he dwells,—whom late I noted
In tatter'd weeds, with overwhelming brows,
Culling of simples; meagre were his looks,
Sharp misery had worn him to the bones;
And in his needy shop a tortoise hung,
An alligator stuff'd, and other skins
Of ill-shaped fishes; and about his shelves
A beggarly account of empty boxes,
Green earthen pots, bladders, and musty seeds,
Remnants of packthread, and old cakes of roses,
Were thinly scatter'd to make up a shew.
Noting this penury, to myself I said—
An if a man did need a poison now,
Whose sale is present death in Mantua,
Here lives a caitiff wretch would sell it him.
O, this same thought did but fore-run my need;
And this same needy man must sell it me.
As I remember, this should be the house:
Being holyday, the beggar's shop is shut.—
What, ho! apothecary!

Poison.

Enter APOTHECARY.

Ap. Who calls so loud?

Rom. Come hither, man.—I see that thou art
     poor;
Hold, there is forty ducats: let me have
A dram of poison; such soon-speeding gear
As will disperse itself through all the veins,
That the life-weary taker may fall dead;
And that the trunk may be discharged of breath
As violently, as hasty powder fired
Doth hurry from the fatal cannon's womb.

Ap. Such mortal drugs I have; but Mantua
     law
Is death, to any he that utters them.

Rom. Art thou so bare, and full of wretchedness,
And fear'st to die? famine is in thy cheeks,
Need and oppression starveth in thy eyes,
Upon thy back hangs ragged misery,
The world is not thy friend, nor the world's law:
The world affords no law to make thee rich.
Then be not poor, but break it and take this.

Ap. My poverty, but not my will, consents.

Rom I pay thy poverty, and not thy will.

Ap. Put this in any liquid thing you will,
And drink it off; and, if you had the strength
Of twenty men, it would despatch you straight.

Rom. There is thy gold, worse poison to men's
     souls,
Doing more murders in this loathsome world,
Than these poor compounds, that thou may'st not
     sell:

I sell thee poison, thou hast sold me none,
Farewell; buy food, and get thyself in flesh.
Come, cordial, and not poison; go with me
To Juliet's grave, for there must I use thee.

Death of Romeo.

Enter Romeo *and* Balthazar *with a torch, mattock, &c.*

Rom. Give me that mattock, and the wrenching
      iron.
Hold, take this letter; early in the morning
See thou deliver it to my lord and father.
Give me the light: Upon thy life, I charge thee;
Whate'er thou hear'st or seest, stand all aloof.
And do not interrupt me in my course.
Why I descend into this bed of death,
Is, partly, to behold my lady's face:
But, chiefly, to take thence from her dead finger
A precious ring; a ring, that I must use
In dear employment: therefore hence, be gone:—
But if thou, jealous, dost return to pry
In what I farther shall intend to do,
By Heaven, I will tear thee joint by joint,
And strew this hungry churchyard with thy limbs:
The time and my intents are savage-wild;
More fierce, and more inexorable far,
Than empty tigers, or the roaring sea.
A grave? O no; a lantern, slaughter'd youth,
For here lies Juliet, and her beauty makes
This vault a feasting presence full of light.
Death, lie thou here, by a dead man interr'd.
How oft, when men are at the point of death,
Have they been merry? which their keepers
      call

A lightning before death: O, how may I
Call this a lightning?—O, my love! my wife!
Death, that hath suck'd the honey of thy breath,
Hath had no power yet upon thy beauty:
Thou art not conquer'd; beauty's ensign yet
Is crimson in thy lips, and in thy cheeks,
And death's pale flag is not advanced there.—
Tybalt, liest thou there in thy bloody sheet?
O, what more favour can I do to thee,
Than with that hand, that cut thy youth in
         twain,
To sunder his, that was thine enemy?
Forgive me, cousin?—Ah, dear Juliet,
Why art thou yet so fair?   Shall I believe
That unsubstantial death is amorous;
And that the lean abhorred monster keeps
Thee here in dark to be his paramour?
For fear of that, I will stay with thee;
And never from this palace of dim night
Depart again: here, here will I remain
With worms that are thy chamber maids; O,
         here
Will I set up my everlasting rest;
And shake the yoke of inauspicious stars
From this world-wearied flesh.—Eyes, look your
         last!
Arms, take your last embrace! and lips, O you
The doors of breath, seal with a righteous kiss
A dateless bargain to engrossing death!—
Come, bitter conduct, come, unsavoury guide!
Thou desperate pilot, now at once run on
The dashing rocks thy sea-sick weary bark!
Here's to my love! (*Drinks.*)   O, true apothecary!

Thy drugs are quick.—Thus with a kiss I die.

(Dies.)

 Prince. Give me the letter, I will look on it.—
Where is the county's page, that raised the watch?
Sirrah, what made your master in this place?

 Page. He came with flowers to strew his lady's
   grave;
And bid me stand aloof, and so I did:
Anon comes one with light to ope the tomb;
And, by and by, my master drew on him;
And then I ran away to call the watch.

 Prince. This letter doth make good the friar's
   words,
Their course of love, the tidings of her death:
And here he writes—that he did buy a poison
Of a poor 'pothecary, and therewithal
Came to this vault to die, and lie with Juliet.—
Where be these enemies? Capulet! Montague!—
See, what a scourge is laid upon your hate,
That Heaven finds means to kill your joys with
   love!
And I, for winking at your discords too,
Have lost a brace of kinsmen:—all are punish'd.

 Cap. O brother Montague, give me thy hand:
This is my daughter's jointure, for no more
Can I demand.

 Mon. But I can give thee more:
For I will raise her statue in pure gold;
That, while Verona by that name is known,
There shall no figure at such rate be set,
As that of true and faithful Juliet.

 Cap. As rich shall Romeo by his lady lie;
Poor sacrifices of our enmity!

Prince. A gloomy peace this morning with it
       brings;
The sun for sorrow, will not shew his head:
Go hence, to have more talk of these sad things;
   Some shall be pardon'd and some punished:
For never was a story of more wo,
Than this of Juliet and her Romeo.   [*Exeunt.*

MACBETH.

ACT I—Scene I.

Thunder and lightning.

Enter Three Witches—*their chant.*

1 *Witch.* When shall we three meet again,
In thunder, lightning, or in rain?
    2 *Witch.* When the hurlyburly's done,
When the battle's lost and won:
    3 *Witch.* That will be ere set of sun.
    1 *Witch.* Where the place?
    2 *Witch.* Upon the heath:
    3 *Witch.* There to meet with Macbeth.
    1 *Witch.* I come, Graymalkin!
    All. Paddock calls:—Anon.—
Fair is foul, and foul is fair:
Hover through the fog and filthy air.

[*Witches vanish.*

Scene II.

Multiplying villainies.

Sold. Doubtfully it stood;
As two spent swimmers, that do cling together,
And choke their art. The merciless Macdonwald,
(Worthy to be a rebel; for, to that,

The multiplying villianies of nature
Do swarm upon him,) from the western isles
Of Kernes and Gallowglasses is supplied;
And fortune, on his damned quarrel smiling.

Discomfort.

Sold. As whence the sun 'gins his reflection,
Shipwrecking storms and direful thunders break;
So from that spring, whence comfort seem'd to
      come,
Discomfort swells..

Comparison of bravery of Macbeth and Banquo.

Dun. Dismay'd not this
Our captains, Macbeth and Banquo?
  Sold. Yes;
As sparrows, eagles; or the hare, the lion.
If I say sooth, I must report they were
As cannons overcharged with double cracks;
So they
Doubly redoubled strokes upon the foe:

Macbeth's valor.

But all's too weak;
For brave Macbeth (well he deserves that name,)
Disdaining fortune, with his brandish'd steel,
Which smoked with bloody execution,
Like valour's minion,
Carved out his passage, till he faced the slave;
And ne'er shook hands, nor bade farewell to him,
Till he unseam'd him from the nave to th' chaps,
And fix'd his head upon our battlements.

Scene III.

Insanity.

Banquo. Were such things here as we do speak about, or
have we eaten of the insane root that takes the reason
prisoner?

Scene IV.

Macbeth's soliloquy.

Macb. The prince of Cumberland !—That is a step,
On which I must fall down, or else o'erleap,
For in my way it lies.   Stars, hide your fires!
Let not light see my black and deep desires!
The eye wink at the hand! yet let that be,
Which the eye fears, when it is done, to see.

Scene V.

Lady Macbeth's soliloquy and dreadful resolution.

Lady M. Give him tending,
He brings great news.—The raven himself is hoarse,

[Exit attendant.

That croaks the fatal entrance of Duncan
Under my battlements.   Come, come, you spirits
That tend on mortal thoughts, unsex me here;
And fill me from the crown to the toe, top-full
Of direst cruelty! make thick my blood,
Stop up the access and passage to remorse,
That no compunctious visitings of nature
Shake my fell purpose, nor keep peace between
The effect and it!   Come to my woman's breasts,
And take my milk for gall, you murd'ring ministers,
Wherever in your sightless substances
5

You wait on nature's mischief!   Come, thick night
And pall thee in the dunnest smoke of hell!
That my keen knife see not the wound it makes:
Nor Heaven peep through the blanket of the dark,
To cry, *Hold, hold!*—Great Glamis! worthy
          Cawdor!

Enter MACBETH.

   Macb. My dearest love,
Duncan comes here to-night.
   Lady M. And when goes hence?
   Macb. To-morrow, as he purposes.
   Lady M. O, never
Shall sun that morrow see!
Your face, my thane, is as a book, where men
May read strange matters.—To beguile the time,
Look like that time: bear welcome in your eye,
Your hand, your tongue: look like the innocent
          flower,
But be the serpent under it.   He that's coming
Must be provided for: and you shall put
This night's great business into my despatch;
Which shall to all our nights and days to come
Give solely sovereign sway and masterdom.

Scene VII.

MACBETH CONTEMPLATING THE CONSEQUENCES OF ASSASSINATION.

*A Room in the Castle.   Hautboys and torches.   Enter and pass over the
stage, a Sewer, and divers Servants with dishes and service.   Then
enter* MACBETH.

   Macb. If it were done, when 'tis done, then 'twere well
It were done quickly: If the assassination
Could trammel up the consequence, and catch,

With his surcease, success; that but this blow
Might be the be-all and the end-all here,
But here, upon this bank and shoal of time,—
We'd jump the life to come.—But, in these cases,
We still have judgment here; that we but teach
Bloody instructions, which, being taught, return
To plague the inventor: This even-handed justice
Commends the ingredients of our poison'd chalice
To our own lips. He's here in double trust:
First, as I am his kinsman and his subject,
Strong both against the deed; then, as his host,
Who should against his murderer shut the door,
Not bear the knife myself. Besides, this Duncan
Hath borne his faculties so meek, hath been
So clear in his great office, that his virtues
Will plead like angels, trumpet-tongued, against
The deep damnation of his taking-off:
And pity, like a naked new-born babe,
Striding the blast or Heaven's cherubin horsed
Upon the sightless couriers of the air,
Shall blow the horrid deed in every eye,
That tears shall drown the wind—I have no spur
To prick the sides of my intent, but only
Vaulting ambition, which o'erleaps itself,
And falls on the other side.—

LADY MACBETH TO HER HUSBAND.

Lady M. *We fail!* But screw your courage to the sticking
place, and we'll not fail.

Macb. I dare do all that may become a man;
Who dares do more is none.

ACT II.—Scene I.

The assassination.

Macb. **Go,** bid my mistress, when my drink is
　　　ready,
She strike upon the bell.　Get thee to bed.—

[Exit Servant.

Is this a dagger which I see before me,
The handle toward my hand?　Come, let me clutch thee:—
I have thee not, and yet I see thee still.
Art thou not, fatal vision, sensible
To feeling, as to sight? or art thou but
A dagger of the mind; a false creation,
Proceeding from the heat-oppressed brain?
I see thee yet, in form as palpable
As this which now I draw.
Thou marshal'st me the way that I was going;
And such an instrument I was to use.
Mine eyes are made the fools o' the other senses,
Or else worth all the rest: I see thee still;
And on thy blade, and dudgeon, gouts of blood,
Which was not so before.—There's no such thing:
It is the bloody business, which informs
Thus to mine eyes.—Now o'er the one half world
Nature seems dead, and wicked dreams abuse
The curtain'd sleep; now witchcraft celebrates
Pale Hecate's offerings; and wither'd murder,
Alarm'd by his sentinel, the wolf,
Whose howl's his watch, thus with his stealthy
　　　　pace,
With Tarquin's ravishing strides, towards his design
Moves like a ghost.—Thou sure and firm set earth,
Hear not my steps, which way they walk, for fear

The very **stones prate of** my whereabout,
And take the present horror from the time,
Which **now** suits with it.—While I threat, he lives;
Words to the heat of deeds too cold breath gives.

(A bell rings.)

I go, and it is done; the bell invites me.
Hear it not, Duncan; for it is a knell
That summons thee to heaven or to hell. [Exit.

Scene II.

Macbeth's definition of sleep.

Macb. Methought I heard a voice cry, "Sleep no more!"
Macbeth does murder sleep, the innocent sleep;
Sleep, that knits up the ravell'd sleeve of care,
The death of each day's life, sore labour's bath,
Balm of hurt minds, great nature's second course,
Chief nourisher in life's feast,—"

Lady M. What do you mean?

Macb. Still it cried, "Sleep no more!" to all the house:
"Glamis hath murder'd sleep; and therefore Cawdor
Shall sleep no more,—Macbeth shall sleep no more!"

Lady M. Who was it that thus cried? Why, worthy
You do unbend your noble strength, to think   [thane,
So brainsickly of things.—Go get some water,
And wash this filthy witness from your hand.—
Why did you bring these daggers from the place?
They must lie there: go carry them; and smear
The sleepy grooms with blood.

Macbeth's fears.

Macb. I'll go no more:
I am afraid to think what I have done;
Look on't again, I dare not.

Lady M. Infirm of purpose!
Give me the daggers: the sleeping, and the dead,
Are but as pictures: 'tis the eye of childhood,
That fears a painted devil.　If he do bleed,
I'll gild the faces of the grooms withal,
For it must seem their guilt.

[Exit. Knocking within.

Macb. Whence is that knocking?
How is't with me, when every noise appals me?
What hands are here?　Ha! they pluck out mine
　　　　eyes!
Will all great Neptune's ocean wash this blood
Clean from my hand? No? this my hand will rather
The multitudinous seas incarnardine,
Making the green—one red.

SCENE III.

MACDUFF'S HORROR ON DISCOVERY OF THE MURDER.

Macd. O horror! horror! horror!　Tongue, nor heart,
Cannot conceive, nor name thee!

Macb. & Len. What's the matter?

Macd. Confusion now hath made his masterpiece!
Most sacrilegious murder hath broke ope
The Lord's anointed temple, and stole thence
The life 'o the building.

Macb. What is't you say? the life?

Len. Mean you his majesty?

Macd. Approach the chamber, and destroy your sight
With a new Gorgon.—Do not bid me speak,
See, and then speak yourselves.—Awake! awake!—

[Exeunt Macbeth and Lenox.

Ring the alarum-bell.—Murder! and treason!

Banquo, and Donalbain! Malcolm! awake!
Shake off this downy sleep, death's counterfeit,
And look on death itself!—up, up, and see
The great doom's image!—Malcolm! Banquo!
As from your graves rise up, and walk like
      sprites,
To countenance this horror!

MACBETH'S PHILOSOPHY.

Macb. Who can be wise, amazed, temperate and furious,
Loyal and neutral, in a moment? No man:
The expedition of my violent love
Outran the pauser reason.—Here lay Duncan,
His silver skin laced with his golden blood;
And his gash'd stabs look'd like a breach in nature,
For ruin's wasteful entrance: there, the murderers,
Steep'd in colours of their trade, their daggers
Unmannerly breech'd with gore: who could refrain,
That had a heart to love, and in that heart
Courage to make his love known?

FLIGHT OF THE CONSPIRITORS.

Don. To Ireland, I; our separate fortune
Shall keep us both the safer: where we are,
There's dagger's in men's smiles; the near in blood,
The nearer bloody.
   Mal. This murderous shaft that's shot,
Hath not yet lighted; and our safest way
Is, to avoid the aim. Therefore, to horse;
And let us not be dainty of leave-taking,
But shift away. There's warrant in that theft,
Which steals itself, when there's no mercy left.

Scene IV.

Unnatural murder.

Enter Rosse *and an* Old Man.

Old M. Threescore and ten I can remember well:
Within the volume of which time I have seen
Hours dreadful, and things strange; but this sore night
Hath trifled former knowings.

Rosse. Ah, good father,
Thou see'st the heavens, as troubled with man's act,
Threaten his bloody stage: by the clock 'tis day,
And yet dark night strangles the travelling lamp;
Is it night's predominance; or the day's shame
That darkness does the face of earth entomb,
When living light should kiss it?

Old M. 'Tis unnatural,
Even like the deed that's done. On Tuesday last,
A falcon, tow'ring in her pride of place,
Was by a mousing owl hawk'd at, and kill'd.

Rosse. And Duncan's horses, (a thing most strange
and certain,)
Beauteous and swift, the minions of their race,
Turn'd wild in nature, broke their stalls, flung out,
Contending 'gainst obedience, as they would make
War with mankind.

Old M. 'Tis said they eat each other.

Rosse. They did so; to the amazement of mine eyes,
That look'd upon't.—Here comes the good Macduff.—

ACT III.—Scene I.

Macbeth's fears of Banquo.

Macb. Bring them before us.—[*Exit Attendant.*]
     To be thus, is nothing;
But to be safely thus.—Our fears in Banquo
Stick deep; and in his royalty of nature
Reigns that, which would be fear'd. 'Tis much he dares;
And, to that dauntless temper of his mind,
He hath a wisdom that doth guide his valour
To act in safety. There is none but he
Whose being I do fear: and, under him,
My genius is rebuked; as, it is said,
Mark Antony's was by Cæsar. He chid the sisters,
When first they put the name of king upon me,
And bade them speak to him; then, prophet-like,
They hail'd him father to a line of kings:
Upon my head they placed a fruitless crown,
And put a barren sceptre in my gripe,
Thence to be wrench'd with an unlineal hand,
No son of mine succeeding. If it be so,
For Banquo's issue have I filed my mind;
For them the gracious Duncan have I murder'd,
Put rancours in the vessel of my peace
Only for them; and mine eternal jewel
Given to the common enemy of man,
To make them kings, the seed of Banquo kings!

Scene II.

Macbeth's remorse.

Lady M. How, now, my lord? why do you keep alone,
Of sorriest fancies your companions making?

Using those thoughts, which should indeed have
  died
When them they think on?　Things without remedy,
Should be without regard: what's done, is done.

 Macb. We have scotch'd the snake, not kill'd it;
She'll close, and be herself; whilst our poor malice
Remains in danger of her former tooth,
But let
The frame of things disjoint, both the worlds suffer,
Ere we will eat our meal in fear, and sleep
In the affliction of these terrible dreams,
That shake us nightly: Better be with the dead,
Whom we, to gain our place, have sent to peace,
Then on the torture of the mind to lie
In restless ecstasy.　Duncan is in his grave;
After life's fitful fever, he sleeps well;
Treason has done his worst: nor steel, nor poison,
Malice domestic, foreign levy, nothing,
Can touch him farther!

 Lady M. What's to be done?

 Macb. Be innocent of the knowledge, dearest chuck.
Till thou applaud the deed.　Come seeling night,
Scarf up the tender eye of pitiful day;
And, with thy bloody and invisible hand,
Cancel, and tear to pieces, that great bond
Which keeps me pale!—Light thickens; and the crow
Makes wing to the rooky wood;
Good things of day begin to droop and drowse;
While night's black agents to their prey do rouse.
Then marvell'st at my words: but hold thee still;
Things, bad begun, make strong themselves by ill,

 Macb. Then comes my fit again: I had else been perfect:
Whole as the marble, founded as the rock;

As broad, and general, as the casing air:
But now, I am cabin'd, cribb'd confined, bound in
To saucy doubts and fears. But Banquo's safe?

Mur. Ay, my good lord: safe in a ditch he bides,
With twenty trenched gashes on his head;
The least a death to nature.

Macb. Thanks for that.—
There the grown serpent lies; the worm, that's fled,
Hath nature that in time will venom breed,
No teeth for the present.—Get thee gone: to-morrow
We'll hear ourselves again.   [*Exit Murderer.*

Good digestion and appetite.

Lady M. My royal lord,
You do not give the cheer: the feast is sold
That is not often vouch'd, while 'tis a making,
'Tis given with welcome: To feed were best at
        home:
From thence, the sauce to meat is ceremony;
Meeting were bare without it.

Macb. Sweet remembrancer!—
Now, good digestion wait on appetite,
And health on both!

Lady Macbeth upbraiding her husband.

Lady M. O proper stuff!
This is the very painting of your fear:
This is the air-drawn dagger, which, you said,
Led you to Duncan. O, these flaws and starts,
(Impostors to true fear,) would well become
A woman's story, at a winter's fire,
Authorized by her grandam. Shame itself!

Macbeth to Banquo's Ghost.

Macb. Avaunt! and quit my sight! Let the earth
      hide thee!
Thy bones are marrowless, thy blood is cold;
Thou hast no speculation in those eyes
Which thou dost glare with!

Lady M. Think of this, good peers,
But as a thing of custom: 'tis no other;
Only it spoils the pleasure of the time.

Macb. What man dare, I dare:
Approach thou like the rugged Russian bear,
The arm'd rhinoceros, or the Hyrcan tiger,
Take any shape but that, and my firm nerves
Shall never tremble.

Macbeth's terror.

Macb. Can such things be,
And overcome us like a summer's cloud,
Without our special wonder. You make me strange,
Even to the disposition that I owe,
When now I think you can behold such sights,
And keep the natural ruby of your cheeks,
When mine are blanch'd with fear.

Rosse. What sights, my lord?

Lady M. I pray you, speak not; he grows worse and worse;
Question enrages him: at once, good night:—
Stand not upon the order of your going,
But go at once.

Macbeth to the Witches.

Macb. I conjure you, by that which you profess,
(Howe'er you come to know it,) answer me:
Though you untie the winds, and let them fight
Against the churches; though the yesty waves

Confound and swallow navigation up;
Though bladed corn be lodged, and trees blown down!
Though castles topple on their warders' heads;
Though palaces and pyramids do slope
Their heads to their foundations; though the treasure
Of nature's germins tumble all together,
Even till destruction sicken, answer me
To what I ask you.

Spirit speaking to Macbeth.

  App. Be bloody, bold,
And resolute; laugh to scorn the power of man,
For none of woman born shall harm Macbeth.

[*Descends.*

  Macb. Then live, Macduff: what need I fear of thee,
But yet I'll make assurance doubly sure,
And take a bond of fate: thou shalt not live;
That I may tell pale-hearted fear, it lies,
And sleep in spite of thunder.—What is this,

Thunder. An Apparition of a Child crowned, with a tree in his hand, rises.

That rises like the issue of a king,
And wears upon his baby brow the round
And top of sovereignty?
  App. Be lion-mettled, proud; and take no care
Who chafes, who frets, or where conspirers are;
Macbeth, will never vanquish'd be, until
Great Birnam wood to high Dunsinane hill
Shall come against him.   (*Descends.*
  Macb. That will never be:
Who can impress the forest; bid the tree
Unfix his earth-bound root? sweet bodements! good!
Rebellion's head rise never, till the wood

Of Birnam rise, and our high-placed Macbeth
Shall live the lease of nature, pay his breath
To time and mortal custom.

SCENE III.

INTEMPERANCE IN NATURE A TYRANNY.

Macd. Boundless intemperance
In nature is a tyranny; it hath been
The untimely emptying of the happy throne,
And fall of many kings.

ACT V.—SCENE I,

LADY MACBETH'S REMORSE.

Enter LADY MACBETH, *with a taper.*

Lo you, here she comes! This is her very guise, and,
upon my life, fast asleep. Observe her; stand close.

Doct. How came she by that light?

Gent. Why, it stood by her: she has light by her con-
tinually; 'tis her command.

Doct. You see, her eyes are open.

Gent. Ay, but their sense is shut.

Doct. What is it she does now? Look, how she rubs her
hands.

Gent. It is an accustomed action with her to seem thus
washing her hands; I have known her continue in this a
quarter of an hour.

Lady M. Yet here's a spot.

Doct. Hark, she speaks: I will set down what comes from
her, to satisfy my remembrance the more strongly.

Lady M. Out, damned spot! out, I say!—One!

  *   *   *   *   *

Lady M. Here's the smell of the blood still: all the perfumes of Arabia will not sweeten this little hand. Oh! oh! oh!

Doct. What a sigh is there! The heart is sorely charged.

Gent. I would not have such a heart in my bosom, for the dignity of the whole body.

Doct. Well, well, well,—

Gent. 'Pray God, it be sir.

Doct. This disease is beyond my practice: Yet I have known those which have walked in their sleep, who have died holily in their beds.

Lady M. Wash your hands, put on your nightgown, look not so pale:—I tell you yet again, Banquo's buried; he cannot come out of his grave.

SCENE III.

SICKNESS OF LADY MACBETH.

Doct. Not so sick, my lord,
As she is troubled with thick-coming fancies,
That keep her from her rest.

Macb. Cure her of that:
Canst thou not minister to a mind diseased;
Pluck from the memory a rooted sorrow;
Raze out the written troubles of the brain;
And, with some sweet oblivious antidote,
Cleanse the stuff'd bosom of that perilous stuff,
Which weighs upon the heart?

Doct. Therein the patient
Must minister to himself.

Macb. Throw physic to the dogs,—I'll none of it.—

SCENE V.—*Dunsinane.* *Within the Castle*

MACBETH'S DEFIANCE TO THE ENEMY.

Enter with drums and colours, MACBETH, SEYTON, *and Soldiers.*

Macb. Hang out our banners on the outward walls;
The cry is still, *They come:* Our castle's strength
Will laugh a siege to scorn: here let them lie,
Till famine, and the ague eat them up:
Were they not forced with those that should be ours,
We might have met them dareful, beard to beard,
And beat them backward home.   What is that noise?

(*A cry within of women.*)

Sey.   It is the cry of women, my good lord.
Macb. I have almost forgot the taste of fears:
The time has been, my senses would have cool'd
To hear a night-shriek; and my fell of hair
Would at a dismal treatise rouse, and stir
As life were in't: I have supp'd full with horrors;
Direness, familiar to my slaught'rous thoughts,
Cannot once start me.—Wherefore was that cry?

MACBETH ON THE DEATH OF HIS WIFE.

Sey. The queen, my lord, is dead.
Macb. She should have died hereafter;
There would have been a time for such a word.—
To-morrow, and to-morrow, and to-morrow,
Creeps in this petty pace from day to day,
To the last syllable of recorded time;
And all our yesterdays have lighted fools
The way to dusty death.   Out, out, brief candle!
Life's but a walking shadow; a poor player,
That struts and frets his hour upon the stage,

And then is heard no more: it is a tale
Told by an idiot, full of sound and fury,
Signifying nothing.—

FIGHT OF MACDUFF AND MACBETH.

Re-enter MACDUFF.

Macd. Turn, hell-hound, turn.

Macb. Of all men else I have avoided thee:
But get thee back, my soul is too much charged
With blood of thine already.

Macd. I have no words,
My voice is in my sword; thou bloodier villian
Than terms can give thee out! (*They fight.*)

Macb. Thou losest labour:
As easy may'st thou the intrenchant air
With thy keen sword impress, as make me bleed:
Let fall thy blade on vulnerable crests;
I bear a charmed life, which must not yield
To one of woman born.

Macd. Then yield thee, coward,
And live to be the show and gaze 'o the time.
We'll have thee, as our rarer monsters are,
Painted upon a pole; and underwrit,
Here you may see the tyrant.

Macb. I'll not yield,
To kiss the ground before young Malcolm's feet,
And to be baited with the rabble's curse.
Though Birnam wood be come to Dunsinane,
And thou opposed, being of no woman born,
Yet I will try the last: Before my body

6

I throw my warlike shield: lay on, Macduff;
And damn'd be him that first cries, *Hold, enough.*

                              (*Exeunt, fighting.*

MACDUFF'S TRIUMPH.

Re-enter MACDUFF, *and Macbeth's head on a pole.*

Macd. Hail, king! for so thou art: Behold, where
    stands
The usurper's cursed head: the time is free:
I see thee compass'd with thy kingdom's pearl,
That speak my salutation in their minds;
Whose voices I desire aloud with mine,—
Hail, king of Scotland!

    All. King of Scotland, hail!   (*Flourish.*)

KING LEAR.

ACT I.—Scene I.

King Lear's gifts to his daughters.

        —Tell me, my daughters,
(Since now we will divest us both of rule,
Interest of territory, cares of state,)
Which of you, shall we say, doth love us most?
That we our largest bounty may extend
Where merit doth most challenge it.—Goneril,
Our eldest-born, speak first.
 Gon. Sir, I
Do love you more than words can wield the mat-
   ter,
Dearer than eyesight, space, and liberty;
Beyond what can be valued, rich or rare;
No less than life, with grace, health, beauty,
   honour;
As much as child e're loved, or father found.
A love, that makes breath poor, and speech un-
   able;
Beyond all manner of so much I love you.

Cor. What shall Cordelia do? Love, and be
 silent.

              (*Aside.*)

Lear. Of all these bounds, even from this line to
 this,
With shadowy forests and with champains rich'd;
With plenteous rivers, and wide-skirted meads,
We make thee lady. To thine and Albany's issue
Be this perpetual—What says our second daughter,
Our dearest Regan, wife to Cornwall? Speak.

 Reg. I am made of that self metal as my sister,
And prize me at her worth. In my true heart
I find, she names my very deed of love;
Only she comes too short,—that I profess
Myself an enemy to all other joys,
Which the most precious square of sense pos-
   sesses;
And find, I am alone felicitate
In your dear highness' love.

 Cor. Then poor Cordelia!—

              (*Aside.*)

And yet not so; since, I am sure, my love's
More richer than my tongue.

 Lear. To thee, and thine, hereditary ever,
Remain this ample third of our fair kingdom;
No less in space, validity, and pleasure,
Then that confirm'd on Goneril.—Now our joy,
Although the last, not least; to whose young love
The vines of France and milk of Burgundy,
Strive to be interess'd; what can you say, to draw
A third more opulent than your sisters? Speak.

 Cor. Nothing, my lord.

 Lear. Nothing?

Cor. Nothing.

Lear. Nothing can come of nothing: speak
    again.

Cor. Unhappy that I am; I cannot heave
My heart into my mouth: I love your majesty
According to my bond; nor more, nor less.

    Lear. How, how, Cordelia? mend your speech a
    little,
Lest it may mar your fortunes

    Cor. Good, my lord,
You have begot me, bred me, loved me: I
Return those duties back as are right fit,
Obey you, love you, and most honour you.
Why have my sisters husbands, if they say,
They love you all? Haply, when I shall wed,
That lord, whose hand must take my plight, shall
       carry
Half my love with him, half my care and duty:
Sure, I shall never marry like my sisters,
To love my father all.

    Lear. But goes this with thy heart?

    Cor. Ay, good my lord.

    Lear. So young, and so untender?

    Cor. So young, my lord, and true.

    Lear. Let it be so. Thy truth, then, be thy
    dower:
For, by the sacred radiance of the sun;
The mysteries of Hecate, and the night;
By all the operations of the orbs
From whom we do exist, and cease to be;
Here I disclaim all my paternal care,
Propinquity and property of blood,
And, as a stranger to my heart and me,

Hold thee from this, for ever.   The barbarous Scythian,
Or he that makes his generation messes
To gorge his appetite, shall to my bosom
Be as well neighbour'd, pitied, and relieved,
As thou my sometime daughter.

   Kent. Good my liege,—

   Lear. Peace, Kent !

Come not between the dragon and his wrath.
I loved her most, and thought to set my rest
On her kind nursery —[*To* Cor.] Hence, and avoid my
       sight!—
So be my grave my peace, as here I give
Her father's heart from her!—Call France;—who stirs ?
Call Burgundy.—Cornwall, and Albany,
With my two daughters' dowers digest this third:
Let pride, which she calls plainness, marry her,
I do invest you jointly with my power,
Pre-eminence, and all the large effects
That troop with majesty.   Ourself, by monthly course,
With reservation of a hundred knights,
By you to be sustain'd, shall our abode
Make with you by due turns.   Only we still retain
The name, and all the additions to a king;
The sway,
Revenue, execution of the rest,
Beloved sons, be yours: which to confirm,
This coronet part between you.   [*Giving the crown.*

   Kent. Royal Lear,
Whom I have ever honour'd as my king,
Loved as my father, as my master follow'd,
As my great patron thought on in my prayers,—

   Lear. The bow is bent and drawn, make from the
      shaft.

Kent. Let it fall rather, though the fork invade
The region of my heart: be Kent unmannerly,
When Lear is mad.   What wouldst thou do, old man?
Think'st thou that duty shall have dread to speak,
When power to flattery bows?   To plainness honour's
        bound,
When majesty stoops to folly.   Reverse thy doom;
And, in thy best consideration, check
This hideous rashness: answer my life my judgment,
Thy youngest daughter does not love thee least;
Nor are those empty-hearted, whose low sound
Reverbs no hollowness.

Lear. Kent, on thy life, no more.

Kent. My life I never held but as a pawn
To wage against thine enemies; nor fear to lose it,
Thy safety being the motive.

Changes on changes.

Glo. These late eclipses in the sun and moon portend no
good to us; though the wisdom of nature can reason it thus
and thus, yet nature finds itself scourged by the sequent
effects: love cools, friendship falls off, brothers divide: in
cities, mutinies; in countries, discord; in palaces, treason;
and the bond cracked between son and father.   This villian
of mine comes under the prediction; there's son against
father: the king falls from bias of nature; there's father
against child.   We have seen the best of our time: Machin-
ations, hollowness, treachery, and all ruinous disorders,
follow us disquietly to our graves!—Find out this villian,
Edmund; it shall lose thee nothing; do it carefully.—And
the noble and true-hearted Kent banished! his offence,
honesty!—Strange! strange!

Scene IV.

Ingratitude.

Is it your will? (*To Alb.*) Speak, sir.—Prepare my
    horses.
Ingratitude ! thou marble-hearted fiend,
More hideous, when thou shew'st thee in a child,
Then the sea-monster!

ACT II.—Scene II.

Obsequiousness.

Kent. That such a slave as this should wear a
    sword,
Who wears no honesty. Such smiling rogues as
    these
Like rats, oft bite the holy chords atwain
Which are too intrinse t' unloose: smooth every
    passion
That in the natures of their lords rebel;
Bring oil to fire, snow to their colder moods;
Renege, affirm, and turn their halcyon beaks
With every gale and vary of their masters,
As knowing nought, like dogs, but following.—
A plague upon your epileptic visage:

Scene IV.

King Lear's reproach to his daughters.

Reg. I am glad to see your highness.
Lear. Regan, I think you are; I know what reason
I have to think so: if thou should'st not be glad,

I would divorce me from thy mother's tomb,
Sepulch'ring an adultress —O, are you free ?

(*To Kent.*)

Some other time for that.—Beloved Regan,
Thy sister's naught: O Regan, she hath tied
Sharp-tooth'd unkindness, like a vulture, here,—

SAME.

Lear. Never, Regan:
She hath abated me of half my train;
Look'd black upon me; struck me with her tongue,
Most serpent-like, upon the very heart.—
All the stored vengeances of Heaven fall
On her ingrateful top!   Strike her young bones,
You taking airs, with lameness!
   Corn. Fy, fy, fy!
   Lear. You nimble lightnings, dart your blinding
         flames
Into her scornful eyes!   Infect her beauty,
You fen-suck'd fogs, drawn by the powerful sun,
To fall and blast her pride!
   Reg. O the blest gods!
So will you wish on me, when the rash mood's on.

SAME.

Reg. I pray you, father, being weak, seem so.
If, till the expiration of your month,
You will return and sojourn with my sister,
Dismissing half your train, come then to me;
I am now from home, and out of that provision,
Which shall be needful for your entertainment.
   Lear. Return to her, and fifty men dismiss'd ?
No, rather I abjure all roofs, and choose
To wage against the enmity o' the air;

To be a comrade with the wolf and owl,—
Necessity's sharp pinch!—Return with her?
Why, the hot-blooded France, that dowerless took
Our youngest born, I could as well be brought
To knee his throne, and, squire-like, pension beg
To keep base life a-foot:—Return with her?
Persuade me rather to be slave and sumpter
To this detested groom.

(Looking on the Steward.)

Gon. At your choice, sir.

Lear. I pr'ythee, daughter, do not make me
     mad;
I will not trouble thee, my child; farewell;
We'll no more meet, no more see one another:—
But yet thou art my flesh, my blood, my daughter;
Or, rather, a disease that's in my flesh,
Which I must needs call mine: thou art a boil,
A plague-sore, an embossed carbuncle,
In my corrupted blood. But I'll not chide thee;
Let shame come when it will, I do not call it:
I do not bid the thunder-bearer shoot,
Nor tell tales of thee to high-judging Jove:
Mend when thou canst; be better, at thy leisure:
I can be patient; I can stay with Regan,
I, and my hundred knights.

Reg. Not altogether so, sir;
I look'd not for you yet, nor am provided
For your fit welcome: Give ear, sir, to my sister;
For those that mingle reason with your passion,
Must be content to think you old, and so—
But she knows what she does.

Gon. Hear me, my lord,
What need you five and twenty, ten, or five,

To follow in a house, where twice so many
Have a command to tend you?

   Reg. What need one?

   Lear. O, reason not the need: our basest beggars
Are in the poorest thing superfluous:
Allow not nature more than nature needs,
Man's life is cheap as beast's: thou art a lady;
If only to go warm were gorgeous,
Why, nature needs not what thou gorgeous wear'st,
Which scarcely keeps the warm.—But, for true need,—
You heavens, give me that patience, patience I need!
You see me here, you gods, a poor old man,
As full of grief as age; wretched in both!
If it be you that stir these daughters' hearts
Against their father, fool me not so much
To bear it tamely; touch me with noble anger!
O, let not women's weapons, water-drops,
Stain my man's cheeks!—No, you unnatural hags.
I will have such revenges on you both,
That all the world shall—I will do such things,—
What they are, yet I know not; but they shall be
The terrors of the earth. You think I'll weep;
No, I'll not weep:—
I have full cause of weeping; but this heart
Shall break into a hundred thousand flaws,
Or ere I'll weep. O fool, I shall go mad!

ACT III.

Scene I.—*A Heath.*

A storm.

A storm is heard, with thunder and lightning. Enter KENT *and a*
Gentleman, *meeting.*

Kent. Who's here, beside foul weather?
Gent. One minded, like the weather, most unquietly.
Kent. I know you; where's the king?
Gent. Contending with the fretful elements:
Bids the wind blow the earth into the sea,
Or swell the curled waters 'bove the main,
That things might change, or cease: tears his white hair;
Which the impetuous blasts, with eyeless rage,
Catch in their fury, and make nothing of:
Strives in his little world of man to outscorn
The to-and-fro-coflicting wind and rain.
This night, wherein the cub-drawn bear would couch,
The lion and the belly-pinched wolf
Keep their fur dry, unbonneted he runs,
And bids what will take all.

Scene II.—*Another part of the Heath. Storm continues.*

King Lear in a storm.

Enter Lear *and* Fool.

Lear. Blow, winds, and crack your cheeks! rage! blow!
You cataracts and hurricanes, spout
Till you have drench'd our steeples, drown'd the cocks!
You sulphurous and thought-executing fires,
Vaunt-couriers to oak-cleaving thunder-bolts,
Singe my white head! and thou, all-shaking thunder,

Strike flat the thick rotundity o' the world!
Crack nature's moulds, all germins spill at once,
That make ingrateful man!

Fool. O nuncle, court holy-water in a dry house is better
than this rain-water out o' door. Good nuncle, in, and ask
thy daughter's blessing: here's a night pities neither wise
men nor fools.

Lear. Rumble thy bellyful! Spit, fire! spout, rain!
Nor rain, wind, thunder, fire, are my daughters:
I tax not you, you elements, with unkindness;
I never gave you kingdom, call'd you children,
You owe me no subscription; why then, let fall
Your horrible pleasure; here I stand, your slave,
A poor, infirm, weak, and despised old man:—
But yet I call you servile ministers,
That have with two pernicious daughters join'd
Your high engender'd battles, 'gainst a head
So old and white as this. O! O! 'tis foul!

DESCRIPTION OF A STORM.

Enter KENT.

Lear. No, I will be the pattern of all patience; I will say
nothing.

Kent. Who's there?

Fool. Marry, here's grace, and a cod-piece; that's a wise
man and a fool.

Kent. Alas, Sir, are you here? things that love night
Love not such nights as these; the wrathful skies
Gallow the very wanderers of the dark,
And make them keep their caves: since I was man,
Such sheets of fire, such bursts of horrid thunder,
Such groans of roaring wind and rain, I never

Remember to have heard: man's nature cannot carry
The affliction, nor the fear.

    Lear. Let the great gods,
That keep this dreadful pother o'er our heads,
Find out their enemies now. Tremble, thou wretch,
That hast within thee undivulged crimes,
Unwhipp'd of justice: hide thee, thou bloody hand;
Thou perjured, and thou simular man of virtue
That art incestuous: caitiff, to pieces shake,
That under covert and convenient seeming
Hast practised on man's life!—Close pent-up guilts,
Rive your concealing continents, and cry
These dreadful summoners grace.—I am a man
More sinn'd against than sinning.

CONTEMPTIBLE PERSECUTION.

    Lear. The little dogs and all,
Tray, Blanch, and Sweetheart, see, they bark at me.

SCENE VII.

THE DAUGHTERS' INGRATITUDE TO LEAR.

    Glo. Because I would not see thy cruel nails
Pluck out his poor eyes; nor thy fierce sister
In his anointed flesh stick boarish fangs.
The sea, with such a storm as his bare head
In hell-black night endured, would have buoy'd up,
And quench'd the stelled fires: yet, poor old heart,
He holp the heavens to rain.
If wolves had at thy gate howl'd that stern time,
Thou shouldst have said, *Good porter turn the key;*
All cruels else subscribed.—But I shall see
The winged vengeance overtake such children.

ACT IV—Scene II.

Goneril's ingratitude.

Alb. O Goneril?
You are not worth the dust which the rude wind
Blows in your face.—I fear your disposition:
That nature, which contemns its origin,
Cannot be border'd certain in itself;
She that herself will silver and disbranch
From her material sap, perforce must wither,
And come to deadly use.

Gon. No more; the text is foolish.

Alb. Wisdom and goodness to the vile seem vile:
Filths savour but themselves.   What have you done?
Tigers, not daughters, what have you performed?
A father, and a gracious aged man,
Whose reverence the head-lugg'd bear would lick,
Most barbarous, most degenerate ! have you madded.
Could my good brother suffer you to do it?
A man, a prince, by him so benefited?
If that the heavens do not their visible spirits
Send quickly down to tame these vile offences,
'Twill come,
Humanity must perforce prey on itself,
Like monsters of the deep.

Alb. Thou changed and self-cover'd thing, for shame,
Be-monster not thy feature.   Were it my fitness
To let these hands obey my blood,
They are apt enough to dislocate and tear
Thy flesh and bones:—howe'er thou art a fiend,
A woman's shape doth shield thee.

Scene III.

Cordelia's sorrow for her father.

Kent. Did your letters pierce the queen to any demon-
stration of grief?

 Gent. Ay, sir; she took them, read them in my
    presence;
And now and then an ample tear trill'd down
Her delicate cheek: it seem'd she was a queen
Over her passion; who, most rebel-like,
Sought to be king o'er her.

 Kent. O, then it moved her.

 Gent. Not to a rage: patience and sorrow
    strove
Who should express her goodliest. You have
    seen
Sunshine and rain at once; her smiles and
    tears
Were like a better day: Those happy smiles,
That play'd on her ripe lip, seem'd not to know
What guests were in her eyes; which parted
    thence,
As pearls from diamonds dropp'd.—In brief, sorrow
Would be a rarity most beloved, if all
Could so become it.

 Kent. Made she no verbal question?

 Gent. 'Faith, once or twice she heaved the name
    of *father*
Pantingly forth, as if it pressed her heart;
Cried, *Sisters! sisters! Shame of ladies! sisters!*
Kent! father! sisters! What? i' the storm? i' the
    night?

Let pity not be believed!—There she shook
The holy water from her heavenly eyes,
And clamour moisten'd: then away she started
To deal with grief alone.

    Kent. It is the stars,
The stars above us, govern our conditions;
Else one self mate and mate could not beget
Such different issues. You spoke not with her
      since ?

    Gent. No.

    Kent. Was this before the king return'd ?

    Gent. No, since.

    Kent. Well, sir; the poor distressed Lear is i' the
      town:
Who sometime, in his better tune, remembers
What we are come about, and by no means
Will yield to see his daughter.

    Gent. Why, good sir ?

    Kent. A sovereign shame so elbows him: his own
      unkindness.
That stripp'd her from his benediction, turn'd her
To foreign casualities, gave her dear rights
To his dog-hearted daughters,—these things
      sting
His mind so venomously, that burning shame
Detains him from Cordelia.

Scene IV.

Cordelia's anxiety for her father.

Enter Cordelia, Physician, *and* Soldiers.

    Cor. Alack, 'tis he: why, he was met even now
As mad as the vex'd sea; singing aloud;

7

Crown'd with rank fumiter, and furrow weeds,
With harlocks, hemlock, nettles, cuckoo-flowers,
Darnel, and all the idle weeds that grow
In our sustaining corn.—A century send forth;
Search every acre in the high-grown field,
And bring him to our eye.—   [*Exit an Officer.*
What can man's wisdom do
In the restoring his bereaved sense?
He that helps him take all my outward worth.

   Phys. There is means, Madam:
Our foster-nurse of nature is repose,
The which he lacks; and to provoke in him,
Are many simples operative, whose power
Will close the eye of anguish.

   Cor. All bless'd secrets,
All you unpublish'd virtues of the earth,
Spring with my tears! be aidant and remediate
In the good man's distress!—Seek, seek for him;
Lest his ungovern'd rage dissolve the life
That wants the means to lead it.

Scene VI.

A cliff.

   Edg. Come on, Sir; here's the place: stand still.—
And dizzy 'tis to cast one's eye so low! [How fearful
The crows and choughs, that wing the midway air,
Shew scarce so gross as beetles: half way down
Hangs one that gathers samphire,—dreadful trade!
Methinks he seems no bigger than his head:
The fishermen that walk upon the beach
Appear like mice;
Almost too small for sight: the murmuring surge

That on the unnumber'd idle pebbles chafes,
Cannot be heard so high.—I'll look no more,
Lest my brain turn, and the deficient sight
Topple down headlong.

LEAR'S RAVINGS OF **GOLD'S** POWER OVER JUSTICE

Lear. **What, art mad?** A man may see how this world
goes, with no eyes. Look with thine **ears: see** how yon
justice rails upon yon simple thief. **Hark, in** thine **ear:**
change places; and, handy-dandy, which **is** the **justice,**
which is the thief?—Thou hast seen a farmer's dog bark at a
beggar?

Glo. Ay, Sir.

Lear. And the creature run from the cur? **There** thou
mightst behold the great image of authority: a dog's obeyed
in office.—

The usurer hangs the
cozener.
Through tatter'd **clothes small** vices do appear;
Robes and furr'd gowns hide all. Plate sin with gold,
And the strong **lance of** justice hurtless breaks;
Arm it in **rags,** a pigmy's straw doth **pierce it.**
None does offend, **none,—I say, none;** I'll able 'em:
Take that of me, my friend, who have the power
To seal the accuser's lips. Get thee glass eyes;
And, like a scurvy politician, **seem**
To see the things thou dost not.—Now, now, now, now;
Pull off my boots:—Harder, harder; so.

Edg. O, matter and impertinency mix'd!
Reason in madness!

Scene VII.

Cordelia's warm affection.

Cor. O my dear father! Restoration, hang
Thy medicine on my lips; and let this kiss
Repair those violent harms that my two sisters
Have in thy reverence made!

Kent. Kind and dear princess!

Cor. Had you not been their father, these white flakes
Had challenged pity of them. Was this a face
To be exposed against the warring winds?
To stand against the deep dread-bolted thunder?
In the most terrible and nimble stroke
Of quick, cross lightning? to watch (poor perdu!)
With this thin helm? Mine enemy's dog,
Though he had bit me, should have stood that night
Against my fire; and wast thou fain, poor father,
To hovel thee with swine and rogues forlorn,
In short and musty straw? Alack, alack!
'Tis wonder that thy life and wits at once
Had not concluded all.—He wakes; speak to him.

Phys. Madam, do you; 'tis fittest.

Cor. How does my royal lord? How fares your majesty?

Lear. You do me wrong, to take me out 'o the grave:—
Thou art a soul in bliss; but I am bound
Upon a wheel of fire, that mine own tears
Do scald like molten lead.

JULIUS CÆSAR.

ACT I.—Scene I.

Brutus and Cassius' views of Cæsar.

Bru. What means this shouting?   I do fear, the people
Choose Cæsar for their king.
   Cas. Ay, do you fear it?
Then must I think you would not have it so.
   Bru. I would not, Cassius; yet I love him well:—
But wherefore do you hold me here so long?
What is that you would impart to me?
If it be aught toward the general good,
Set honour in one eye, and death i' the other,
And I will look on both indifferently:
For, let the gods so speed me, as I love
The name of honour more than I fear death.
   Cas I know that virtue to be in you, Brutus,
As well as I do know your outward favour.
Well, honour is the subject of my story—
I cannot tell, what you and other men
Think of this life; but, for my single self,
I had as lief not be, as live to be
In awe of such a thing as I myself.
I was born free as Cæsar; so were you:

We both have fed as well; and we can both
Endure the winter's cold, as well as he.
For once, upon a raw and gusty day,
The troubled Tiber chafing with her shores,
Cæsar said to me, *Dar'st thou, Cassius, now*
Leap in with me into this angry flood,
And swim to yonder point?—Upon the word,
Accouter'd as I was, I plunged in,
And bade him follow: so, indeed, he did.
The torrent roared; and we did buffet it
With lusty sinews; throwing it aside
And stemming it with hearts of controversy.
But ere we could arrive the point proposed,
Cæsar cried, *Help me, Cassius, or I sink.*
I, as Æneas, our great ancestor,
Did from the flames of Troy upon his shoulder
The old Anchises bear, so, from the waves of Tiber
Did I the tired Cæsar: And this man
Is now become a god; and Cassius is
A wretched creature, and must bend his body,
If Cæsar carelessly but nod on him.
He had a fever when he was in Spain,
And, when the fit was on him, I did mark
How he did shake: 'tis true, this god did shake:
His coward lips did from their colour fly;
And that same eye, whose bend doth awe the
             world,
Did lose his lustre: I did hear him groan:
Ay, and that tongue of his, that bade the Romans
Mark him, and write his speeches in their books,
Alas! it cried, *Give me some drink, Titinius,*
As a sick girl. Ye gods, it doth amaze me,
A man of such a feeble temper should

So get the start of the majestic world,
And bear the palm alone.   .   (*Shout. Flourish.*)
   Bru. Another general shout!
I do believe, that these applauses are
For some new honours that are heap'd on Cæsar.
   Cas. Why, man, he doth bestride the narrow
        world,
Like a Colossus, and we petty men
Walk under his huge legs, and peep about
To find ourselves dishonourable graves.
Men at some time are masters of their fates:
The fault, dear Brutus, is not in our stars,
But in ourselves, that we are underlings.
Brutus, and Cæsar: What should be in that Cæsar?
Why should that name be sounded more than
        yours?
Write them together, yours is as fair a name;
Sound them, it doth become the mouth as well;
Weigh them, it is as heavy; conjure with them,
Brutus will start a spirit as soon as Cæsar.   (*Shout.*)
Now in the names of all the gods at once,
Upon what meat doth this our Cæsar feed,
That he is grown so great? Age, thou art ashamed!
Rome, thou hast lost the breed of noble bloods!
When went there by an age, since the great flood,
But it was famed with more than with one man:
When could they say, till now, that talk'd of Rome,
That her wide walks encompass'd but one man?
Now is it Rome indeed, and room enough,
When there is in it but one only man.
O! you and I have heard our fathers say,
There was a Brutus once, that would have brook'd
The eternal devil to keep his state in Rome,
As easily as a king.

Scene II.

Cæsar's caution against Cassius.

Bru. The games are done, and Cæsar is returning.

Cas. As they pass by, pluck Casca by the sleeve;
And he will, after his sour fashion, tell you
What hath proceeded, worthy note, to-day.

Bru. I will do so:—but, look you, Cassius,
The angry spot doth glow on Cæsar's brow,
And all the rest look like a chidden train:
Calphurnia's cheek is pale; and Cicero
Looks with such ferret and such fiery eyes,
As we have seen him in the Capitol,
Being cross'd in conference by some senators.

Cas. Casca will tell us what the matter is.

Cæs. Antonius.

Ant. Cæsar.

Cæs. Let me have men about me that are fat;
Sleek-headed men, and such as sleep o'nights:
Yond Cassius has a lean and hungry look;
He thinks too much: such men are dangerous.

Ant. Fear him not, Cæsar, he's not dangerous;
He is a noble Roman, and well given.

Cæs. 'Would he were fatter:—But I fear him
　　　　not:
Yet if my name were liable to fear,
I do not know the man I should avoid,
So soon as that spare Cassius. He reads much;
He is a great observer, and he looks
Quite through the deeds of men: he loves no plays,
As thou dost, Antony; he hears no music;
Seldom he smiles; and smiles in such a sort,

As if he mock'd himself, and scorn'd his spirit
That could be moved to smile at any thing.
Such men as he be never at heart's ease,
Whiles they behold a greater than themselves;
And therefore are **they very dangerous.**
I rather tell thee what is to be fear'd,
Than what I fear; for always I am Cæsar.
Come on my right hand, for this ear is deaf,
And tell me truly what thou think'st of him.

SCENE III.—*The same.* **A Street.**

EVIL OMENS ABOUT CÆSAR.

Thunder and lightning. *Enter from opposite sides,* CASCA, *with his sword drawn and* CICERO.

Cic. Good even, Casca: Brought you Cæsar
  home?
Why are you breathless? and why stare you so?
  Casca. Are not you moved, when all the sway of
    earth
Shakes like a thing unfirm? O Cicero,
I have seen tempests, when the scolding winds
Have rived the knotty oaks; and I have seen
The ambitious ocean swell, and rage, and foam,
To be exalted with the threat'ning clouds:
But never till to-night, never till **now,**
Did I go through a tempest dropping fire.
Either there is a **civil** strife in heaven;
Or else the world, too saucy with the gods,
Incenses them to send destruction   .
  Cic Why, saw you anything more wonderful?
  Casca. A common slave (you know him well by
    sight)

Held up his left hand, which did flame and burn
Like twenty torches, join'd; and yet his hand,
Not sensible of fire, remain'd unscorch'd.
Besides, (I have not since put up my sword,)
Against the Capitol I met a lion,
Who glared upon me, and went surly by,
Without annoying me: and there were drawn
Upon a heap a hundred ghastly women,
Transformed with their fear; who swore, they saw
Men, all in fire, walk up and down the streets.
And, yesterday, the bird of night did sit,
Even at noon-day, upon the market-place,
Hooting and shrieking.   When these prodigies
Do so conjointly meet, let not men say,
These are their reasons,—They are natural;
For, I believe, they are portentous things
Unto the climate that they point upon.

  Cic. Indeed, it is a strange-disposed time:
But men may construe things after their fashion,
Clean from the purpose of the things themselves.
Comes Cæsar to the Capitol to-morrow?

  Casca. He doth; for he did bid Antonius
Send word to you, he would be there to-morrow.

  Cic. Good night then, Casca: this disturbed sky
Is not to walk in.

  Casca. Farewell, Cicero.   [*Exit Cicero.*

ACT II.—SCENE I.

AMBITIOUS INGRATITUDE.

                        But 'tis a common proof,
That lowliness is young ambition's ladder,
Whereto the climber upward turns his face:

But when he once attains the upmost round,
He then unto the ladder turns his back,
Looks in the clouds, scorning the base degrees
By which he did ascend.

SUFFERINGS OE UNCERTAINTY.

Bru. 'Tis good.   Go to the gate; somebody knocks.
Since Cassius first did whet me against Cæsar,
I have not slept.
Between the acting of a dreadful thing
.And the first motion, all the interim is
Like a phantasma, or a hideous dream:
The Genius and the mortal instruments
Are then in council; and the state of man,
Like to a little kingdom, suffers then
The nature of an insurrection.

PORTENTOUS SIGNS OF EVIL.

Cal. Cæsar, I never stood on ceremonies,
Yet now they fright me.   There is one within,
Besides the things that we have heard and seen,
Recounts most horrid sights seen by the watch.
And graves have yawn'd, and yielded up their dead:
Fierce fiery warriors fought upon the clouds,
In ranks, and squadrons, and right form of war,
Which drizzled blood upon the Capitol:
The noise of battle hurtled in the air,
Horses did neigh, and dying men did groan;
And ghosts did shriek, and squeal about the streets.
O Cæsar! these things are beyond all use,
And I do fear them.

ACT III.—Scene I.

Cæsar's resolution.

Met. Most high, most mighty, and most puissant
     Cæsar,
Metellus Cimber throws before thy seat
In humble heart:—   (*Kneeling.*)
  Cæs. I must prevent thee, Cimber.
These couchings, and these lowly courtesies,
Might fire the blood of ordinary men;
And turn pre-ordinance, and first decree,
Into the law of children. Be not fond,
To think that Cæsar bears such rebel blood,
That will be thaw'd from the true quality
With that which melteth fools; I mean, sweet
        words.
Low-crooked curt'sies, and base spaniel fawning.
Thy brother by decree is banished;
If thou dost bend, and pray, and fawn for him,
I spurn thee like a cur out of my way.
Know, Cæsar doth not wrong; nor without cause
Will he be satisfied.
  Met. Is there no voice more worthy than my own,
To sound more sweetly in great Cæsar's ear,
For the repealing of my banish'd brother?
  Bru. I kiss thy hand, but not in flattery, Cæsar;
Desiring thee, that Publius Cimber may
Have an immediate freedom of repeal.
  Cæs. What, Brutus!
  Cas. Pardon, Cæsar; Cæsar, pardon
As low as to thy foot doth Cassius fall,
To beg enfranchisement for Publius Cimber.

Cæs. I could be well moved, if I were as you;
If I could pray to move, prayers would move me:
But I am constant as the northern star,
Of whose true-fix'd, and resting quality,
There is no fellow in the firmament.
The skies are painted with unnumber'd sparks,
They are all fire, and every one doth shine;
But there's but one in all doth **hold his place:**
So, in the world,   'Tis furnish'd well with men;
And men are flesh and blood, and apprehensive;
Yet, in the number, I do know but one.

CONVERSATIONS OF BRUTUS, CASSIUS AND ANTONY OVER CÆSAR'S
DEATH.

Re-enter ANTONY.

Bru. But here comes Antony.—Welcome, Mark
    Antony.
Ant. O mighty Cæsar ! Dost thou lie so low ?
Are all thy conquests, glories, triumphs, spoils,
Shrunk to this little measure ?—Fare thee well.—
I know not, gentlemen, what you intend,
Who else must be let blood, who else is rank:
If I myself, there is no hour so fit
As Cæsar's death hour; nor no instrument
Of half that worth as those your swords, made
    rich
With the most noble blood of all this world.
I do beseech ye, if ye bear me hard,
Now, whilst your purple hands do reek and smoke,
Fulfil your pleasure.   Live a thousand years,
I shall not find myself so apt to die:
No place will please me so, no mean of death,

As here by Cæsar, and by you cut off,
The choice and master spirits of this age.

Bru. O Antony! beg not your death of us,
Though now we must appear bloody and cruel,
As, by our hands, and this our present act,
You see we do; yet see you but our hands,
And this the bleeding business they have done:
Our hearts you see not, they are pitiful;
And pity to the general wrong of Rome
(As fire drives out fire, so pity, pity,)
Hath done this deed on Cæsar.   For your part,
To you our swords have leaden points, Mark
            Antony:
Our arms, in strength of malice, and our hearts,
Of brothers' temper, do receive you in
With all kind love, good thoughts, and reverence.

Cas. Your voice shall be as strong as any man's
In the disposing of new dignities.

Bru. Only be patient, till we have appeased
The multitude, beside themselves with fear,
And then we will deliver you the cause,
Why I, that did love Cæsar when I struck him,
Have thus proceeded.

Ant. I doubt not of your wisdom.
Let each man render me his bloody hand:
First, Marcus Brutus, will I shake with you;—
Next, Caius Cassius, do I take your hand;—
Now, Decius Brutus, yours:—now yours, Metellus;
Yours, Cinna;—and, my valiant Casca, yours;—
Though last, not least in love, yours, good
            Trebonius.
Gentlemen, all,—alas! what shall I say?
My credit now stands on such slippery ground,

That one of two bad ways you must conceit me,
Either a coward or a flatterer.--
That I did love thee, Cæsar, O, 'tis true:
If then thy spirit look upon us now,
Shall it not grieve thee, dearer than thy death,
To see thy Antony making his peace,
Shaking the bloody fingers of thy foes,
Most noble! in the presence of thy corse?
Had I as many eyes as thou hast wounds,
Weeping as fast as they stream forth thy blood,
It would become me better, than to close
In terms of friendship with thine enemies.
Pardon me, Julius!— Here wast thou bay'd, brave
        hart:
Here didst thou fall; and here thy hunters stand,
Sign'd in thy spoil, and crimson'd in thy lethe.
O world! thou wast the forest to this hart;
And this, indeed, O world, the heart of thee.—
How like a deer, stricken by many princes,
Dost thou here lie!

ANTONY'S APOSTROPHE AND PROPHESY TO CÆSAR'S BODY.

Bru. Prepare the body then, and follow us.
                     [*Exeunt all but* ANTONY.
  Ant. O, pardon me, thou piece of bleeding earth,
That I am meek and gentle with these butchers!
Thou art the ruins of the noblest man
That ever lived in the tide of times.
Woe to the hand that shed this costly blood!
Over thy wounds now do I prophesy,—
Which, like dumb mouths, do ope their ruby lips,
To beg the voice and utterance of my tongue,—

A curse shall light upon the limbs of men;
Domestic fury and fierce civil strife
Shall cumber all the parts of Italy;
Blood and destruction shall be so in use,
And dreadful objects so familiar.

Scene II.

Brutus' oration over Cæsar's body.

3 Cit. The noble Brutus is ascended: silence!

Bru. Be patient till the last.

Romans, countrymen, and lovers! hear me for my cause; and be silent, that you may hear: believe me for mine honour; and have respect to mine honour, that you may believe: censure me in your wisdom; and awake your senses, that you may the better judge. If there be any in this assembly, any dear friend of Cæsar's, to him I say, that Brutus' love to Cæsar was no less than his. If then that friend demand why Brutus rose against Cæsar, this is my answer,—not that I loved Cæsar less, but that I loved Rome more. Had you rather Cæsar was living, and die all slaves; than that Cæsar were dead, to live all free men? As Cæsar loved me, I weep for him; as he was fortunate, I rejoice at it; as he was valiant, I honour him: but, as he was ambitious, I slew him: there are tears for his love; joy for his fortune; honour for his valor; and death for his ambition. Who is here so base, that would be a bondsman? If any, speak; for him have I offended. Who is here so rude, that would not be a Roman? If any, speak; for him have I offended. Who is here so vile, that will not love his country? If any, speak; for him have I offended. I pause for a reply.

Cit. None, Brutus, none. [*Several speaking at once.*

Bru. Then none have I offended. I have done no more to Cæsar, than you should do to Brutus. The question of his death is enrolled in the Capitol: his glory not extenuated, wherein he was worthy; nor his offences enforced, for which he suffered death.

Enter ANTONY *and others, with* CÆSAR's *body.*

Here comes his body, mourned by Mark Antony: who, though he had no hand in his death, shall receive the benefit of his dying, a place in the commonwealth; as which of you shall not? With this I depart,—that, as I slew my best lover for the good of Rome, I have the same dagger for myself, when it shall please my country to need my death.

Cit. Live, Brutus! live, live!

1 *Cit.* Bring him with triumph home unto his house.

2 *Cit.* Give him a statue with his ancestors.

3 *Cit.* Let him be Cæsar.

4 *Cit.* Cæsar's better parts
Shall now be crown'd in Brutus.

1 *Cit.* We'll bring him to his house with shouts and
clamours.

Bru. My countrymen,—

2 *Cit.* Peace, silence! Brutus speaks.

1 *Cit.* Peace, ho!

Bru. Good countrymen, let me depart alone,
And, for my sake, stay here with Antony:
Do grace to Cæsar's corse, and grace his speech
Tending to Cæsar's glories; which Mark Antony,
By our permission, is allow'd to make.
I do entreat you, not a man depart,
Save I alone, till Antony have spoke. [*Exit.*

1 *Cit.* Stay, ho! and let us hear Mark Antony.

8

3 *Cit.* Let him go up into the public chair;
We'll hear him.—Noble Antony, go up.

 Ant. For Brutus' sake, I am beholden to you.

 4 *Cit.* What does he say of Brutus?

 3 *Cit.* He says, for Brutus' sake,
He finds himself beholden to us all.

 4 *Cit.* 'Twere best he speak no harm of Brutus here.

 1 *Cit.* This Cæsar was a tyrant.

 3 *Cit.* Nay, that's certain:
We are bless'd that Rome is rid of him.

 2 *Cit.* Peace! let us hear what Antony can say.

 Ant. You gentle Romans,—

 Cit. Peace, ho! let us hear him.

 Ant. Friends, Romans, countrymen, lend me yours ears;
I come to bury Cæsar, not to praise him.
The evil that men do lives after them;
The good is oft interred with their bones;
So let it be with Cæsar.   The noble Brutus
Hath told you Cæsar was ambitious:
If it were so, it was a grievous fault;
And grievously hath Cæsar answer'd it.
Here, under leave of Brutus and the rest,
(For Brutus is an honourable man;
So are they all, all honourable men;)
Come I to speak in Cæsar's funeral.
He was my friend, faithful and just to me:
But Brutus says he was ambitious;
And Brutus is an honourable man.
He hath brought many captives home to Rome,
Whose ransoms did the general coffers fill:
Did this in Cæsar seem ambitious?
When that the poor have cried, Cæsar hath wept;
Ambition should be made of sterner stuff:

Yet Brutus says he was ambitious;
And Brutus is an honourable man.
You all did see that on the Lupercal
I thrice presented him a kingly crown,
Which he did thrice refuse.   Was this ambition ?
Yet Brutus says he was ambitious;
And, sure, he is an honourable man.
I speak not to disprove what Brutus spoke,
But here I am to speak what I do know.
You all did love him once,—not without cause;
What cause withholds you, then, to mourn for him?
O judgment, thou art fled **to brutish beasts,**
And men have lost their reason!—Bear;with me:
My heart is in the coffin there with Cæsar,
And I must pause till it come back to me.

   1 *Cit.* Methinks there is much reason in his sayings.

   2 *Cit.* If thou consider rightly of the matter,
Cæsar has had great wrong.

   3 *Cit.* Has he, masters?
I fear there will a worse come in his place.

   4 *Cit.* Mark'd ye his words? He would not take the crown;
Therefore 'tis certain he was not ambitious.

   1 *Cit.* If it be found so, some will dear abide it.

   2 *Cit.* **Poor** soul! his eyes are red as fire with weeping.

   3 *Cit.* There's not a nobler man in Rome than Antony.

   4 *Cit.* Now mark him, he begins again to speak.

   Ant. But yesterday, the word of Cæsar might
Have stood **against the world: now lies** he there,
And none so poor to do him reverence.
O masters! if I were disposed to stir
Your hearts and minds to mutiny and rage,
I should do Brutus wrong, and Cassius wrong,
Who, you all know, are honourable men:

I will not do them wrong; I rather choose
To wrong the dead, to wrong myself, and you,
Than I will wrong such honourable men.
But here's a parchment, with the seal of Cæsar,
I found it in his closet, 'tis his will:
Let but the commons hear this testament.
(Which, pardon me, I do not mean to read,)
And they would go and kiss dead Cæsar's wounds,
And dip their napkins in his sacred blood;
Yea, beg a hair of him for memory,
And, dying, mention it within their wills,
Bequeathing it, as a rich legacy,
Unto their issue.

    4 Cit. We'll hear the will: Read it, Mark Antony.
    Cit. The will, the will; we will hear Cæsar's
        will.
    Ant. Have patience, gentle friends, I must not
        read it;
It is not meet you know how Cæsar loved you.
You are not wood, you are not stones, but men;
And, being men, hearing the will of Cæsar,
It will inflame you, it will make you mad:
'Tis good you know not that you are his heirs,
For if you should, O, what would come of it!

    4 Cit. Read the will; we will hear it, Antony:
You shall read us the will; Cæsar's will.
    Ant. Will you be patient? Will you stay a
        while?
I have o'ershot myself, to tell you of it.
I fear, I wrong the honourable men,
Whose daggers have stabb'd Cæsar: I do fear it.

    4 Cit. They were traitors: Honourable men!
    Cit. The will! the testament!
    2 Cit. They were villains, murderers: The will! read the
will!

Ant. You will compel me then to read the will?
Then make a ring about the corpse of Cæsar,
And let me shew you him that made the will.
Shall I descend? And will you give me leave?
  Cit. Come down.
  2 *Cit.* Descend.   (*He comes down from the pulpit.*)
  3 *Cit.* You shall have leave.
  4 *Cit.* A ring; stand round.
  1 *Cit.* Stand from the hearse, stand from the
      body.
  2 *Cit.* Room for Antony;—most noble Antony.
  Ant. Nay, press not so upon me; stand far off.
  Cit. Stand back! room! bear back!
  Ant. If you have tears, prepare to shed them
      now.
You all do know this mantle: I remember
The first time ever Cæsar put it on;
'Twas on a summer's evening, in his tent;
That day he overcame the Nervii:—
Look! In this place ran Cassius' dagger through:
See, what a rent the envious Casca made:
Through this, the well-beloved Brutus stabb'd;
And, as he pluck'd his cursed steel away,
Mark how the blood of Cæsar follow'd it;
As rushing out of doors, to be resolved
If Brutus so unkindly knock'd, or no;
For Brutus, as you know, was Cæsar's angel:
Judge, O you gods, how dearly Cæsar loved him!
This was the most unkindest cut of all:
For when the noble Cæsar saw him stab,
Ingratitude, more strong than traitors' arms,
Quite vanquish'd him: then burst his mighty heart;
And, in his mantle muffling up his face,

Even at the base of Pompey's statua,
Which all the while ran blood, great Cæsar fell.
O, what a fall was there, my countrymen!
Then I, and you, and all of us fell down,
Whilst bloody treason flourish'd over us.
O, now you weep; and, I perceive, you feel
The dint of pity: these are gracious drops.
Kind souls, what, weep you, when you but behold
Our Cæsar's vesture wounded? Look you here,
Here is himself, marr'd, as you see, with traitors.

Same.

Good friends, sweet friends, let me not stir you up
To such a sudden flood of mutiny.
They that have done this deed are honourable;—
What private griefs they have, alas, I know not,
That made them do it;—they are wise and honourable,
And will, no doubt, with reasons answer you.
I come not, friends, to steal away your hearts:
I am no orator, as Brutus is;
But, as you know me all, a plain blunt man,
That love my friend; and that they know full well
That gave me public leave to speak of him:
For I have neither wit, nor words, nor worth,
Action, nor utterance, nor the power of speech,
To stir men's blood: I only speak right on;
I tell you that which you yourselves do know;
Shew you sweet Cæsar's wounds, poor, poor dumb mouths
And bid them speak for me: but were I Brutus,
And Brutus Antony, there were an Antony
Would ruffle up your spirits, and put a tongue
In every wound of Cæsar, that should move
The stones of Rome to rise and mutiny.

ACT IV.—Scene II.

False ceremony in love.

Bru. Thou has described
A hot friend cooling: ever note, Lucilius,
When love begins to sicken and decay,
It useth an enforced ceremony.
There are no tricks in plain and simple faith:
But hollow men, like horses hot at hand,
Make gallant show and promise of their mettle;
But when they should endure the bloody spur,
They fall their crests, and, like deceitful jades,
Sink in the trial.

Scene III.

Brutus' defiance.

Bru. Remember March, the ides of March remember:
Did not great Julius bleed for justice's sake?
What villain touch'd his body, that did stab,
And not for justice? What, shall one of us,
That struck the foremost man of all this world,
But for supporting robbers,—shall we now
Contaminate our fingers with base bribes?
And sell the mighty space of our large honours,
For so much trash as may be grasped thus?—
I had rather be a dog, and bay the moon,
Than such a Roman.

Anger and reconciliation of Cassius and Brutus.

Bru. You have done that you should be sorry for.
There is no terror, Cassius, in your threats;
For I am arm'd so strong in honesty,

That they pass by me as the idle wind,
Which I respect not.   I did send to you
For certain sums of gold, which you denied me;—
For I can raise no money by vile means:
By heaven, I had rather coin my heart,
And drop my blood for drachmas, than to wring
From the hard hands of peasants their vile trash,
By any indirection.   I did send
To you for gold to pay my legions.
Which you denied me;   Was that done like Cassius?
Should I have answer'd Caius Cassius so?
When Marcus Brutus grows so covetous,
To lock such rascal counters from his friends,
Be ready, gods, with all your thunderbolts,
Dash him to pieces.

   Cas. I denied you not.

   Bru. You did.

   Cas. I did not:—he was but a fool,
That brought my answer back.—Brutus hath rived
      my heart:
A friend should bear his friend's infirmities,
But Brutus makes mine greater than they are.

   Bru. I do not, till you practise them on me.

   Cas. You love me not.

   Bru. I do not like your faults.

   Cas. A friendly eye would never see such faults.

   Bru. A flatterer's would not, though they do
      appear
As huge as high Olympus.

   Cas. Come, Antony, and young Octavius, come,
Revenge yourselves alone on Cassius,
For Cassius is a-weary of the world:
Hated by one he loves; braved by his brother;

Check'd like a bondman; all his faults observed,
Set in a note-book, learn'd and conn'd by rote,
To cast into my teeth. O, I could weep
My spirit from mine eyes!—There is my dagger,
And here my naked breast; within, a heart
Dearer than Plutus' mine, richer than gold:
If that thou be'st a Roman, take it forth;
I, that denied thee gold, will give my heart:
Strike, as thou didst at Cæsar; for, I know,
When thou didst hate him worst, thou lov'dst him
            better
Than ever thou lov'dst Cassius.
 Bru. Sheathe your dagger:
Be angry when you will, it shall have scope;
Do what you will, dishonour shall be humour.
O Cassius, you are yoked with a lamb,
That carries anger, as the flint bears fire;
Who, much enforced, shews a hasty spark,
And straight is cold again.
 Cas. Hath Cassius lived
To be but mirth and laughter to his Brutus,
When grief, and blood ill-temper'd, vexeth him?
 Bru. When I spoke that, I was ill-temper'd too.
 Cas. Do you confess so much? Give me your hand.
 Bru. And my heart too.
 Cas. O Brutus!—
 Bru. What's the matter?
 Cas. Have you not love enough to bear with me,
When that rash humour, which my mother gave me,
Makes me forgetful?
 Bru. Yes, Cassius; and, henceforth,
When you are over-earnest with your Brutus,
He'll think your mother chides, and leave you so.

FORTUNE'S FLOODS AND SHALLOWS.

Bru. Well, to our work alive.—What do you think
Of marching to Philippi presently?

Cas. I do not think it good.

Bru. Your reason?

Cas. This it is:
'Tis better that the enemy seek us:
So shall he waste his means, weary his soldiers,
Doing himself offence; whilst we, lying still,
Are full of rest, defence, and nimbleness.

Bru. Good reasons must, of force, give place to better.
The people 'twixt Philippi and this ground
Do stand but in a forced affection;
For they have grudged us contribution:
The enemy, marching along by them,
By them shall make a fuller number up,
Come on refresh'd, new-added, and encouraged;
From which advantage shall we cut him off,
If at Philippi we do face him there,
These people at our back.

Cas. Hear me, good brother,—

Bru. Under your pardon.—You must note beside,
That we have tried the utmost of our friends;
Our legions are brim-full, our cause is ripe:
The enemy increaseth every day;
We, at the height, are ready to decline.
There is a tide in the affairs of men,
Which, taken at the flood, leads on to fortune;
Omitted, all the voyage of their life
Is bound in shallows and in miseries.
On such a full sea are we now afloat;
And we must take the current when it serves,
Or lose our ventures.

CÆSAR'S GHOST APPEARS TO BRUTUS.

[*He sits down.*]

Enter the Ghost of CÆSAR.

How ill this taper burns!—Ha! who comes here?
I think it is the weakness of mine eyes,
That shapes this monstrous apparition.
It comes upon me:—Art thou any thing?
Art thou some god, some angel, or some devil,
That makest my blood cold, and my hair to stare?
Speak to me, what thou art.
   Ghost. Thy evil spirit, Brutus.
   Bru. Why comest thou?
   Ghost. To tell thee, thou shalt see me at Philippi.
   Bru. Well;
Then I shall see thee again?
   Ghost. Ay, at Philippi.

ACT V.—SCENE I.

ANTONY'S ELOQUENCE.

   Ant. In your bad strokes, Brutus, you give good
      words:
Witness the hole you made in Cæsar's heart,
Crying, *Long live! hail, Cæsar!*
   Cas. Antony,
The posture of your blows are yet unknown;
But for your words, they rob the Hybla bees,
And leave them honeyless.
   Ant. Not stingless too.
   Bru. O, yes, and soundless too;
For you have stolen their buzzing, Antony,
And very wisely, threat before you sting.

EVIL OMENS TO CASSIUS.

Cas. Why now, blow, wind; swell, billow; and swim,
The storm is up, and all is on the hazzard.   [bark!
   Bru. Ho,
Lucilius! hark, a word with you.
   Lucil. My lord? [BRUTUS *and* LUCILIUS *converse apart.*
   Cas. Messala,—
   Mes. What says my general?
   Cas. Messala,
This is my birthday; as this very day
Was Cassius born. Give me thy hand, Messala:
Be thou my witness, that, against my will,
As Pompey was, am I compell'd to set
Upon one battle all our liberties.
You know that I held Epicurus strong,
And his opinion: now I change my mind,
And partly credit things that do presage.
Coming from Sardis, on our former ensign
Two mighty eagles fell; and there they perch'd,
Gorging and feeding from our soldiers' hands;
Who to Philippi here consorted us:
This morning are they fled away and gone;
And in their steads do ravens, crows, and kites
Fly o'er our heads, and downward look on us,
As we were sickly prey: their shadows seem
A canopy most fatal, under which
Our army lies, ready to give up the ghost.
   Mes. Believe not so.
   Cas. I but believe it partly;
For I am fresh of spirit, and resolved
To meet all perils very constantly.
   Bru. Even so, Lucilius.

Cas. Now, most noble Brutus,
The gods to-day stand friendly, that we may,
Lovers in peace, lead on our days to age!
But, since the affairs of men rest still uncertain,
Let's reason with the worst that may befall.
If we do lose this battle, then is this
The very last time we shall speak together·
What are you, then, determined to do?

Bru. Even by the rule of that philosophy,
By which I did blame Cato for the death
Which he did give himself:—I know not how,
But I do find it cowardly and vile,
For fear of what might fall, so to prevent
The time of life:—arming myself with patience,
To stay the providence of some high powers
That govern us below.

Cas. Then, if we lose this battle,
You are contented to be led in triumph
Through the streets of Rome?

Bru. No, Cassius, no: think not, thou noble Roman,
That ever Brutus will go bound to Rome;
He bears too great a mind. But this same day
Must end that work the ides of March begun;
And whether we shall meet again, I know not.

Scene III.

Death of Cassius.

Re-enter TITINIUS, *with* MESSALA.

Mes. It is but change, Titinius; for Octavius
Is overthrown by noble Brutus' power,
As Cassius' legions are by Antony.

Tit. These tidings will well comfort Cassius.

Mes. Where did you leave him?

Tit. All disconsolate,
With Pindarus, his bondman, on this hill.

   Mes. Is not that he, that lies upon the ground?

   Tit. He lies not like the living. O my heart!

   Mes. Is not that he?

   Tit. No, this was he, Messala,
But Cassius is no more.—O setting sun!
As in thy red rays thou dost sink to-night,
So in his red blood Cassius' day is set;
The sun of Rome is set; Our day is gone;
Clouds, dews, and dangers come; our deeds are done!
Mistrust of my success hath done this deed.

PRESENTIMENT OF BRUTUS AND HIS DEATH.

   Bru. Come hither, good Volumnius, list a word.

   Vol. What says my lord?

   Bru. Why, this, Volumnius:
The ghost of Cæsar hath appear'd to me
Two several times by night: at Sardis, once;
And, this last night, here in Philippi fields.
I know, my hour is come.

   Vol. Not so, my lord.

   Bru. Nay, I am sure it is, Volumnius.
Thou see'st the world, Volumnius, how it goes;
Our enemies have beat us to the pit:
It is more worthy to leap in ourselves,
Than tarry till they push us. Good Volumnius,
Thou know'st that we two went to school together;
Even for that our love of old, I pray thee,
Hold thou my sword-hilts, whilst I run on it.

   Vol. That's not an office for a friend, my lord.

                             (*Alarum still.*)

Cli. Fly, fly, my lord; there is no tarrying here.

Bru. Farewell to you;—and you;—and you,
Volumnius.—
Strato, thou hast been all this while asleep;
Farewell to thee too, Strato.—Countrymen,
My heart doth joy, that yet, in all my life,
I found no man, but he was true to me.
I shall have glory by this losing day,
More than Octavius, and Mark Antony,
By this vile conquest shall attain unto.
So, fare you well at once; for Brutus' tongue
Hath almost ended his life's history:
Night hangs upon mine eyes; my bones would rest,
That have but labour'd to attain this hour.
I pr'ythee, Strato, stay thou by thy lord:
Thou art a fellow of a good respect;
Thy life hath had some smack of honour in it:
Hold then my sword, and turn away thy face,
While I do run upon it. Wilt thou, Strato?

Stra. Give me your hand first: Fare you well, my
lord.

Bru. Farewell, good Strato.—Cæsar, now be still
I kill'd not thee with half so good a will.

(*He runs on his sword, and dies.*)

Alarum. Retreat. Enter OCTAVIUS, ANTONY, MESSALA, LUCILIUS,
and their army.

Oct. What man is that?

Mes. My master's man—Strato, where is thy
master?

Stra. Free from the bondage you are in, Messala;
The conquerors can but make a fire of him
For Brutus only overcome himself,
And no man else hath honour by his death.

Luc. So Brutus should be found.—I thank thee,
    Brutus,
That thou hast proved Lucilius' saying true.

Oct. All that served Brutus, I will entertain them.
Fellow, wilt thou bestow thy time with me?

Stra. Ay, if Messala will prefer me to you.

Oct. Do so, Messala.

Mes. How died, my master, Strato?

Stra. I held the sword, and he did run on it.

Mes. Octavius, then take him to follow thee,
That did the latest service to my master.

Ant. This was the noblest Roman of them all:
All the conspirators, save only he,
Did that they did in envy of great Cæsar;
He, only, in a general honest thought,
And common good to all, made one of them.
His life was gentle; and the elements
So mix'd in him, that Nature might stand up,
And say to all the world, *This was a man!*

Oct. According to his virtue let us use him,
With all respect, and rites of burial.
Within my tent his bones to-night shall lie,
Most like a soldier, order'd honourably.—
So call the field to rest; and let's away,
To part the glories of this happy day.

HAMLET.

ACT I.—Scene I.

Waiting for the apparition.

Hor. What, has this thing appear'd again to-
    night?

Ber I have seen nothing.

Mar. Horatio says, 'tis but our fantasy;
And will not let belief take hold of him,
Touching this dreaded sight, twice seen of us:
Therefore I have entreated him, along
With us to watch the minutes of this night;
That, if again this apparition come,
He may approve our eyes, and speak to it.

  Hor. Tush! tush! 'twill not appear.

  Ber. Sit down awhile;
And let us once again assail your ears,
That are so fortified against our story,
What we two nights have seen.

  Hor. Well, sit we down,
And let us hear Bernardo speak of this.

  Ber. Last night of all,
When yon same star, that's westward from the pole,
Had made his course to illume that part of heaven
Where now it burns, Marcellus, and myself,
The bell then beating one,—

Mar. Peace, break thee off; look, where it comes
      again!

Enter Ghost.

Ber. In the same figure, like the king's that's dead.

Mar. Thou art a scholar, speak to it, Horatio.

Ber. Looks it not like the king? mark it, Horatio.

Hor. Most like:—it harrows me with fear and
      wonder.

Ber. It would be spoke to.

Mar. Speak to it, Horatio.

Hor. What art thou, that usurp'st this time of
      night,

Together with that fair and warlike form

In which the majesty of buried Denmark

Did sometimes march? by heaven I charge thee,
       speak.

Mar. It is offended.

Ber. See! it stalks away.

Hor. Stay; speak: speak, I charge thee, speak.

[Exit Ghost.

Mar. 'Tis gone, and will not answer,

Ber. How now, Horatio? you tremble, and look
      pale:

Is not this something more than fantasy?

What think you of it?

Hor. Before my God, I might not this believe,

Without the sensible and true avouch

Of my own eyes.

Mar. Is it not like the king?

Hor. As thou art to thyself:

Such was the very armour he had on,

When he the ambitious Norway combated;

So frown'd he once, when, in an angry parle,

He smote the sledded Polack on the ice.
'Tis strange.
   Mar. Thus twice before, and jump at this dead
       hour,
With martial stalk hath he gone by our watch.
   Hor. In what particular thought to work, I know
       not;
But, in the gross and scope of mine opinion, ·
This bodes some strange eruption to our state.
   Mar. Good now, sit down, and tell me, he that
       knows,
Why this same strict and most observant watch
So nightly toils the subject of the land?
And why such daily cast of brazen cannon,
And foreign mart for implements of war;
Why such impress of shipwrights, whose sore task
Does not divide the Sunday from the week:
What might be toward, that this sweaty haste
Doth make the night joint labourer with the day;
Who is't that can inform me?

Wonders.

   Hor. O day and night, but this is wondrous
      strange?
   Ham. And therefore as a stranger give it welcome.
There are more things in heaven and earth,
      Horatio,
Than are dreamt of in your philosophy.

Portentous omens.

   Hor. A mote it is, to trouble the mind's eye.
In the most high and palmy state of Rome,
A little ere the mightiest Julius fell,

The graves stood tenantless, and the sheeted dead
Did squeak and gibber in the Roman streets.

  *   *   *   *   *   *   *

As, stars with trains of fire, and dews of blood,
Disasters in the sun; and the moist star,
Upon whose influence Neptune's empire stands,
Was sick almost to doomsday with eclipse.
And even the like precurse of fierce events,—
As harbingers preceding still the fates,
And prologue to the omen coming on,
Have heaven and earth together demonstrated
Unto our climatures and countrymen.—

Re-enter Ghost.

But, soft; behold! lo, where it comes again!
I'll cross it, though it blast me.—Stay, illusion!
If thou hast any sound, or use of voice,
Speak to me:
If there be any good thing to be done,
That may to thee do ease, and grace to me,
Speak to me:
If thou art privy to thy country's fate,
Which, happily, foreknowing, may avoid.
O, speak!
Or, if thou hast uphoarded in thy life,
Extorted treasure in the womb of earth,
For which, they say, you spirits oft walk in death,

           (*Cock crows.*)

Speak of it:—stay, and speak.—Stop it, Marcellus.
 Mar. Shall I strike at it with my partizan ?
 Hor. Do, if it will not stand.
 Ber. 'Tis here!
 Hor. 'Tis here!
 Mar. 'Tis gone!   [*Exit Ghost.*

The ghost's action.

We do it wrong, being so majestical,
To offer it the show of violence;
For it is, as the air, invulnerable,
And our vain blows malicious mockery.

Ber. It was about to speak, when the cock crew.

Hor. And then it started, like a guilty thing
Upon a fearful summons.   I have heard,
The cock, that is the trumpet to the morn,
Doth with his lofty and shrill-sounding throat
Awake the god of day; and, at his warning,
Whether in sea or fire, in earth or air,
The extravagant and erring spirit hies
To his confine: and of the truth herein
This present object made probation.

Mar. It faded on the crowing of the cock.
Some say, that ever 'gainst that season comes,
Wherein our Saviour's birth is celebrated,
This bird of dawning singeth all night long:
And then, they say, no spirit dares stir abroad;
The nights are wholesome; then no planets strike,
No fairy takes, nor witch hath power to charm,
So hallow'd and so gracious is the time.

Hor. So have I heard, and do in part believe it.
But, look, the morn, in russet mantle clad,
Walks o'er the dew of yon high eastern hill:
Break we our watch up;

Scene II.

Excessive grief a fault.

King. 'Tis sweet and commendable in your
     nature, Hamlet,

To give these mourning duties to your father:
But you must know, your father lost a father;
That father lost his; and the survivor bound
In filial obligation, for some term
To do obsequious sorrow: But to persevere
In obstinate condolement, is a course
Of impious stubbornness; 'tis unmanly grief:
It shows a will most incorrect to heaven;
A heart unfortified, a mind impatient;
An understanding simple and unschool'd:
For what, we know, must be, and is as common
As any the most vulgar thing to sense,
Why should we, in our peevish opposition,
Take it to heart; Fie! 'tis a fault to heaven,
A fault against the dead, a fault to nature,
To reason most absurd; whose common theme
Is death of fathers, and who still hath cried,
From the first corse, till he that died to-day,
This must be so.

HAMLET'S SOLILOQUY ON HIS MOTHER'S MARRIAGE.

Ham. O, that this too too solid flesh would melt,
Thaw, and resolve itself into a dew!
Or that the Everlasting had not fix'd
His canon 'gainst self-slaughter! O God! O God!
How weary, stale, flat, and unprofitable
Seem to me all the uses of this world!
Fie on 't! O fie! 'tis an unweeded garden,
That grows to seed; things rank and gross in nature
Possess it merely. That it should come to this!
But two months dead!—nay, not so much, not two:
So excellent a king; that was, to this,
Hyperion to a satyr: so loving to my mother,

That he might not beteem the winds of heaven
Visit her face too roughly. Heaven and earth!
Must I remember? why, she would hang on him,
As if increase of appetite had grown
By what it fed on; and yet, within a month,—
Let me not think on 't,—Frailty, thy name is woman!—
A little month; or ere those shoes were old
With which she follow'd my poor father's body,
Like Niobe, all tears;—why she, even she,—
O heaven! a beast, that wants discourse of reason,
Would have mourn'd longer,—married with my uncle,
My father's brother; but no more like my father
Than I to Hercules: within a month;
Ere yet the salt of most unrighteous tears
Had left the flushing in her galled eyes
She married;

Same.

Description of Hamlet's Father.

Ham. He was a man, take him for all in all, I shall not
look upon his like again.

Scene III.

Caution to Ophelia.

Fear it, Ophelia, fear it, my dear sister;
And keep you in the rear of your affection,
Out of the shot and danger of desire.
The chariest maid is prodigal enough,
If she unmask her beauty to the moon.
Virtue itself scapes not columnious strokes:

Correct deportment described.

Pol. Yet here, Laertes? aboard, aboard, for
        shame;
The wind sits in the shoulder of your sail,
And you are staid for: There,—my blessing with
        you:
                    (*Laying his hand on Laertes' head.*)
And these few precepts in thy memory
Look thou character.   Give thy thoughts no tongue,
Nor any unproportioned thought his act.
Be thou familiar, but by no means vulgar.
The friends thou hast, and their adoption tried,
Grapple them to thy soul with hooks of steel;
But do not dull thy palm with entertainment
Of each new-hatch'd, unfledg'd comrade.   Beware
Of entrance to a quarrel; but, being in,
Bear it, that the opposer may beware of thee.
Give every man thine ear, but few thy voice:
Take each man's censure, but reserve thy judgment.
Costly thy habit as thy purse can buy,
But not express'd in fancy; rich, not gaudy;
For the apparel oft proclaims the man;
And they in France, of the best rank and station,
Are most select and generous, chief in that.
Neither a borrower, nor a lender be:
For loan oft loses both itself and friend;
And borrowing dulls the edge of husbandry.
This above all,—To thine ownself be true;
And it must follow, as the night the day,
Thou canst not then be false to any man.

Scene IV.

Custom.

Hor. Is it a custom?

Ham. Ay, marry, is't;
But to my mind,—though I am native here,
And to the manner born,—it is a custom
More honour'd in the breach, than the observance.

Hamlet's soliloquy.

Enter Ghost.

Hor. Look, my lord, it comes!

Ham. Angels and ministers of grace defend us! -
Be thou a spirit of health, or goblin damn'd.
Bring with thee airs from heaven, or blasts from hell,
Be thy intents wicked, or charitable,
Thou comest in such a questionable shape,
That I will speak to thee; I'll call thee, Hamlet,
King, father: Royal Dane, O, answer me:
Let me not burst in ignorance! but tell,
Why thy canonized bones, hearsed in death,
Have burst their cerements! why the sepulcher,
Wherein we saw thee quietly in urn'd,
Hath ope'd his ponderous and marble jaws,
To cast thee up again! What may this mean,
That thou, dead corse, again in complete steel,
Revisit'st thus the glimpses of the moon,
Making night hideous; and we fools of nature,
So horridly to shake our disposition,
With thoughts beyond the reaches of our souls?
Say, why is this? wherefore? what should we do?

Hor. It beckons you to go away with it,
As if it some impartment did desire
To you alone.

Scene IV.

Hamlet resolves to go to the ghost.

Mar. Look, with what courteous action
It waves you to a more removed ground:
But do not go with it.
   Hor. No, by no means.
   Ham. It will not speak; then I will follow it.
   Hor. Do not, my lord.
   Ham. Why, what would be the fear?
I do not set my life at a pin's fee:
And, for my soul, what can it do to that,
Being a thing immortal as itself?
It waves me forth again;—I'll follow it.
   Hor. What, if it tempt you toward the flood, my
        lord,
Or to the dreadful summit of the cliff,
That beetles o'er his base into the sea:
And there assume some other horrible form,
Which might deprive your sovereignty of reason,
And draw you into madness? think of it:
The very place puts toys of desperation,
Without more motive, into every brain,
That looks so many fathoms to the sea,
And hears it roar beneath.
   Ham. It waves me still:
.Go on, I'll follow thee.
   Mar. You shall not go, my lord.
   Ham. Hold off your hands.
   Hor. Be ruled, you shall not go.
   Ham. My fate cries out,
And makes each petty artery in this body

As hardy as the Nemean lion's nerve.—

(Ghost beckons.)

Still am I call'd:—unhand me, gentlemen;—

(Breaking from them)

By heaven, I'll make a ghost of him that lets me:—
I say, away:—Go on, I'll follow thee.

(Exeunt Ghost and Hamlet.

Hor He waxes desperate with imagination.
Mar. Let's follow; 'tis not fit thus to obey him.
Hor. Have after:—To what issue will this come?
Mar. Something is rotten in the state of Denmark.
Hor. Heaven will direct it.
Mar. Nay, let's follow him. 　　　　 *[Exeunt.*

Scene V.

The ghost talks with Hamlet about his murder.

R-enter Ghost and Hamlet.

Ham. Whither wilt thou lead me? speak, I'll go
　　　no farther.
Ghost. Mark me.
Ham. I will.
Ghost. My hour is almost come,
When I to sulphurous and tormenting flames
Must render up myself.
Ham. Alas, poor ghost!
Ghost. Pity me not, but lend thy serious hearing
To what I shall unfold.
Ham. Speak, I am bound to hear.
Ghost. So art thou to revenge, when thou shalt
　　　hear.
Ham. What?

Ghost. I am thy father's spirit;
Doom'd for a certain term to walk the night,
And, for the day, confined to fast in fires,
Till the foul crimes, done in my days of nature,
Are burnt and purged away.   But that I am forbid
To tell the secrets of my prison house,
I could a tale unfold, whose lightest word
Would harrow up thy soul; freeze thy young blood;
Make thy two eyes, like stars, start from their
          spheres;
Thy knotted and combined locks to part,
And each particular hair to stand an-end,
Like quills upon the fretful porcupine:
But this eternal blazon must not be
To ears of flesh and blood:—List, list, O list!—
If thou didst ever thy dear father love,—

   Ham. O heaven!

   Ghost. Revenge his foul and most unnatural
          murder.

   Ham. Murder?

   Ghost. Murder most foul, as in the best it is;
But this most foul, strange, and unnatural.

   Ham. Haste me to know it; that I, with wings as
          swift
As meditation, or the thoughts of love,
May sweep to my revenge.

   Ghost. I find thee apt;
And duller shouldst thou be than the fat weed
That rots itself in ease on Lethe wharf,
Wouldst thou not stir in this?   Now, Hamlet, hear:
'Tis given out, that, sleeping in mine orchard,
A serpent stung me; so the whole ear of Denmark
Is by a forged process of my death

Rankly abused: but know, thou noble youth,
The serpent, that did sting thy father's life,
Now wears his crown.
  *   *   *   *   *   *   •
O Hamlet, what a falling-off was there!
From me, whose love was of that dignity,
That it went hand in hand even with the vow
I made to her in marriage; and to decline
Upon a wretch, whose natural gifts were poor
To those of mine!
But virtue, as it never will be moved,
Though lewdness court it in a shape of heaven;
So lust, though to a radiant angel link'd,
Will state itself in a celestial bed,
And prey on garbage.
But, soft! methinks I scent the morning air;
Brief let me be:—Sleeping within mine orchard,
My custom always of the afternoon,
Upon my secure hour thy uncle stole,
With juice of cursed hebenon in a vial,
And in the porches of mine ears did pour
The leperous distilment: whose effect
Holds such an enmity with blood of man,
That, swift as quicksilver, it courses through
The natural gates and alleys of the body;
And, with a sudden vigor, it doth posset
And curd, like eager droppings into milk,
The thin and wholesome blood: so did it mine;
And a most instant tetter bark'd about,
Most lazar-like, with vile and loathsome crust,
All my smooth body.
Thus was I, sleeping, by a brother's hand,
Of life, of crown, of queen, at once despatch'd:

Cut off even in the blossoms of my sin
Unhousel'd, disappointed, unanel'd;
No reckoning made, but sent to my account
With all my imperfections on my head:
O, horrible! O, horrible! most horrible!

HAMLET'S PROMISE OF REMEMBRANCE.

But bear me stiffly up!—Remember thee?
Ay, thou poor ghost, while memory holds a seat
In this distracted globe.   Remember thee?
Yea, from the table of my memory
I'll wipe away all trivial fond records,
All saws of books, all forms, all pressures past,
That youth and observation copied there;
And thy commandment all alone shall live
Within the book and volume of my brain,
Unmix'd with baser matter: yes, by heaven.—
O most pernicious woman!
O villain, villain, smiling, damned villain!
My tables,—meet it is I set it down,
That one may smile, and smile, and be a villain;
At least I am sure it may be so in Denmark:

| *Writing*

ACT II.—SCENE II.

BREVITY.

Pol. This business is well ended,
My liege, and madam, to expostulate
What majesty should be, what duty is,
Why day is day, night night, and time is time,
Were nothing but to waste night, day, and time,
Therefore,—since brevity is the soul of wit,

And tediousness the limbs and outward flourishes,—
I will be brief: Your noble son is mad:
Mad, call I it; for to define true madness,
What is't, but to be nothing else but mad?
But let that go.

   Queen. More matter, with less art.

   Pol. Madam, I swear, I use no art at all.
That he is mad, 'tis true, 'tis true, 'tis pity:
And pity 'tis, 'tis true.

DOUBT NOT LOVE.

   Queen. Came this from Hamlet to her?

   Pol. Good madam, stay awhile; I will be faithful.—

> *Doubt thou, the stars are fire ;*
> *Doubt, that the sun doth move ;*
> *Doubt truth to be a liar :*
> *But never doubt. I love.*

*O dear Ophelia, I am ill at these numbers, I have not art to
reckon my groans: but that I love thee best, O most best, believe
it. Adieu.*

> *Thine evermore, most dear lady, whilst
> this machine is to him.* HAMLET.

DREAMS, AMBITION, BEGGARS.

   Ros. Why, then your ambition makes it one; 'tis too narrow for your mind.

   Ham. O God! I could be bounded in a nut-shell, and count myself a king of infinite space; were it not that I have bad dreams.

   Guil. Which dreams, indeed, are ambition; for the very substance of the ambitious is merely the shadow of a dream.

   Ham. A dream itself is but a shadow.

Ros. Truly, and I hold ambition of so airy and light a quality, that it is but a shadow's shadow.

Ham. There are our beggars, bodies; and our monarchs, and outstretch'd heroes, the beggars' shadows.

How to use men.

Ham. 'Tis well; I'll have thee speak out the rest of this soon.—Good, my lord, will you see the players well bestowed? Do you hear, let them be well used; for they are the abstract, and brief chronicles of the time: After your death you were better have a bad epitaph, than their ill report while you live.

Pol. My lord, I will use them according to their desert.

Ham. Odd's bodikin, man, much better: Use every man after his desert, and who shall 'scape whipping? Use them after your own honour and dignity: The less they deserve, the more merit is in your bounty. Take them in.

Man's character.

Ham. I will tell you why; so shall my anticipation prevent your discovery, and your secresy to the king and queen moult no feather. I have of late (but wherefore I know not) lost all my mirth, foregone all custom of exercises; and, indeed, it goes so heavily with my disposition, that this goodly frame, the earth, seems to me a sterile promontory; this most excellent canopy, the air, look you, this brave o'erhanging firmament, this majestical roof fretted with golden fire,—why, it appears no other thing to me than a foul and pestilent congregation of vapours. What a piece of work is a man! How noble in reason! how infinite in faculties! in form and moving, how express and admirable! in action, how like an angel! in apprehension, how like a god! the beauty of the world! the paragon of animals! And yet, to me, what is this quintessence of dust? man delights not me, nor woman neither; though, by your smiling, you seem to say so.

HAMLET PLEASED WITH A PLAYER'S SPEECH.

1 *Play.* What speech, my lord?

Ham. I heard thee speak me a speech once,—but it was never acted; or, if it was, not above once; for the play, I remember, pleased not the million; 'twas caviare to the general: but it was (as I received it, and others, whose judgments in such matters cried in the top of mine) an excellent play; well digested in the scenes; set down with as much modesty as cunning. I remember, one said, there was no salads in the lines, to make the matter savoury, nor no matter in the phrase, that might indite the author of affectation; but called it an honest method, as wholesome as sweet, and by very much more handsome than fine. One speech in it I chiefly loved: 'twas Æneas' tale to Dido; and thereabout of it especially, where he speaks of Priam's slaughter. If it live in your memory, begin at this line;—let me see, let me see:—

" The rugged Pyrrhus, like the Hyrcanian beast,"—
'Tis not so; it begins with Pyrrhus:—
" The rugged Pyrrhus,—he, whose sable arms,
Black as his purpose, did the night resemble
When he lay couched in the ominous horse,—
Hath now this dread and black complexion smear'd
With heraldry more dismal; head to foot
Now is he total gules; horribly trick'd
With blood of fathers, mothers, daughters, sons;
Baked and impasted with the parching streets,
That lend a tyrannous and a damned light
To their lord's murder: roasted in wrath and fire,

10

And thus o'er-siezd with coagulate gore,
With eyes like carbuncles, the hellish Pyrrhus
Old grandsire Priam seeks;"—
So proceed you.

　　Pol. 'For God, my lord, well spoken, with good accent
and good discretion.

　　1 *Play.* "Anon he finds him
Striking too short at Greeks; his antique sword,
Rebellious to his arm, lies where it falls,
Repugnant to command: unequal match'd,
Pyrrhus at Priam drives; in rage, strikes wide;
But with the whiff and wind of his fell sword
The unnerved father falls.　Then senseless Ilium,
Seeming to feel this blow, with flaming top
Stoops to his base, and with a hideous crash
Takes prisoner Pyrrhus' ear: for, lo! his sword,
Which was declining on the milky head
Of reverend Priam, seem'd i' the air to stick:
So, as a painted tyrant, Pyrrhus stood;
And, like a neutral to his will and matter,
Did nothing.
But, as we often see against some storm
A silence in the heaven, the rack stand still,
The bold winds speechless, and the orb below
As hush as death, anon the dreadful thunder
Doth rend the region; so, after Pyrrhus' pause,
A roused vengance sets him new a-work;
And never did the Cyclops' hammers fall
On Mar's armour, forged for proof eterne,
With less remorse than Pyrrhus' bleeding sword
Now falls on Priam.—
Out, out, Fortune!　All you gods,

In general synod, take away her power;
Break all the spokes and fellies from her wheel,
And bowl the round nave down the hill of heaven,
As low as to the fiends!"

ACT III.

Scene I.—*A Room in the Castle.*

To be or not to be.

Ham. To be, or not to be, that is the question:
Whether 'tis nobler in the mind to suffer
The slings and arrows of outrageous fortune;
Or to take arms against a sea of troubles,
And, by opposing, end them?—To die,—to sleep,—
No more;—and, by a sleep, to say we end.
The heart-ache, and the thousand natural shocks
That flesh is heir to,—'tis a consummation
Devoutly to be wish'd.   To die—to sleep;—
To sleep! perchance to dream;—ay, there's the
          rub;
For in that sleep of death what dreams may come,
When we have shuffled off this mortal coil,
Must give us pause: there's the respect,
That makes calamity of so long life:
For who would bear the whips and scorns of time,
The oppressor's wrong, the proud man's contumely,
The pangs of despised love, the law's delay,
The insolence of office, and the spurns
That patient merit of the unworthy takes,
When he himself might his quietus make
With a bare bodkin? who would fardels bear,
To grunt and sweat under a weary life,

But that the dread of something after death,—
The undiscover'd country, from whose bourn
No traveller returns,—puzzles the will,
And makes us rather bear those ills we have,
Than fly to others that we know not of?
Thus conscience does make cowards of us all;
And thus the native hue of resolution
Is sicklied o'er with the pale cast of thought;
And enterprises of great pith and moment,
With this regard, their currents turn awry,
And lose the name of action.—Soft you now!
The fair Ophelia.—Nymph, in thy orisons
Be all my sins remember'd.

CALUMNY.

Be thou as chaste as ice, as pure as snow, thou
shalt not escape calumny.

HAMLET'S ECSTATIC CRAZE.

Oph. O, what a noble mind is here o'erthrown!
The courtier's, soldier's, scholar's, eye, tongue, sword:
The expectancy and rose of the fair state,
The glass of fashion, and the mould of form,
The observed of all observers,—quite, quite down!
And I, of ladies most deject and wretched,
That suck'd the honey of his music vows,
Now see that noble and most sovereign reason,
Like sweet bells jangled, out of tune and harsh,
That unmatch'd form and feature of blown youth,
Blasted with ecstacy.

Scene II.

How to speak.

Enter Hamlet, *and certain players.*

Ham. Speak the speech, I pray you, as I pronounced it to you, trippingly on the tongue: but if you mouth it, as many of your players do, I had as lief the town-crier spoke my lines. Nor do not saw the air too much with your hand, thus; but use all gently: for in the very torrent, tempest, and (as I may say) whirlwind of your passion, you must acquire and beget a temperance, that may give it smoothness. O, it offends me to the soul, to hear a robustious, periwig-pated fellow tear a passion to tetters, to very rags, to split the ears of the groundlings; who, for the most part, are capable of nothing but inexplicable dumb shews, and noise: I would have such a fellow whipped for o'er-doing Termagant; it out-herods Herod: Pray you, avoid it.

1 Play. I warrant your honour.

Ham. Be not too tame neither, but let your own discretion be your tutor: suit the action to the word, the word to the action; with this special observance, that you o'er-step not the modesty of nature: for anything so overdone is from the purpose of playing, whose end, both at the first, and now, was, and is, to hold, as 'twere, the mirror up to nature; to shew virtue her own feature, scorn her own image, and the very age and body of the time, is form and pressure. Now, this overdone, or come tardy off, though it make the unskilful laugh, cannot but make the judicious grieve; the censure of which one, must, in your allowance, o'erweigh a whole theatre of others. O, there be players, that I have seen play,— and heard others praise, and that highly,—not to speak it profanely, that, neither having the accent of Christians, nor the gait of Christians, Pagan, nor man, have

so strutted, and bellowed, that I have thought some of
nature's journeymen had made men, and not made them
well, they imitated humanity so abominably.

HAMLET'S IDEA OF FLATTERY.

Hor. Here, sweet lord, at your service.

Ham. Horatio, thou art e'en as just a man,
As e'er my conversation coped withal.

Hor. O, my dear lord,—

Ham. Nay, do not think I flatter:
For what advancement may I hope from thee,
That no revenue hast, but thy good spirits,
To feed, and clothe thee ?   Why should the poor be
        flatter'd ?
No, let the candied tongue lick absurd pomp;
And crook the pregnant hinges of the knee,
Where thrift may follow fawning.   Dost thou
        hear ?
Since my dear soul was mistress of her choice,
And could of men distinguish her election,
She hath seal'd thee for herself: for thou hast
        been
As one, in suffering all, that suffers nothing;
A man, that fortune's buffets and rewards
Hast ta'ed with equal thanks; and blessed are
        those
Whose blood and judgment are so well co-mingled,
That they are not a pipe for fortune's finger
To sound what stop she pleases: Give me that
        man,
That is not passion's slave, and I will wear him
In my heart's core, ay, in my heart of heart,
As I do thee.—

Obsequiousness.

Ham. Do you see yonder cloud that's almost in shape of a camel?

Pol. By the mass, and 'tis like a camel, indeed.

Ham. Methinks, it is like a weasel.

Pol. It is back'd like a weasel.

Ham. Or, like a whale?

Pol. Very like a whale.

Hamlet's soliloquy on his mother.

'Tis now the very witching time of night;
When churchyards yawn, and hell itself breathes
   out
Contagion to this world: Now could I drink hot
   blood,
And do such bitter business as the day
Would quake to look on. Soft; now to my
   mother.—
O, heart, lose not thy nature; let not ever
The soul of Nero enter this firm bosom:
Let me be cruel, not unnatural:
I will speak daggers to her, but use none;
My tongue and soul in this be hypocrites:
How in my words soever she be shent,
To give them seals, never, my soul, consent!

Scene III.

The King's remorse and Hamlet's soliloquy about him.

Enter Polonius.

Pol. My lord, he's going to his mother's closet:
Behind the arras I'll convey myself,

To hear the process; I'll warrant she'll tax him home:
And, as you said, and wisely was it said,
'Tis meet that some more audience than a mother,
Since nature makes them partial, should o'erhear
The speech of vantage.   Fare you well, my liege:
I'll call upon you ere you go to bed,
And tell you what I know.

    King. Thanks, dear my lord.   [*Exit* POLONIUS.
O, my offence is rank, it smells to heaven;
It hath the primal eldest curse upon't,—
A brother's murder!—Pray can I not,
Though inclination be as sharp as will:
My stronger guilt defeats my strong intent;
And, like a man to double business bound,
I stand in pause where I shall first begin,
And both neglect.   What if this cursed hand
Were thicker than itself with brother's blood,—
Is there not rain enough in the sweet heavens
To wash it white as snow ?   Whereto serves mercy,
But to confront the visage of offence?
And what's in prayer, but this twofold force,—
To be forestalled ere we come to fall,
Or pardon'd, being down?   Then I'll look up;
My fault is past.   But, O, what form of prayer
Can serve my turn?   Forgive me my foul murder!—
That cannot be; since I am still possess'd
Of those effects for which I did the murder,—
My crown, mine own ambition, and my queen.
May one be pardon'd and retain the offence?
In the corrupted currents of this world,
Offence's gilded hand may shove by justice;
And oft 'tis seen the wicked prize itself
Buys out the law: but 'tis not so above;

There is no shuffling,—there the action lies
In his true nature; and we ourselves compell'd,
Even to the teeth and forehead of our faults,
To give in evidence. What then? what rests?
Try what repentance can: what can it not?
Yet what can it, when one cannot repent?
O wretched state! O bosom, black as death!
O limed soul, that, struggling to be free,
Art more engaged. Help, angels! make assay:
Bow, stubborn knees? and, heart, with strings of steel,
Be soft as sinews of the new-born babe!
All may be well.   *[Retires and kneels.*

Enter HAMLET.

Ham. Now might I do it, pat, now he is praying;
And now I'll do't:—and so he goes to heaven;
And so am I revenged? That would be scann'd:
A villian kills my father; and, for that,
I, his sole son, do this same villian send
To heaven
Why, this is hire and salary, not revenge.
He took my father grossly, full of bread;
With all his crimes broad blown, as flush as May;
And how his audit stands, who knows, save heaven?
But, in our circumstance and course of thought,
'Tis heavy with him: and am I then revenged
To take him in the purging of his soul,
When he is fit and season'd for his passage?
No.
Up, sword; and know thou a more horrid hent:
When he is drunk, asleep, or in his rage;
At gaming, swearing; or about some act
That hath no relish of salvation in't:
Then trip him, that his heels may kick at heaven;

And that his soul may be as damn'd and black
As hell, whereto it goes. My mother stays:
This physic but prolongs thy sickly days.   [*Exit.*

Scene IV.

Hamlet reproaching his mother.

Queen. What have I done, that thou darest wag
   thy tongue
In noise so rude against me ?
 Ham. Such an act,
That blurs the grace and blush of modesty;
Calls virtue, hypocrite; takes off the rose
From the fair forehead of an innocent love
And sets a blister there; makes marriage vows
As false as dicers' oaths: O, such a deed
As from the body of contraction plucks
The very soul; and sweet religion makes
A rhapsody of words: Heaven's face doth glow;
Yea, this solidity and compound mass,
With tristful visage, as against the doom,
Is thought-sick at the act.
 Queen. Ah me, what act,
That roars so loud, and thunders in the index ?
 Ham. Look here, upon this picture, and on this;
The counterfeit presentment of two brothers.
See, what a grace was seated on this brow:
Hyperion's curls; the front of Jove himself:
An eye like Mars, to threaten and command;
A station like the herald Mercury
New-lighted on a heaven-kissing hill;
A combination, and a form, indeed,

Where every god did seem to set his seal,
To give the world assurance of a man:
This was your husband.—Look you now what
      follows:
Here is your husband, like a mildew'd ear,
Blasting his wholesome brother. Have you eyes?
Could you on this fair mountain leave to feed,
And batten on this moor?

Hamlet's advice to his mother.

Queen. This is the very coinage of your brain:
This bodiless creation ecstasy
Is very cunning in.
    Ham. Ecstasy!
My pulse, as yours, doth temperately keep time,
And makes as healthful music: it is not madness
That I have utter'd: bring me to the test,
And I the matter will re-word; which madness
Would gambol from. Mother, for love of grace,
Lay not that flattering unction to your soul,
That not your trespass, but my madness speaks:
It will but skin and film the ulcerous place,
While rank corruption, mining all within,
Infects unseen. Confess yourself to heaven;
Repent what's past; avoid what is to come;
And do not spread the compost on the weeds,
To make them ranker. Forgive me this my virtue;
For in the fatness of these pursy times,
Virtue itself of vice must pardon beg,
Yea, curb and woo, for leave to do him good.
    Queen. O Hamlet! thou hast cleft my heart in twain.
    Ham. O, throw away the worser part of it,
And live the purer with the other half.

Good night:
Assume a virtue, if you have it not.
That monster, custom, who all sense doth eat,
Of habits, devil, is angel yet in this,—
That to the use of actions fair and good
He likewise gives a frock or livery,
That aptly is put on.   Refrain to-night;
And that shall lend a kind of easiness
To the next abstinence: the next more easy;
For use almost can change the stamp of nature,
And either curb the devil, or throw him out
With wondrous potency.

ACT IV.

To avoid slander.

Come, Gertude, we'll call up our wisest friends;
And let them know, both what we mean to do,
And what's untimely done: so haply, slander,—
Whose whisper o'er the world's diameter,
As level as the cannon to his blank,
Transports his poison'd shot,—may miss our name,
And hit the woundless air.

Hamlet's philosophy and angry resolve.

How all occasions do inform against me,
And spur my dull revenge!   What is a man,
If his chief good and market of his time
Be but to sleep and feed? A beast, no more.
Sure, He that made us with such large discourse,
Looking before and after, gave us not
That capability and godlike reason

To fust in us unused.   Now, whether it be
Bestial oblivion, or some craven scruple
Of thinking too precisely on the event,—
A thought which, quarter'd, hath but one part wisdom,
And ever three parts coward,—I do not know
Why yet I live to say, " This thing's to do;"
Sith I have cause and will, and strength and means,
To do 't.   Examples, gross as earth, exhort me:
Witness this army of such mass and charge,
Led by a delicate and tender prince;
Whose spirit, with divine ambition puff'd,
Makes mouths at the invisible event;
Exposing what is mortal and unsure
To all that fortune, death, and danger dare,
Even for an egg-shell.   Rightly to be great,
Is not to stir without great argument,
But greatly to find quarrel in a straw,
When honour's at the stake.   How stand I, then,
That have a father kill'd, a mother stain'd,
Excitements of my reason and my blood,
And let all sleep? while, to my shame, I see
The imminent death of twenty thousand men,
That, for a fantasy and trick of fame,
Go to their graves like beds; fight for a plot
Whereon the numbers cannot try the cause,
Which is not tomb enough and continent
To hide the slain!—O, from this time forth
My thoughts be bloody, or be nothing worth!

Scene V.

King. When sorrows come, they come not single spies,
But in battalions!

DIVINITY OF KINGS.

King. What is the cause, Laertes,
That thy rebellion looks so giant-like?—
Let him go, Gertude; do not fear our person;
There's such divinity doth hedge a king.

Scene VII.

DEATH OF OPHELIA.

Queen. There is a willow grows askant the brook,
That shews his hoar leaves in the glassy stream;
Therewith fantastic garlands did she make
Of crowflowers, nettles, daisies, and long purples,
That liberal shepherds give a grosser name,
But our cold maids do dead men's fingers call them:
There on the pendent boughs her coronet weeds
Clambering to hang, an envious sliver broke;
When down her weedy trophies and herself
Fell in the weeping brook.   Her clothes spread wide;
And, mermaid-like, a while they bore her up:
Which time she chanted snatches of old tunes,
As one incapable of her own distress,
Or like a creature native and indued
Unto that element: but long it could not be,
Till that her garments, heavy with their drink,
Pull'd the poor wretch from her melodious lay
To muddy death.
    Laer. Alas, then she is drown'd?
    Queen. Drow'd, drown'd.
    Laer. Too much of water hast thou, poor Ophelia,
And therefore I forbid my tears: but yet
It is our trick; nature her custom holds,

Let shame say what it will: when these are gone,
The woman will be out.—Adieu, my lord:
I have a speech of fire, that fain would blaze,
But that this folly drowns it.

ACT V.—Scene II.

Reflections on a skull.

Ham. Alas, poor Yorick!—I knew him, Horatio; a fellow of infinite jest, of most excellent fancy: he hath borne me on his back a thousand times! and now, how abhorred in my imagination it is! my gorge rises at it. Here hung those lips, that I have kissed I know not how oft. Where be your gibes now? your gambols? your songs? your flashes of merriment, that were wont to set the table on a roar? Not one now, to mock your own grinning? quite chap-fallen? Now get you to my ladies chamber, and tell her, let her paint an inch thick, to this favour she must come: make her laugh at that.—Pr'ythee, Horatio, tell me one thing.

Hor. What's that, my lord?

Ham. Dost thou think, Alexander looked 'o this fashion i' the earth?

Hor. E'en so.

Ham. And smelt so? pah!

(*Throws down the skull.*)

Hor. E'en so, my lord.

Ham. To what base uses we may return, Horatio? Why may not imigination trace the noble dust of Alexander, till he find it stopping a bung-hole?

Hor. 'Twere to consider too curiously, to consider so.

Ham. No, faith, not a jot; but to follow him thither with modesty enough, and likelihood to lead it: As thus: Alex-

ander died, Alexander was buried, Alexander returneth to
dust: the dust is earth; of earth we make loam: And why
of that loam, whereto he was converted, might they not
stop a beer-barrel ?
Imperious Cæsar, dead, and turn'd to clay;
Might stop a hole to keep the wind away:
O that that earth, which kept the world in awe,
Should patch a wall to expel the winter's flaw!

Burial of Ophelia.

Laer. Lay her in the earth:—
And from her fair and unpolluted flesh,
May violets spring!—I tell thee, churlish priest,
A minist'ring angel shall my sister be,
When thou liest howling.

ACT V.—Scene II.

Fate.

Our indiscretion sometimes serves us well,
When our deep plots do pall; and that should teach
            us,
There's a divinity that shapes our ends,
Rough-hew them how we will.

Conceited Value cannot be computed.

Ham. Sir, his definement suffers no perdition in you;—
though, I know, to divide him inventorially, would dizzy the
arithmetic of memory.

THE KING'S WISH FOR HAMLET.

King. Set me the stoups of wine upon that
        table :—
If Hamlet give the first or second hit,
Or quit in answer of the third exchange,
Let all the battlements their ordnance fire;
The king shall drink to Hamlet's better breath;
And in the cup an union shall he throw,
Richer than that which four successive kings
In Denmark's crown have worn: Give me the
        cups:
And let the kettle to the trumpet speak,
The trumpet to the cannoneer without,
The cannons to the heavens, the heavens to earth.

OTHELLO.

ACT I.—Scene III.

Brabantio's lament for his daughter.

Bra. So did I yours: Good your grace, pardon
    me;
Neither my place, nor aught I heard of business,
Hath raised me from thy bed; nor doth the general
    care
Take hold on me; for my particular grief
Is of so flood-gate and o'erbearing nature,
That it engluts and swallows other sorrows,
And it is still itself.

    Duke. Why, what's the matter?

    Bra. My daughter! O my daughter!

    Sen. Dead?

    Bra. Ay, to me;
She is abused, stolen from me, and corrupted
By spells and medicines bought of mountebanks:
For nature so preposterously to err,
Being not deficient, blind, or lame of sense,
Sans witchcraft could not—

    Duke. Whoe'er he be, that, in this foul proceeding,
Hath thus beguiled your daughter of herself,
And you of her, the bloody book of law

You shall yourself read in the bitter **letter,**
After your own sense; yea, though **our proper**
son
Stood in **your** action.

OTHELLO'S DEFENCE.

Duke. Say it, Othello.

Oth. **Her father loved me; oft invited me;**
Still question'd me the story **of my** life,
From year to year; the battles, sieges, fortunes,
That I have pass'd.
I ran it through, even from my boyish days,
To the very moment **that he bade me tell it.**
Wherein I spoke of most disastrous chances,
Of moving accidents, by flood and field;
Of hair-breadth 'scapes i' the imminent **deadly**
breach;
Of being taken by the insolent foe,
And sold to slavery; of my redemption thence,
And portance **of my** travel's history:
Wherein **of antres vast, and deserts wild,**
Rough quarries, rocks, and hills whose heads touch
heaven,
It was my hint to speak, such was the process;
And of the Cannibals that each other eat,
The Anthropophagi, and men whose heads
Do grow beneath their shoulders. These things to
hear,
Would Desdemona seriously incline:
But still the house affairs would draw her thence:
Which ever as she could with haste despatch,
She'd come again, and with a **greedy ear**
Devour up my discourse: Which I observing,

Took once a pliant hour; and found good means
To draw from her a prayer of earnest heart,
That I would all my pilgrimage dilate,
Whereof by parcels she had something heard,
But not intentively: I did consent;
And often did beguile her of her tears,
When I did speak of some distressful stroke,
That my youth suffer'd. My story being done,
She gave me for my pains a world of sighs:
She swore.—In faith, 'twas strange, 'twas passing
       strange;
'Twas pitiful, 'twas wondrous pitiful:
She wish'd she had not heard it, yet she wish'd
That Heaven had made her such a man: she
       thank'd me,
And bade me, if I had a friend that loved her,
I should but teach him how to tell my story,
And that would woo her. Upon this hint, I spake;
She loved me for the dangers I had pass'd;
And I loved her, that she did pity them.
This only is the witchcraft I have used;
Here comes the lady, let her witness it.

OURSELVES RESPONSIBLE FOR OUR FORTUNES.

Iago. Virtue? a fig! 'tis in ourselves, that we are thus, or thus. Our bodies are our gardens; to the which, our wills are gardeners: so that if we will plant nettles, or sow lettuce; set hyssop, and weed up thyme; supply it with one gender of herbs, or distract it with many; either to have it steril with idleness, or manured with industry; why, the power and corrigible authority of this lies in our wills. If the balance of our lives had not one scale of reason to poise another of sensuality, the blood and baseness of our natures would conduct us to most preposterous conclusions: But we have reason to cool our raging motions, our carnal stings.

Put money in thy purse.

Iago. It is merely a lust of the blood, and a permission of the will. Come, be a man: Drown thyself? drown cats, and blind pupies I have professed me thy friend, and I confess me knit to thy deserving with cables of perdurable toughness; I could never better stead thee than now. Put money in thy purse; follow these wars; defeat thy favour with an usurped beard; I say, put money in thy purse. It cannot be, that Desdemona should long continue her love to the Moor,—put money in thy purse;—nor he his to her; it was a violent commencement, and thou shalt see an answerable sequestration;—put but money in thy purse.—These Moors are changeable in their wills:—fill thy purse with money: the food, that to him now is as luscious as locusts, shall be to him shortly as bitter as coloquintida.

ACT II—Scene I.

Description of a storm on the ocean.

2 *Gent.* A segregation of the Turkish fleet:
For do but stand upon the foaming shore,
The chiding billow seems to pelt the clouds;
The wind-shaked surge, with high and monstrous
      main,
Seems to cast water on the burning bear,
And quench the guards of th' ever fixed pole:
I never did, like molestation view
On the enchafed flood.

BEAUTY OF DESDEMONA.

Mon. But, good lieutenant, is your general
       wived ?
Cas. Most fortunately; he hath achieved a maid,
That paragons description, and wild fame;
One, that excels the quirks of blazoning pens,
And in the essential vesture of creation.
Does bear all excellency.—How now ? who has put
      in ?

        Re-enter Second Gentleman.

  2 *Gent.* 'Tis one Iago, ancient to the general.
  Cas. He has had most favourable and happy
      speed:
Tempests themselves, high seas, and howling
      winds.
The gutter'd rocks, and congregated sands,—
Traitors ensteep'd to clog the guiltless keel,
As having sense of beauty, do omit
Their mortal natures, letting go safely by
The divine Desdemona.

DESDEMONA'S JOY AT MEETING OTHELLO.

     Enter OTHELLO, *and attendants.*

  Oth. O my fair warrior!
  Des. My dear Othello!
  Oth. It gives me wonder, great as my content,
To see you here before me.   O my soul's joy!
If after every tempest come such calms,
May the winds blow till they have awaken'd
      death!
And let the labouring bark climb hills of seas,
Olympus-high; and duck again as low

As hell's from heaven! If it were now to die,
'Twere now to be most happy; for, I fear,
My soul hath her content so absolute,
That not another comfort like to this
Succeeds in unknown fate.

Des. The heavens forbid,
But that our loves and comforts should increase,
Even as our days do grow!

Oth. Amen to that, sweet powers!
I cannot speak enough of this content,
It stops me here: it is too much of joy:
And this, and this, the greatest discords be,

(Kissing her.)

That e'er our hearts shall make!

Scene III.

Self control,

Oth. Good Michael, look you to the guard to-
      night;
Let's teach ourselves that honourable stop
Not to outsport discretion.

Custom of drinking regretted.

Cas. Not to-night, good Iago; I have very poor and unhappy brains for drinking: I could well wish courtesy
would invent some other custom of entertainment.

Iago. O, they are our friends; but one cup: I'll drink for
you.

Cas. I have drunk but one cup to-night, and that was
craftily qualified too, and, behold, what innovation it makes
here; I am unfortunate in the infirmity, and dare not task
my weakness with any more.

REPUTATION.

Iago. What, are you hurt, lieutenant?

Cas. Ay, past all surgery.

Iago. Marry, Heaven forbid!

Cas. Reputation, reputation, reputation! O, I have lost my reputation! I have lost the immortal part, sir, of myself, and what remains is bestial—My reputation, Iago, my reputation.

Iago. As I am an honest man, I thought you had received some bodily wound; there is more offence in that, than in reputation Reputation is an idle and most false imposition; oft got without merit, and lost without deserving: You have lost no reputation at all, unless you repute yourself such a loser. What, man! there are ways to recover the general again: You are but now cast in his mood, a punishment more in policy than in malice; even so as one would beat his offenceless dog, to affright an imperious lion: sue to him again, and he's yours.

Cas. I will rather sue to be despised, than to deceive so good a commander, with so slight, so drunken, and indiscreet an officer. Drunk? and speak parrot? and squabble? swagger? swear? and discourse fustian with one's own shadow?—O thou invisible spirit of wine, if thou hast no name to be known by, let us call thee—devil!

Iago. What was he that you followed with your sword? What had he done to you?

Cas. I know not.

Iago. Is it possible?

Cas. I remember a mass of things, but nothing distinctly; a quarrel, but nothing wherefore,—O, that men should put an enemy in their mouths, to steal away their brains! that we should, with joy, revel, pleasure, and applause, transform ourselves into beasts!

Iago. Why, but you are now well enough. How came you thus recovered?

Cas. It hath pleased the devil, drunkenness, to give place to the devil, wrath: one imperfectness shews me another, to make me frankly despise myself.

ACT III.

Scene III.—A good name.

Oth. What dost thou mean?

Iago. Good name, in man and woman, dear my
        lord,
Is the immediate jewel of their souls;
Who steals my purse, steals trash; 'tis something,
        nothing;
'Twas mine, 'tis his, and has been slave to
        thousands:
But he, that filches from me my good name,
Robs me of that, which not enriches him,
And makes me poor indeed.

Beware of jealousy.

Iago O, beware, my lord, of jealousy;
It is the green-eyed monster, which doth mock
The meat it feeds on: That cuckold lives in bliss,
Who, certain of his fate, loves not his wronger;
But, O, what damned minutes tells he o'er,
Who dotes, yet doubts; suspects, yet strongly
        loves!

Oth. O misery!

Iago, Poor and content, is rich, and rich enough;
But riches, fineless, is as poor as winter,

To him that ever fears he shall be poor:—
Good Heaven, the souls of all my tribe defend
From jealousy!

WEIGHT OF LIGHT EVIDENCE AND CONCEITS.

Trifles, light as air,
Are, to the jealous, confirmations strong
As proofs of holy writ.   This may do something,
The Moor already changes with my poison:—
Dangerous conceits are, in their natures, poisons,
Which, at the first, are scarce found to distaste;
But, with a little act upon the blood,
Burn like some mines of sulphur.—

NO MEDICINE FOR SLEEP.

Not poppy, nor mandragora,
Nor all the drowsy syrups of the world,
Shall ever medicine thee to that sweet sleep,
Which though ow'dst yesterday.

OTHELLO'S WISH FOR IGNORANCE, AND FAREWELL TO WAR.

He that is robb'd, not wanting what is stolen,
Let him not know it, and he's not robb'd at all.
    Iago. I an sorry to hear this.
    Oth. I had been happy, if the general camp,
Pioneers and all, had tasted her sweet body,
So I had nothing known: O, now, for ever,
Farewell the tranquil mind: farewell the content!
Farewell the plumed troop, and the big wars,
That makes ambition virtue!   O, farewell!
Farewell the neighing steed, and the shrill trump,
The spirit-stirring drum, the ear-piercing fife,
The royal banner; and all quality,

Pride, pomp, and circumstance of glorious war!
And O you mortal engines, whose rude throats
The immortal Jove's dread clamours counterfeit,
Farewell!   Othello's occupation gone!

IMPRECATION.

Oth. If thou dost slander her, and torture me,
Never pray more: abandon all remorse:
On horror's head, horrors accumulate:
Do deeds to make heaven weep, all earth amazed,
For nothing canst thou to damnation add,
Greater than that.

ACT IV.—SCENE I.

A NOBLE NATURE.

Lod. Is this the noble Moor whom our full
     senate
Call—all-in-all sufficient?—This the noble nature,
Whom passion could not shake? whose solid virtue,
The shot of accident, nor dart of chance,
Could neither graze nor pierce?

DESDEMONA'S CHASTITY.

Oth. That's strange.
Emil. I durst, my lord, to wager she is honest,
Lay down my soul at stake: if you think other,
Remove your thought: it doth abuse your bosom.
If any wretch hath put this in your head,
Let Heaven requite it with the serpent's curse!
For, if she be not honest, chaste, and true,
There's no man happy; the purest of their wives
Is foul as slander.

To be scorned and deceived.

Oth. Had it pleased Heaven
To try me with affliction; had he rain'd
All kinds of sores, and shames, on my bare head;
Steep'd me in poverty to the very lips;
Given to captivity me and my utmost hopes;
I should have found in some part of my soul
A drop of patience: but (alas!) to make me
A fixed figure, for the time of scorn
To point his slow unmoving finger at,—
O! O!
Yet could I bear that too; well, very well:
But there, where I have garner'd up my heart;
Where either I must live, or bear no life;
The fountain, from the which my current runs,
Or else dries up; to be discarded thence!
Or keep it as a cistern, for foul toads
To knot and gender in!—turn thy complexion
          there!
Patience, thou young and rose-lipp'd cherubin.

Scene II.

Desdemona's fidelity.

Des. O good Iago,
What shall I do to win my lord again?
Good friend, go to him; for, by the light of heaven,
I know not how I lost him. Here I kneel:—
If e'er my will did trespass 'gainst his love,
Either in discourse of thought or actual deed;
Or that mine eyes, mine ears, or any sense,
Delighted them in any other form;

Or that I do not yet, and ever did,
And ever will,—though he do shake me off
To beggarly divorcement,—love him dearly,
Comfort forswear me: Unkindness may do much;
And his unkindness may defeat my life,
But never taint my love.
To do the act that might the addition earn,
Not the world's mass of vanity could make me.

ACT V.

Othello's soliloquy on the murder of his wife.

Scene II.—*A Bedchamber: Desdemona in bed, asleep.*
A light burning.

Enter Othello.

Oth. It is the cause, it is the cause, my soul,—
Let me not name it to you, you chaste stars!—
It is the cause.—Yet I'll not shed her blood;
Nor scar that whiter skin of hers than snow,
And smooth as monumental alabaster.
                              (*Takes off his sword.*)
Yet she must die, else she'll betray more men.
Put out the light, and then—Put out the light!
If I quench thee, thou flaming minister,
I can again thy former light restore,
Should I repent me: but once put out thine,
Thou cunning'st pattern of excelling nature,
I know not where is that Promethean heat,
That can thy light relume.   When I have pluck'd
        thy rose,
I cannot give it vital growth again,

It needs must wither:—I'll smell it on the tree —

(*Kissing her.*)

O balmy breath, that dost almost persuade
Justice to break her sword!—One more, one more.—
Be thus when thou art dead, and I will kill thee,
And love thee after:—One more, and this the last:
So sweet was ne'er so fatal. I must weep,
But they are cruel tears; This sorrow's heavenly;
It strikes where it doth love.—She wakes—

HORROR.

My wife! my wife! what wife?—I have no wife:
O, insupportable! O heavy hour!
Methinks it should be now a huge eclipse
Of sun and moon; and that the affrighted globe
Should yawn at alteration.

PRICELESS VALUE OF DESDEMONA.

Oth. Ay, with Cassio.
Nay, had she been true,
If heaven would make me such another world
Of one entire and perfect chrysolite,
I'd not have sold her for it.
Emil. My husband?
Oth. Ay, 'twas he that told me first;
An honest man he is, and hates the slime
That sticks on filthy deeds.

OTHELLO'S REMORSE.

Re-enter GRATIANO.

Gra. What is the matter?
Oth. Behold! I have a weapon;
A better never did itself sustain

Upon a soldier's thigh: I have seen the day,
That, with this little arm, and this good sword,
I have made my way through more impediments
Than twenty times your stop:—But, O vain boast
Who can control his fate? 'tis not so now.—
Be not afraid, though you do see me weapon'd;
Here is my journey's end,
And very sea-mark of my utmost sail.
Do you go back dismay'd? 'tis a lost fear;
Man but a rush against Othello's breast,
And he retires:—Where should Othello go?
Now, how dost thou look now? O ill-starr'd wench!
Pale as thy smock! when we shall meet at compt,
This look of thine will hurl my soul from heaven,
And fiends will snatch at it Cold, cold, my girl?
Even like thy chastity.—
O cursed, cursed slave!—Whip me, ye devils,
From the possession of this heavenly sight!
Blow me about in winds! roast me in sulphur!
Wash me in steep-down gulfs of liquid fire!
O Desdemona! Desdemona! dead?
Dead? O! O! O!

OTHELLO'S REFLECTIONS AND DEATH,

Oth. Soft you; a word or two, before you go.
I have done the state some service, and they know
   it;
No more of that:—I pray you, in your letters,
When you shall these unlucky deeds relate,
Speak of me as I am; nothing extenuate,
Nor set down aught in malice: then must you
   speak
Of one, that loved not wisely, but too well;

Of one, not easily jealous, but, being wrought,
Perplex'd in the extreme, of one, whose hand,
Like the base Judean, threw a pearl away,
Richer than all his tribe; of one, whose subdued
      eyes,
Albeit unused to the melting mood,
Drop tears as fast as the Arabian trees
Their medicinal gum: Set you down this;
And, say besides,—that in Aleppo once,
Where a malignant and a turban'd Turk
Beat a Venetian, and traduced the state,
I took by the throat the circumcised dog,
And smote him—thus.   *(Stabs himself.)*

   Lod. O bloody period!
   Gra. All, that's spoke is marr'd.
   Oth. I kiss'd thee, ere I kill'd thee:—No way but
      this,   *(Falling upon Desdemona.)*
Killing myself, to die upon a kiss.   *(Dies.)*

CORIOLANUS.

ACT I.—Scene I.

Power of the Roman state.

Men. I tell you, friends, most charitable care
Have the patricians of you.   For your wants,
Your suffering in this dearth, you may as well
Strike at the heaven with your staves, as lift them
Against the Roman state; whose course will on
The way it takes, cracking ten thousand curbs
Of more strong link asunder, than can ever
Appear in your impediment; for the dearth,
Of this most wise rebellion, thou go'st foremost;
Thou rascal, that art worst in blood to run,
Lead'st first to win some vantage,—
But make you ready your stiff bats and clubs;
Rome and her rats are at the point of battle;
The one side must have bale.—Hail, noble Marcius!

Instability of the Romans.

Enter Caius Marcius.

Mar. Thanks.—What's the matter, you dissentious rogues,
That, rubbing the poor itch of your opinion,
Make yourselves scabs?

1 *Cit.* We have ever your good word.

12

Mar. He that will give good words to thee, will flatter
Beneath abhorring.—What would you have, you curs,
That like nor peace nor war? the one affrights you,
The other makes your proud.   He that trusts you,
Where he should find you lions, finds you hares;
Where foxes, geese: you are no surer, no,
Than is the coal of fire upon the ice,
Or hailstone in the sun.   Your virtue is,
To make him worthy whose offence subdues him,
And curse that justice did it.   Who deserves greatness,
Deserves your hate: and your affections are
A sick man's appe ite, who desires most that
Which would increase his evil.   He that depends
Upon your favours, swims with fins of lead,
And hews down oaks with rushes.   Hang ye! Trust ye?
With every minute you do change a mind;
And call him noble that was now your hate,
Him vile that was your garland.   What's the matter,
That in these several places of the city
You cry against the noble senate, who,
Under the gods, keep you in awe, which else
Would feed on one another?—What's their seeking?

Scene III.

A mother's praise.

Vol. Indeed, you shall not,
Methinks I hear hither your husband's drum;
See him pluck Aufidius down by the hair;
As children from a bear, the Volsces shunning him:
Methinks I see him stamp thus, and call thus,—
" Come on, you cowards!
Though you were born in Rome:" his bloody brow

With his mail'd hand then wiping, forth he goes;
Like to a harvest-man, that's task'd to mow
Or all, or lose his hire.

   Vir. His bloody brow! O Jupiter, no blood!

Scene IV.

Coriolanus' looks and power.

   Lart. O noble fellow!
Who, sensible, outdares his senseless sword,
And, when it bows, stands up! Thou art left, Marcius:
A carbuncle entire, as big as thou art,
Were not so rich a jewel. Thou wast a soldier
Even to Cato's wish, not fierce and terrible
Only in stroke; but, with thy grim looks and
The thunder-like percussion of thy sounds,
Thou mad'st thine enemies shake, as if the world
Were feverous, and did tremble.

Scene X.

Character of Coriolanus.

   Bru. All tongues speak of him, and the bleared sights
Are spectacled to see him: your prattling nurse
Into a rapture lets her baby cry,
While she chats him: the kitchen malkin pins
Her richest lockram 'bout her reechy neck,
Clambering the walls to eye him: stalls, bulks, windows,
Are smother'd up, leads fill'd, and ridges horsed
With variable complexions; all agreeing
In earnestness to see him: seld-shewn flamens
Do press among the popular throngs, and puff
To win a vulgar station: our veil'd dames

Commit the war of whites and damask, in
Their nicely-gawded cheeks, to the wanton spoil
Of Phœbus' burning kisses: such a pother,
As if that whatsoever god who leads him,
Were slily crept into his human powers,
And gave him graceful posture.

   Com. I shall lack voice: the deeds of Coriolanus
Should not be utter'd feebly.—It is held
That valour is the chiefest virtue, and
Most dignifies the haver: if it be,
The man I speak of cannot in the world
Be singly counterpoised. At sixteen years,
When Tarquin made a head for Rome, he fought
Beyond the mark of others; our then dictator,
Whom with all praise I point at, saw him fight,
When with his Amazonian chin he drove
The bristled lips before him: he bestrid
An o'er-press'd Roman, and i' the consul's view
Slew three opposers: Tarquin's self he met,
And struck him on his knee: in that day's feats,
When he might act the woman in the scene,
He proved best man i' the field, and for his meed
Was brow-bound with the oak. His pupil age
Man-enter'd thus, he waxed like a sea;
And, in the brunt of seventeen battles since,
He lurch'd all swords o' the garland. For this last,
Before and in Corioli, let me say,
I cannot speak him home: he's stopp'd the fliers;
And, by his rare example, made the coward
Turn terror into sport: as waves before
A vessel under sail, so men obey'd,
And fell below his stem: his sword, (death's stamp,)
Where it did mark, it took; from face to foot

He was a thing of blood, whose every motion
Was timed with dying cries: alone he enter'd
The mortal gate of the city, which he painted
With shunless destiny, aidless came off,
And with a sudden re-enforcement struck
Corioli like a planet: now all's his:
When by and by the din of war 'gan pierce
His ready sense: then straight his doubled spirit
Re-quicken'd what in flesh was fatigate,
And to the battle came he; where he did
Run reeking o'er the lives of men, as if
'Twere a perpetual spoil: and till we call'd
Both field and city ours, he never stood
To ease his breast with panting.

Scene III.

Ingratitude.

3 *Cit.* We have power in ourselves to do it, but it is a power that we have no power to do: for if he shew us his wounds, and tell us his deeds, we are to put our tongues into those wounds, and speak for them; so, if he tells us his noble deeds, we must also tell him our noble acceptance of them. Ingratitude is monstrous: and for the multitude to be ingrateful, were to make a monster of the multitude; of the which, we being members, should bring ourselves to be monstrous members.

Custom.

Cor. Most sweet voices!—
Better it is to die, better to starve,
Than crave the hire which first we do deserve.
Why in this woolvish gown should I stand here,
To beg of Hob and Dick, that do appear,

Their needless vouches ?   Custom calls me to't:—
What custom wills, in all things should we do't,
The dust on antique time would lie unswept,
And mountainous error be too highly heap'd
For truth to over-peer.—Rather than fool it so,
Let the high office and the honour go
To one that would do thus.—I am half through;
The one part suffer'd, the other will 1 do.

ACT III.—Scene I.

Fears of the plebian's power.

The senate's courtesy ?   Let deeds express
What's like to be their words:— *We did request it :*
We are the greater poll, and in true fear
They gave us our demands :—Thus we debase
The nature of our seats, and make the rabble
Call our cares, fears: which will in time break ope
The locks o' the senate, and bring in the crows
To peck the eagles.—

Public policy.

Cor. No, take more:
What may be sworn by, both divine and human,
Seal what I end withal!—This double worship,—
Where one part does disdain with cause, the other
Insult without all reason; where gentry, title, wisdom,
Cannot conclude, but by the yea and no
Of general ignorance,—it must omit
Real necessities, and give way the while
To unstable slightness: purpose so barr'd, it follows,
Nothing is done to purpose: Therefore, beseech
          you,—
You that will be less fearful than discreet;

That love the fundamental part of state,
More than you doubt the change of 't; that prefer
A noble life before a long, and wish
To jump a body with a dangerous physic,
That's sure of death without it,—at once pluck out
The multitudinous tongue, let them not lick
The sweet which is their poison: your dishonour
Mangles true judgment, and bereaves the state
Of that integrity which should become it;   .
Not having the power to do the good it would,
For the ill which doth control it.

Coriolanus' courage.

1 *Pat*. This man has marr'd his fortune.
Men. His nature is too noble for the world:
He would not flatter Neptune for his trident,
Or Jove for his power to thunder.   His heart's his
            mouth:
What his breast forges, that his tongue must vent;
And being angry, does forget that ever
He heard the name of death.

Scene II.

Defiance.

Cor. Let them pull all about mine ears; present
            me
Death on the wheel, or at the wild horses' heels;
Or pile ten hills on the Tarpeian rock,
That the precipitation might down stretch
Below the beam of sight, yet will I still
Be thus to them.

HONOUR.

Vol. If it be honour, in your wars, to seem
The same you are not, (which, for your best ends,
You adopt your policy,) how is it less, or worse,
That it shall hold companionship in peace
With honour, as in war; since that to both
It stands in like request?

SCENE III.

Cor. I'll know no farther:
Let them pronounce the steep Tarpeian death,
Vagabond exile, flaying: Pent to linger
But with a grain a day, I would not buy
Their mercy at the price of one fair word;
Nor check my courage for what they can give,
To have 't with saying, Good morrow.

DEFIANCE.

Cor. You common cry of curs! whose breath I
       hate
As reek o' the rotten fens; whose loves I prize
As the dead carcasses of unburied men
That do corrupt my air, I banish you;
And here remain with your uncertainty!
Let every feeble rumour shake your hearts!
Your enemies, with nodding of their plumes,
Fan you into despair! Have the power still
To banish your defenders; till, at length,
Your ignorance, (which finds not, till it feels,)
Making not reservation of yourselves,
(Still your own foes,) deliver you, as most
Abated captives, to some nation

That won you without blows! Despising,
For you, the city, thus I turn my back:
There is a world elsewhere.

ACT IV.—SCENE IV.

Cor. A goodly city is this Antium.—City,
'Tis I that made thy widows: many an heir
Of these fair edifices 'fore my wars
Have I heard groan and drop: then knew me not;
Lest that thy wives with spits, and boys with stone,

Enter a CITIZEN.

In punny battle slay me.—Save you, Sir.
    Cit. And you.
    Cor. Direct me, if it be your will,
Where great Aufidius lies: is he in Antium?
    Cit. He is, and feasts the nobles of the state
At his house this night.
    Cor. Which is the house, 'beseech you?
    Cit. This, here, before you.
    Cor. Thank you, Sir: farewell.   [*Exit* CITIZEN.
O world, thy slippery turns! Friends now fast sworn,
Whose double bosoms seem to wear one heart,
Whose hours, whose bed, whose meal and exercise,
Are still together, who twin, as 'twere, in love
Unseparable, shall within this hour,
On a dissension of a doit, break out
To bitterest enmity: so, fellest foes,
Whose passions and whose plots have broke their sleep
To take the one the other, by some chance,
Some trick not worth an egg, shall grow dear friends,
And interjoin their issues. So with me:
My birthplace hate I, and my love's upon

This enemy town. I'll enter: if he slay me,
He does fair justice; if he give me way,
I'll do his country service.

Scene V.

Auf. Where is this fellow ?

2 Serv. Here, sir; I'd have beaten him like a dog, but for
disturbing the lords within.

Auf. Whence comest thou ? What wouldst
      thou ? Thy name ?
Why speak'st not ? Speak, man: What's thy
      name ?

Cor. If Tullus,   (*Unmuffling.*)
Not yet thou know'st me, and seeing me, dost not
Think me for the man I am, necessity
Commands me name myself.

Auf. What is thy name ?   (*Servants retire.*)

Cor. A name unmusical to the Volscians' ears,
And harsh in sound to thine.

Auf. Say, what's thy name ?
Thou hast a grim appearance, and thy face
Bears a command in 't; though thy tackle's torn,
Thou shew'st a noble vessel: What's thy name ?

Cor. Prepare thy brow to frown: Know'st thou
      me yet ?

Auf. I know thee not:—Thy name ?

Cor. **My** name is Caius Marcius, who hath done
To thee particularly, and to all the Volces,
Great hurt and mischief; thereto witness may
My surname, Coriolanus: The painful service,
The extreme dangers, and the drops of blood

Shed for my thankless country, are requited
But with that surname; a good memory,
And witness of the malice and displeasure
Which thou shouldst bear me: only that name
  remains;
The cruelty and envy of the people,
Permitted by our dastard nobles, who
Have all forsook me, hath devoured the rest;
And suffer'd me by the voice of slaves to be
Whoop'd out of Rome. Now, this extremity
Hath brought me to thy hearth: Not out of hope,
Mistake me not, to save my life; for if
I had fear'd death, of all the men i' the world
I would have 'voided thee: but in mere spite,
To be full quit of those my banishers,
Stand I before thee here.   •

ADMIRATION FOR VALOR.

Auf. O Marcius, Marcius,
Each word thou hast spoke hath weeded from my
  heart
A root of ancient envy. If Jupiter
Should from yon cloud speak divine things, and
  say,
'Tis true; I'd not believe them more than thee,
All noble Marcius.—O, let me twine
Mine arms about that body, where against,
My grained ash an hundred times hath broke,
And scared the moon with splinters! Here I clip
The anvil of my sword; and do contest
As hotly and as nobly with thy love,
As ever in ambitious strength I did
Contend against thy valor. Know thou first,

I loved the maid I married; never man
Sigh'd truer breath; but that I see thee here,
Thou noble thing! more dances my wrapt heart.
Then when I first my wedded mistress saw
Bestride my threshold.

Scene VII

Coriolanus' nobility of nature.

Auf.   All places yield to him, ere he sits down,
And the nobility of Rome are his:
The senators, and patricians, love him too:
The tribunes are no soldiers; and their people
Will be as rash in the repeal, as hasty
To expel him thence   I think, he'll be to Rome,
As is the osprey to the fish, who takes it
By sovereignty of nature.

ACT V.—Scene III.

Coriolanus' soliloquy.

Enter, in mourning habits, Virgilia, Volumnia, *leading young* Marcius, Valeria, *and Attendants.*

My wife comes foremost;

                                    But, out, affection!

All bond and privilege of nature, break!
Let it be virtuous, to be obstinate.—
What is that court'sy worth? or those doves' eyes,
Which can make gods forsworn?—I melt, and am
        not
Of stronger earth than others.—My mother bows;
As if Olympus to a molehill should
In supplication nod: and my young boy
Hath an aspect of intercession, which

Great nature cries, *Deny not.*—Let the Volces
Plough Rome, and harrow Italy; I'll never
Be such a gosling to obey instinct; but stand,
As if man were author of himself,
And knew no other kin.

   Vir. My lord and husband!

   Cor. These eyes are not the same I wore in
      Rome.

   Vir. The sorrow that delivers us thus changed,
Makes you think so.

   Cor. Like a dull actor now,
I have forgot my part, and I am out,
Even to a full disgrace. Best of my flesh,
Forgive my tyranny; but do not say,
For that, *Forgive our Romans.*—O, a kiss
Long as my exile, sweet as my revenge!
Now by the jealous queen of heaven, that kiss
I carried from thee, dear; and my true lip
Hath virgin'd it e'er since.—You gods! I prate,
And the most noble mother of the world
Leave unsaluted: Sink, my knee, i' the earth: (*Kneels.*)
Of thy deep duty more impression shew
Than that of common sons.

   Vol. O, stand up, bless'd!
Whilst, with no softer cushion than the flint,
I kneel before thee; and unproperly
Shew duty, as mistaken all this while
Between the child and the parent.

His surprise.

   Cor. What is this?
Your knees to me? to your corrected son?
Then let the pebbles on the hungry beach

Fillip the stars; then let the mutinous winds
Strike the proud cedars 'gainst the fiery sun;
Murd'ring impossibility, to make
What cannot be, slight work.

PURITY.

Cor. The noble sister of Publicola,
The moon of Rome; chaste as the icicle,
That's curded by the frost from purest snow,
And hangs on Dian's temple: Dear Valeria!

Cor. I beseech you, peace:
Or, if you'd ask, remember this before,—
The things I have forsworn to grant may never
Be held by your denials.   Do not bid me
Dismiss my soldiers, or capitulate
Again with Rome's mechanics: tell me not
Wherein I seem unnatural: desire not
To allay my rages and revenges with
Your colder reasons.

Vol.   O, no more, no more!
You have said you will not grant us anything;
For we have nothing else to ask but that
Which you deny already: yet we will ask;
That, if you fail in our request, the blame
May hang upon your hardness: therefore hear us

Cor. Aufidious and you Volsces, mark; for we'll
Hear naught from Rome in private.—Your request?

Vol. Should we be silent and not speak, our raiment
And state of bodies would bewray what life
We have led since thy exile.   Think with thyself,
How more unfortunate than all living women
Are we come hither: since that thy sight, which should
Make our eyes flow with joy, hearts dance with comforts,

Constrains them weep, and shake with fear and sorrow:
Making the mother, wife, and child, to see
The son, the husband, and the father, tearing
His country's bowels out.   And to poor we
Thine enmity's most capital: thou barr'st us
Our prayers to the gods, which is a comfort
That all but we enjoy; for how can we,
Alas! how can we for our country pray,
Whereto we are bound,—together with thy victory,
Whereto we are bound?   Alack! or we must lose
The country, our dear nurse; or else thy person,
Our comfort in the country.   We must find
An evident calamity, though we had
Our wish, which side should win; for either thou
Must, as a foreign recreant, be led,
With manacles through our streets, or else
Triumphantly tread on thy country's ruin;
And bear the palm for having bravely shed
Thy wife and children's blood.

   Cor. Not of a woman's tenderness to be,
Requires nor child nor woman's face to see.
I have sat too long.   (*Rising.*)

   Vol. Nay, go not from us thus.
If it were so, that our request did tend
To save the Romans, thereby to destroy
The Volces whom you serve, you might condemn us
As poisonous of your honour: No, our suit
Is, that you reconcile them: while the Volces
May say, *This mercy we have shew'd*, the Romans.

A MOTHER'S APPEAL.

Thou know'st great son,
The end of war's uncertain: but this certain,

That, if thou conquer Rome, the benefit
Which thou shalt thereby reap, is such a name,
Whose repetition will be dogg'd with curses;
Whose chronicle thus writ.—*The man was noble,*
But with his last attempt he wiped it out;
Destroy'd his country, and his name remains
To the ensuing age, abhorr'd   Speak to me, son;
Thou hast affected the fine strains of honour.
To imitate the graces of the gods;
To tear with thunder the wide cheeks o' the air,
And yet to charge thy sulphur with a bolt
That should but rive an oak.   Why dost not speak
Think'st thou it honourable for a noble man
Still to remember wrongs?—Daughter, speak you;
He cares not for your weeping.   Speak thou, boy;
Perhaps thy childishness will move him more
Than can our reasons.—There is no man in the
                world
More bound to his mother: yet here he lets me
                prate
Like one i' the stocks.   Thou hast never in thy life
Shew'd thy dear mother any courtesy;
When she, (poor hen!) fond of no second brood,
Has cluck'd thee to the wars, and safely home,
Loaden with honour.   Say, my request's unjust,
And spurn me back: But, if it be not so,
Thou art not honest; and the gods will plague thee,
That thou restrain'st from me the duty, which
To a mother's part belongs.—He turns away:
Down, ladies; let us shame him with our knees.
To his surname Coriolanus 'longs more pride,
Then pity to our prayers.   Down; and end;
This is the last.—So we will home to Rome,

And die among our neighbours.—Nay, behold us;
This boy, that cannot tell what he would have,
But kneels, and holds up his hands, for fellowship,
Does reason our petition with more strength
Than thou hast to deny't.—Come, let us go;
This fellow has a Volscian to his mother;
His wife is in Corioli, and his child
Like him by chance:—Yet give us our dispatch:
I am hush'd until our city be afire,
And then I'll speak a little.

CORIOLANUS' WEAKNESS.

Auf. I was moved withal.
Cor. I dare be sworn, you were:
And sir, it is no little thing to make
Mine eyes to sweat compassion. But, good sir,
What peace you'll make, advise me: For my part,
I'll not to Rome, I'll back with you; and pray you,
Stand to me in this cause.—O mother, wife!
Auf. I am glad, thou hast set thy mercy and thy
honour
At difference in thee: out of that I'll work
Myself a former fortune. (*Aside*.)
(*The Ladies make signs to Coriolanus.*)
Cor. Ay, by and by; (*To Volumnia, Virgilia, &c.*)
But we will drink together; and you shall bear
A better witness back than words, which we,
On like conditions, will have counter-seal'd.
Come, enter with us. Ladies, you deserve
To have a temple built you: all the swords
In Italy, and her confederate arms,
Could not have made this peace.
    13

DEFIANCE.

Cor. Cut me to pieces, Volsces; men and lads,
Stain all your edges on me.—Boy! False hound!
If you have writ your annals true, 'tis there,
That, like an eagle in a dove-cote, I
Flutter'd your Volsces in Corioli:
Alone I did it.—Boy!

NOBILITY.

2 *Lord.* Peace, ho!—no outrages:—peace!
The man is noble, and his fame holds in
This orb o' the earth.

TITUS ANDRONICUS.

ACT I.—Scene II.

Tit. Kind Rome, that hast thus lovingly reserved
The cordial of mine age to glad my heart!—
Lavinia, live; outlive thy father's days,
And fame's eternal date, for virtue's praise!

Mercy.

Wilt thou draw near the nature of the gods?
Draw near them then in being merciful:
Sweet mercy is nobility's true badge.

ACT. II.

Scene I.—*Rome.   Before the Palace.*

Safety on top of Mt. Olympus.

Enter Aaron.

Aar. Now climbeth Tamora Olympus' top,
Safe out of fortune's shot: and sits aloft,
Secure of thunder's crack or lightning's flash;
Advanced above pale envy's threat'ning reach.
As when the golden sun salutes the morn,
And, having gilt the ocean with his beams,

Gallops the zodiac in his glistering coach,
And overlooks the highest-peering hills.

Treachery in Kingly Courts.

The emperor's court is like the house of fame,
The palace full of tongues, of eyes, of ears:
The woods are ruthless, dreadful, deaf, and dull;
There speak, and strike, brave boys, and take your
    turns.

Hunting Morn.

Tit. The hunt is up, the morn is bright and grey,
The fields are fragrant, and the woods are green:
Uncouple here, and let us make a bay,
And wake the emperor and his lovely bride,
And rouse the prince; and ring a hunter's peal,
That all the court may echo with the noise.

Scene III.

Hunting scene.

Tam. My lovely Aaron, wherefore look'st thou
    sad,
When every thing doth make a gleeful boast?
The birds chaunt melody on every bush;
The snake lies rolled in the cheerful sun;
The green leaves quiver in the cooling wind,
And make a chequer'd shadow on the ground:
Under their sweet shade, Aaron, let us sit,
And—whilst the babbling echo mocks the hounds,
Replying shrilly to the well-tuned horns,
As if a double hunt were heard at once,—
Let us sit down, and mark their yelling noise:
And—after conflict, such as was supposed

The wandering prince and Dido once enjoy'd,
When with a happy storm they were surprised,
And curtain'd with a counsel-keeping cave,—
We may, each wreathed in the other's arms,
Our pastimes done, possess a golden slumber.

ACT III.—Scene I.

Titus' defence of Rome.

Mar. Which of your hands hath not defended
    Rome,
And rear'd aloft the bloody battle-axe,
Writing destruction on the enemies' castles?

ACT IV.- Scene VI.

Pride of lofty thoughts.

Tam. King, be thy thoughts imperious like thy
    name.
Is the sun dimm'd, that gnats do fly in it?
The eagle suffers little birds to sing,
And is not careful what they mean thereby;
Knowing that with the shadow of his wings,
He can at pleasure stint their melody:

TIMON OF ATHENS.

ACT I.—Scene I.

Force increases itself.

Poet. A thing slipp'd idly from me.
Our posey, is as a gum, which oozes
From whence 'tis nourished: The fire i' the flint
Shows not, till it be struck; our gentle flame
Provokes itself, and, like the current, flies
Each bound it chafes.

A poet like an eagle.

Poet. You see this confluence, this great flood
I have, in this rough work, shaped out a man,
Whom this beneath world doth embrace and hug
With amplest entertainment: My free drift
Halts not particularly, but moves itself
In a wide sea of wax: no levell'd malice
Infects one comma in the course I hold;
But flies an eagle flight, bold, and forth on,
Leaving no track behind.

Fortune's changes.

Poet. Sir, I have upon a high and pleasant hill
Feign'd Fortune to be throned: The base o' the
      mount

Is rank'd with all deserts, all kind of natures,
That labour on the bosom of this sphere
To propagate their states: amongst them all,
Whose eyes are on this sovereign lady fix'd,
One do I personate of Lord Timon's frame,
Whom Fortune with her ivory hand wafts to her:
Whose present grace to present slaves and servants
Translates his rivals.

    Pain. 'Tis conceived to scope.
This throne, this fortune, and this hill, methinks,
With one man beckon'd from the rest below,
Bowing his head against the sleepy mount
To climb his happiness, would be well express'd
In our condition.

    Poet. Nay, sir, but hear me on:
All those, which were his fellows but of late,
(Some better than his value), on the moment
Follow his strides, his lobbies fill with tendance,
Rain sacrificial whisperings in his ear,
Make sacred even his stirrup, and through him
Drink the free air.

    Pain. Ay, marry, what of these?

    Poet. When Fortune, in her shift and change of mood,
Spurns down her late beloved, all his dependants,
Which labour'd after him to the mountain's top,
Even on their knees and hands, let him slip down,
Not one accompanying his declining foot.

    Pain. 'Tis common:
A thousand moral paintings I can shew,
That shall demonstrate these quick blows of
        fortune
More pregnantly than words.

Scene II.

Ceremony.

Tim. Nay, my lords, ceremony
Was but devised at first, to set a gloss
On faint deeds, hollow welcomes,
Recanting goodness, sorry ere 'tis shewn;
But where there is true friendship, there needs none.
Pray, sit; more welcome are ye to my fortunes,
Than my fortunes to me.   (*They sit.*)

Apem. So;—
Thou'lt not hear me now,—thou shalt not? then,—
  I'll lock
Thy heaven from thee. O, that men's ears should be
To counsel deaf, but not to flattery!

ACT III.—Scene I.

Scene V.

Alcib. Honour, health, and compassion to the
  senate.
Sen. Now, captain?
Alcib. I am an humble suitor to your virtues;
For pity is the virtue of the law,
And none but tyrants use it cruelly.
It pleases time, and fortune, to lie heavy
Upon a friend of mine, who, in hot blood,
Hath stepp'd into the law, which is past depth
To those that, without heed do plunge into it.
He is a man, setting his fate aside,
Of comely virtues:
Nor did he soil the fact with cowardice:
(An honour in him, which buys out his fault,)

But, with a noble fury, and fair spirit,
Seeing his reputation touch'd to death,
He did oppose his foe:
And with such sober and unnoted passion
He did behave his anger, ere 'twas spent,　　　•
As if he had but proved an argument.

　　1 *Sen.* You undergo too strict a paradox,
Striving to make an ugly deed look fair:
Your words have took such pains, as if they labour'd
To bring manslaughter into form, set quarrelling
Upon the head of valour; which, indeed,
Is valour misbegot, and came into the world
When sects and factions were newly born:
He's truly valiant, that can wisely suffer
The worst that man can breathe; and make his
　　　　　wrongs
His outsides; wear them like his raiment,
　　　　　carelessly;
And ne'er prefer his injuries to his heart,
To bring it into danger.
If wrongs be evils, and enforce us kill,
What folly 'tis, to hazard life for ill?

　　Alcib. My lord, ——

　　1 *Sen.* You cannot make gross sins look clear;
To revenge is no valour, but to bear.

　　Alcib. My lords, then, under favour, pardon me,
If I speak like a captain.—
Why do fond men expose themselves to battle,
And not endure all threatnings? sleep upon it,
And let the foes quietly cut their throats
Without repugnancy? but if there be
Such valour in the bearings, what make we
Abroad? why then, women are more valiant,

That stay at home, if bearing carry it;
And the ass more captain than the lion; the felon,
Loaded with irons, wiser than the judge,
If wisdom be in suffering.   O my lords,
As you are great, be pitifully good:
Who cannot condemn rashness in cold blood?
To kill, I grant, is sin's extremest gust;
But, in defence, by mercy, 'tis most just.
To be in anger, is impiety;
But who is man, that is not angry?
Weigh but the crime with this.

ACT IV.--Scene II.

Coldness to misfortune.

2 Serv. As we do turn our backs
From our companion, thrown into his grave;
So his familiars to his buried fortunes
Slink all away: leave their false vows with him,
Like empty purses pick'd: and his poor self,
A dedicated beggar to the air,
With his disease of all-shunn'd poverty,
Walks, like contempt, alone.—

Scene III.

Power of gold.

What is here?
Gold? yellow, glittering, precious gold?   No, gods,
I am no idle votarist.   Roots, you clear heavens!
Thus much of this, will make black, white; foul,
          fair;

Wrong, right; base, noble; old, young; coward,
      valiant.
Ha, you gods! why this? What this, you gods?
      Why this
Will lug your priests and servants from your
      sides;
Pluck stout men's pillows from below their heads:
This yellow slave
Will knit and break religions; bless the accursed;
Make the hoar leprosy adored; place thieves,
And give them title, knee, and approbation,
With senators on the bench: this is it,
That makes the wappen'd widow wed again;
She, whom the spital-house, and ulcerous sores
Would cast the gorge at, this embalms and spices
To the April day again.
O thou sweet king-killer, and dear divorce
                            (*Looking on the gold.*)
'Twixt natural son and sire! thou bright defiler
Of Hymen's purest bed! thou valiant Mars!
Thou ever young, fresh, loved, and delicate wooer
Whose blush doth thaw the consecrated snow
That lies on Dian's lap! thou visible god,
That solder'st close impossibilities,
And makest them kiss! that speak'st with every
      tongue,
To every purpose! O thou touch of hearts!
Think, thy slave man rebels: and by thy virtue
Set them into confounding odds, that beasts
May have the world in empire!

THIEVES.

I'll example you with thievery:
The sun's a thief, and with his great attraction
Robs the vast sea: the moon's an arrant thief,
And her pale fire she snatches from the sun:
The sea's a thief, whose liquid surge resolves
The moon into salt tears: the earth's a thief,
That feeds and breeds by composture stolen
From general excrement: each thing's a thief:
The laws, your curb and whip, in their rough power
Have uncheck'd theft.   Love not yourselves: away!
Rob one another.   There's more gold: cut throats;
All that you meet are thieves.   To Athens go,
Break open shops; nothing can you steal,
But thieves do lose it.   Steal not less, for this
I give you; and gold confound you howsoever!
Amen.

CYMBELINE.

ACT I.—Scene I.

Imogen's sorrow.

Imo. O
Dissembling courtesy! How fine this tyrant
Can tickle where she wounds!—My dearest hus-
   band,
You must be gone;
And I shall here abide the hourly shot
Of angry eyes; not comforted to live,
But that there is this jewel in the world,
That I may see again.

Scene III.

Imogen's adieu.

Imo. Thou shouldst have made him
As little as a crow, or less, ere left
To after-eye him.
 Pis. Madam, so I did.
 Imo I would have broke mine eye-strings,
   crack'd them, but
To look upon him: till the diminution
Of space had pointed him as sharp as my needle:
Nay, follow'd him, till he had melted from

The smallness of a knat to air; and then
Have turn'd mine eye, and wept.—But, good
          Pisanio,
When shall we hear from him?

Pis. Be assured, madam,
With his next vantage.

Imo. I did not take my leave of him, but had
Most pretty things to say: ere I could tell him,
How I would think on him, at certain hours,
Such thoughts, and such; or I could make him
          swear,
The shes of Italy should not betray
Mine interest and his honour; or have charged him
At the sixth hour of morn, at noon, at midnight,
To encounter me with orizons, for then
I am in heaven for him, or ere I could
Give him that parting kiss, which I had set
Betwixt two charming words, comes in my father,
And like the tyrannous breathing of the north,
Shakes all our buds from growing.

Scene VII.

Description of a descended god.

Iach. He sits 'mongst men, like a descended god:
He hath a kind of honour sets him off,
More than a mortal seeming.

ACT II.—Scene I.

Encouraging honour.

The Heavens hold firm
The walls of thy dear honour; keep unshaked

That temple, thy fair mind; that thou may'st
    stand,
To enjoy thy banish'd lord, and his great
    land!

INDELIBLE MEMORY.

Why should I write this down, that's riveted,
Screw'd to my memory?

Scene III.

POWER OF GOLD.

What
If I do line one of their hands? 'Tis gold
Which buys admittance; oft it doth; yea, and
    makes
Diana's rangers, false themselves, yield up
Their deer to stand of the stealer; and 'tis
    gold
Which makes the true man kill'd, and saves the
    thief;
Nay, sometimes hangs both thief and true man:
    What
Can it not do, and undo?

Scene IV.

DESCRIPTION OF IMOGEN'S ROOM.

Iach. First, her bed-chamber
(Where, I confess, I slept not; but, profess,
Had that was well worth watching), it was hang'd
With tapestry of silk and silver; the story
Proud Cleopatra, when she met her Roman,
And Cydnus swell'd above the banks, or for
The press of boats, or pride: A piece of work
So bravely done, so rich, that it did strive

In workmanship and value.
The chimney
Is south the chamber; and the chimney-piece,
Chaste Dian bathing; never saw I figures
So likely to report themselves; the cutter
Was as another nature, dumb; outwent her,
Motion and breath left out.
The roof of the chamber
With golden cherubins is fretted: Her and-irons
(I had forgot them) were two winking Cupids
Of silver, each on one foot standing, nicely
Depending on their brands.

Scene V.

Women's deceits.

Could I find out
The woman's part in me!   For there's no motion,
That tends to vice in man, but I affirm
It is the woman's part: Be it lying, note it,
The woman's; flattering, hers; deceiving, hers;
Lust and rank thoughts, hers, hers; revenges,
          hers;
Ambitions, covetings, change of prides, disdain,
Nice longings, slanders, mutability,
All faults that may be named, nay, that hell
          knows,
Why, hers, in part, or all; but rather, all:
For even to vice
They are not constant, but are changing still
One vice, but of a minute old, for one
Not half so old as that.   I'll write against
          them,

Detest them, curse them.—Yet 'tis greater skill
In a true hate, to pray they have their will:
The very devils cannot plague them better.

ACT III.—Scene I.

Why pay tribute?

Why tribute? why should we pay tribute? If Cæsar can hide the sun from us with a blanket, or put the moon in his pocket, we will pay tribute for light; else, sir, no more tribute, pray you now.

ACT IV.—Scene II.

Boastfulness.

Gui. To who? to thee? What art thou? Have
    not I
An arm as big as thine? a heart as big?
Thy words; I grant, are bigger: for I wear not
My dagger in my mouth. Say, what thou art;
Why I should yield to thee?

Royalty in sons.

Bel. O thou goddess,
Thou divine Nature, how thyself thou blazon'st
In these two princely boys! They are as gentle
As zephyrs, blowing below the violet,
Not wagging his sweet head: and yet as rough,
Their royal blood enchafed, as the rudest wind,
That by the top doth take the mountain pine,
And make him stoop to the vale. 'Tis wonderful,
That an invisible instinct should frame them
To royalty unlearn'd; honour untaught;

14

Civility not seen from other; valour,
That wildly grows in them, but'yields a crop
As if it had been sow'd!

Signs of Roman success.

Sooth. Last night the very gods shew'd me a
   vision:
(I fast and pray'd for their intelligence), thus:—
I saw Jove's bird, the Roman eagle, wing'd
From the spungy south to this part of the
   west,
There vanish'd in the sunbeams: which
   portends
(Unless my sins abuse my divination)
Success to the Roman host.

ACT V—Scene II.

Chagrin for slandering a lady.

Iach. The heaviness and guilt within my
   bosom
Takes off my manhood: I have belied a lady,
The princess of this country, and the air on't
Revengingly enfeebles me; or could this carle,
A very drudge of nature's, have subdued me,
In my profession?

Scene IV.

Jupiter's descent on an eagle.

Sici. He came in thunder: his celestial breath
Was sulphurous to smell: the holy eagle
Stoop'd, as to foot us: his ascension is
More sweet than our bless'd fields: his royal bird

Prunes the immortal wing, and cloys his beak,
As when his god is pleased.

All. Thanks, **Jupiter!**

Sici. The marble pavement closes, he is enter'd
His radiant roof.—Away! and, to be blest,
Let us with care perform his great behest.

Scene V.

Posthumus' remorse for acts to Imogen.

O, give me cord, or knife, or poison,
Some upright justicer! Thou, king, send out
For torturers ingenious; It is I
That all the abhorred things of the earth amend,
By being worse than they.   I am Posthumus,
That kill'd thy daughter:—villian-like, I lie;
That caused a lesser villain than myself,
A sacriligious thief to do't:—the temple
Of virtue was she; yea, and she herself
Spit, and throw stones, cast mire upon me,
   set
The dogs o' the street to bay me: every villain
Be call'd, Posthumus Leonatus; and
Be villainy less than 'twas!—O Imogen!
My queen, my life, my wife!   O Imogen!
Imogen, Imogen!

Description of an uncivil prince.

Gui. A most uncivil one.   The wrongs he did
  me
Were nothing prince-like; for he did provoke
  me,
With language that would make me spurn the
  sea,

If it could so roar to me: I cut off's head;
And am right glad he is not standing here
To tell this tale of mine.

Two noble sons.

But, gracious sir,
Here are your sons again: and I must lose
Two of the sweet'st companions in the world:—
The benediction of these covering heavens
Fall on their heads like dew! for they are worthy
To inlay heaven with stars.

Penitence and forgiveness.

Iach. I am down again,   (*Kneeling.*)
But now my heavy conscience sinks my knee,
As then your force did.   Take that life, 'beseech
          you,
Which I so often owe: but your ring first;
And here the bracelet of the truest princess,
That ever swore her faith.
     Post. Kneel not to me;
The power that I have on you, is to spare you;
The malice towards you, to forgive you: Live,
And deal with others better.

Triumph of the Roman arms.

Sooth. The fingers of the powers above do tune
The harmony of this peace.   The vision
Which I made known to Lucius, ere the stroke
Of this yet scarce-cold battle, at this instant
Is full accomplish'd: For the Roman eagle,
From south to west on wing soaring aloft,
Lessen'd herself, and in the beams o' the sun

So vanish'd: which foreshew'd our princely eagle
The imperial Cæsar, should again unite
His favour with the radiant Cymbeline,
Which shines here in the west.
   Cym. Laud we the gods;
And let our crooked smoke climb to their nos-
        trils
From our bless'd altars! Publish we this
        peace
To all our subjects. Set we forward: Let
A Roman and a British ensign wave
Friendly together: so through Lud's town march
And in the temple of great Jupiter
Our peace we'll ratify; seal it with feasts.—
Set on there:—Never was a war did cease
Ere bloody hands were wash'd, with such a peace.

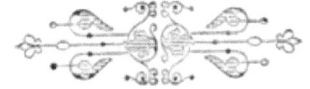

PERICLES, PRINCE OF TYRE.

ACT II—Scene III.

DESCRIPTION OF A KING.

Per. Yon king's to me, like my father's picture,
Which tells me, in that glory once he was;
Had princes sit, like stars, about his throne,
And he the sun, for them to reverence.
None, that beheld him, but, like lesser lights,
Did vail their crowns to his supremacy;
Where now his son's a glow-worm in the night,
The which hath fire in darkness, none in light;
Whereby I see that Time's the king of men,
For he's their parent, and he is their grave,
And gives them what he will, not what they crave.

ACT III—Scene I.

PERICLES PRAYING A STORM WILL CEASE.

Enter PERICLES, *on a ship at sea.*

Per. Thou God of this great vast, rebuke these
    surges,
Which wash both heaven and hell; and thou, that hast
Upon the winds command, bind them in brass,
Having call'd them from the deep! O, still thy
    deaf'ning,

Thy dreadful thunders; gently quench thy nimble,
Sulphurous flashes !—O how, Lychorida,
How does my queen ?—Thou storm, thou! venomously
Wilt thou spit all thyself ?—The seaman's whistle
Is as a whisper in the ears of death,
Unheard.

SCENE II.

THE QUEEN'S RETURN TO LIFE.

The queen will live: nature awakes; a warmth
Breathes out of her, she hath not been entranced
Above five hours.   See, how she gins to blow
Into life's flower again!

   1 Gent. The Heavens, sir,
Through you, increase our wonder, and set up
Your fame for ever.

   Cer. She is alive; behold,
Her eye-lids cases to those heavenly jewels
Which Pericles hath lost,   .
Begin to part their fringes of bright gold;
The diamonds of a most praised water
Appear, to make the world twice rich.   O live,
And make us weep to hear your fate, fair creature,
Rare as you seem to be.   (*She moves.*)

ACT V.—SCENE I.

DESCRIPTION OF PERICLES' QUEEN.

   Per. My dearest wife was like this maid, and such a one
My daughter might have been: my queen's square
       brows;
Her statue to an inch; as wand-like straight;
As silver-voiced: her eyes as jewel-like,

And cased as richly: in pace another Juno;
Who starves the ears she feeds, and makes them
        hungry,
The more she gives them speech.

        *   *   *   *   *   *   *

  Per. Pr'ythee speak;
Falseness cannot come from thee, for thou look'st
Modest as justice, and thou seem'st a palace
For the crown'd truth to dwell in: I'll believe thee,
And make my senses credit thy relation,
To points that seem impossible.

TROILUS AND CRESSIDA.

Joy of expectant love.

Tro. No, Pandarus: I stalk about her door,
Like a strange soul upon the Stygian banks,
Staying for waftage.   O, be thou my Charon,
And give me swift transportance to those fields,
Where I may wallow in the lily beds
Proposed for the deserver!   O, gentle Pandarus,
From Cupid's shoulder pluck his painted wings,
And fly with me to Cressid!

   Pan. Walk here i' the orchard, I'll bring her
     straight.   [*Exit.*

   Tro. I am giddy: expectation whirls me round.
The imaginary relish is so sweet,
That it enchants my sense: What will it be,
When that the watery palate tastes indeed
Love's thrice-reputed nectar? death, I fear me;
Swooning destruction; or some joy too fine,
Too subtle-potent, turned too sharp in sweetness,
For the capacity of my ruder powers:
I fear it much; and I do fear besides,
That I shall lose distinction in my joys;
As doth a battle, when they charge on heaps
The enemy flying.

Scene III.

What time and perseverance do.

Ulyss. Time hath, my lord, a wallet at his back,
Wherein he puts alms for oblivion,
A great-sized monster of ingratitudes
Those scraps are good deeds past; which are
                devour'd
As fast as they are made, forgot as soon
As done: Perserverance, dear my lord,
Keeps honour bright:
O, let not virtue seek
Remuneration for the thing it was!
For beauty, wit,
High birth, vigour of bone, desert in service,
Love, friendship, charity, are subjects all
To envious and calumniating time.
One touch of nature makes the whole world kin--

Omnipotence of providence.

Ulyss. The providence that's in a watchful state,
Knows almost every grain of Plutus' gold;
Finds bottom in the uncomprehensive deeps;
Keeps place with thought, and almost like the gods
Does thoughts unveil in their dumb cradles.
There is a mystery (with whom relation
Durst never meddle) in the soul of state;
Which hath an operation more divine,
Than breath, or pen, can give expressure to.

Scene IV.

Declaration of love.

Tro. Cressid, I love thee in so strain'd a purity,
That the blest gods—as angry with my fancy,

More bright in zeal than the devotion which
Cold lips blow to their deities,—take thee from me.

TIMES HASTE.

Tro. And suddenly; where injury of chance
Puts back leave-taking, justles roughly by
All time of pause, rudely beguiles our lips
Of all rejoindure; forcibly prevents
Our lock'd embrasures; strangles our dear vows
Even in the birth of our own labouring breath;
We two, that with so many thousand sighs
Did buy each other, must poorly sell ourselves
With the rude brevity and discharge of one.
Injurious Time now, with a robber's haste,
Crams his rich thievery up, he knows not how:
As many farewells as be stars in heaven,
With distinct breath and consign'd kisses to them,
He fumbles up in a loose adieu:
And scants us with a single famish'd kiss,
Distasted with the salt of broken tears.

ACT V.—Scene III.

HONOR DEARER THAN LIFE.

Hect. Hold you still, I say;
Mine honour keeps the weather of my fate:
Life every man holds dear; but the dear man
Holds honour far more precious-dear than life.—

MISFORTUNE CAUSES LOSS OF COURAGE.

Full merrily the humble-bee doth sing,
Till he hath lost his honey, and his sting;
And being once subdued in armed tail,
Sweet honey and sweet notes together fail.—

THE WINTER'S TALE.

ACT I.—Scene I.

Revolted wives.

Should all despair
That have revolted wives, the tenth of mankind
Would hang themselves.   Physic for't there is
   none.
It is a bawdy planet, that will strike
Where 'tis predominant; and 'tis powerful, think
   it,
From east, west, north, and south.

Signs of love.

 Leon. Is whispering nothing?
Is leaning cheek to cheek? is meeting noses?
Kissing with inside lip? stopping the career
Of laughter with a sigh? (a note infallible
Of breaking honesty:) horsing foot on foot?
Skulking in corners? wishing clocks more swift?
Hours, minutes? noon, midnight? and all eyes
   blind
With the pin and web, but theirs, theirs only,
That would unseen be wicked? is this nothing?
Why, then the world, and all that's in't, is no-
   thing;

The covering sky is nothing; Bohemia nothing;
My wife is nothing; nor nothing have these no-
        things,
If this be nothing.

STUBBORNNESS OF FOLLY.

Cam. Swear his thought over
By each particular star in heaven; and
By all their influences, you may as well
Forbid the sea for to obey the moon,
As or by oath remove, or counsel shake,
The fabric of his folly; whose foundation
Is piled upon his faith, and will continue
The standing of his body.

ACT V.—SCENE I.

VALUE OF GOOD COUNSEL.

Leon. Good Paulina,—
What hast the memory of Hermione,
I know, in honour.—O, that ever I
Had squared me to thy counsel!—then, even
        now,
I might have look'd upon my queen's full eyes;
Have taken treasure from her lips,—
Paul. And left them
More rich for what they yielded.

COMEDY OF ERRORS.

ACT II.—Scene I.
Everything has limits

Luc. Why, headstrong liberty is lash'd with wo.
There's nothing, situate under heaven's eye,
But hath his bound, in earth, in sea, in sky:
The beasts, the fishes, and the winged fowls,
Are their males' subject, and at their controls:
Men, more divine, the masters of all these,
Lords of the wide world, and wild wat'ry seas,
Indued with intellectual sense and souls,
Of more pre-eminence than fish and fowls,
Are masters to their females, and their lords:
Then let your will attend on their accords.

ACT V.—Scene I.
Jealousy makes madness.

Abb. And thereof came it, that thy man was mad:
The venom clamours of a jealous woman
Poison more deadly than a mad dog's tooth.
It seems, his sleep was hinder'd by thy railing:
And therefore comes it, that his head is light.
Thou say'st, his meat was sauced by thy
            upbraidings:
Unquiet meals make ill digestions,
Thereof the raging fire of fever bred;
And what's a fever but a fit of madness?

MEASURE FOR MEASURE.

ACT I.—Scene IV.

Laws in contempt.

Duke. We have strict statutes, and most biting laws,
(The needful bits and curbs for headstrong steeds,)
Which for these fourteen years we have let sleep;
Even like an o'er-grown lion in a cave,
That goes not out to prey: Now, as fond fathers
Having bound up the threat'ning twigs of birch,
Only to stick it in their children's sight,
For terror, not to use; in time the rod
Becomes more mock'd than fear'd: so our decrees,
Dead to infliction, to themselves we are dead;
And liberty plucks justice by the nose.

Scene IV.

Doubts make weakness.

Lucio. Our doubts are traitors,
And make us lose the good we oft might win,
By fearing to attempt.

ACT II.

Scene I.—*A Hall in Angelo's House.*

Enter Angelo, Escalus, *a Justice, Provost, Officers, and other Attendants.*

The law.

Ang. We must not make a scare-crow of the law,
Setting it up to fear the birds of prey,

And let it keep one shape, till custom make it
Their perch and not their terror.
   Escal. Ay, but yet
Let us be keen, and rather cut a little,
Than fall, and bruise to death: Alas! this
       gentleman,
Whom I would save, had a most noble father.
Let but your honour know,
(Whom I believe to be most straight in virtue,)
That, in the working of your own affections,
Had time cohered with place, or place with
       wishing,
Or that the resolute acting of your blood
Could have attain'd the effect of your own purpose,
Whether you had not, sometime in your life,
Err'd in this point, which now you censure him,
And pull'd the law upon you.
   Ang. 'Tis one thing to be tempted, Escalus,
Another thing to fall. I not deny,
The jury, passing on the prisoner's life,
May, in the sworn twelve, have a thief or two
Guiltier than him they try: What's open made to
      justice,
That justice seizes. What know the laws,
That thieves do pass on thieves? 'Tis very
      pregnant,
The jewel that we find, we stop and take it,
Because we see it.

MERCY AND PARDON ARE OFT MISTAKEN.

   Just. Lord Angelo is severe.
   Escal. It is but needful;

Mercy is not itself, that oft looks so;
Pardon is still the nurse of second woe:
But yet,—

VALUE OF MERCY.

Well believe this,
No ceremony that two great ones 'longs,
Not the king's crown, nor the deputed sword,
The marshal's truncheon, nor the judge's robe,
Become them with one half so good a grace,
As mercy does.

MERCY.

Isab. Alas! alas!
Why, all the souls that were, were forfeit once;
And He, that might the vantage best have took,
Found out the remedy: How would you be,
If He, which is the top of judgment, should
But judge you as you are?   O, think on that;
And mercy then will breathe within your lips,
Like man new made.

JUSTICE.

Isab. Yet, shew some pity.
Ang I shew it most of all, when I shew justice;
For then I pity those I do not know,
Which a dismiss'd offence would after gall;
And do him right, that, answering one foul wrong,
Lives not to act another.   Be satisfied;
Your brother dies to-morrow: be content.
Isab. So you must be the first, that gives this sen-
      tence;
And he, that suffers: O, it is excellent
To have a giant's strength; but it is tyrannous
To use it like a giant.

15

FOLLIES OF MAN'S LITTLE BRIEF AUTHORITY.

Isab. Could great men thunder
As Jove himself does, Jove would ne'er be quiet,
For every pelting, petty officer,
Would use his heaven for thunder: nothing but
         thunder.
Merciful Heaven!
Thou rather, with thy sharp and sulphurous bolt,
Split's the unwedgeable and gnarled oak,
Then the soft myrtle.—O, but men, proud men!
Drest in a little brief authority,
Most ignorant of what he's most assured,
His glassy essence,—like an angry ape,
Plays such fantastic tricks before high Heaven,
As makes the angels weep; who, with our spleens,
Would all themselves laugh mortal

ACT III—Scene I.

FEAR OF DEATH.

Claud. Ay, but to die, and go we know not
         where;
To lie in cold obstruction, and to rot;
This sensible warm motion to become
A kneaded clod; and the delighted spirit
To bathe in fiery floods, or to reside
In thrilling regions of thick-ribbed ice;
To be imprison'd in the viewless winds,
And blown with restless violence round about
The pendent world; or to be worse than worst
Of those, that lawless and uncertain thoughts
Imagine howling?—'tis too horrible!

The weariest and most loathed worldly life,
That age, ache, penury, and imprisonment
Can lay on nature; is a paradise
To what we fear of death.

Scene II.

Calumny and slander.

Duke. No might nor greatness in mortality
Can censure 'scape; back-wounding calumny
The whitest virtue strikes: What king so strong,
Can tie the gall up in the slanderous tongue ?—
But who comes here ?

ACT V—Scene V.

Justice.

F. Peter. Now is your time; speak loud, and
    kneel before him.
Isab. Justice, O royal duke! Vail your regard
Upon a wrong'd, I'd fain have said, a maid!
O worthy prince, dishonour not your eye
By throwing it on any other object,
Till you have heard me in my true complaint,
And given me justice, justice, justice, justice!

Midsummer Night's Dream.

ACT I.

Love's impatience.

Enter Theseus, Hippolyta, Philostrate, *and Attendants.*

The. Now, fair Hippolyta, our nupital hour
Draws on apace; four happy days bring in
Another moon; but, oh, methinks, how slow
This old moon wanes! she lingers my desires,
Like to a step-dame, or a dowager,
Long withering out a young man's revenue.

   Hip. Four days will quickly steep themselves in
       night;
Four nights will quickly dream away the time;
And then the moon, like to a silver bow
New bent in heaven, shall behold the night
Of our solemnities.

   The. What say you, Hermia? be advised fair
       maid:
To you your father should be as a god;
One that composed your beauties; yea, and one
To whom you are but as a form in wax,
By him imprinted, and within his power
To leave the figure, or disfigure it.
Demetrius is a worthy gentleman.

Lovers crosses and pledges.

Lys. Ah me! for aught that ever I could read,
Could ever hear by tale or history,
The course of true love never did run smooth:
But, either it was different in blood,—

   Her. O cross! too high to be enthrall'd to low!

   Lys. Or else misgraffed, in respect of years,—

   Her. O spite! too old to be engaged to young!

   Lys. Or else it stood upon the choice of
       friends,—

   Her. O hell! to choose love by another's eye!

   Lys. Or if there were a sympathy in choice,
War, death, or sickness did lay siege to it;
Making it momentary as a sound,
Swift as a shadow, short as any dream;
Brief as the lightning in the cooly'd night,
That, in a spleen, unfolds both heaven and earth,
And ere a man hath power to say,—Behold!
The jaws of darkness do devour it up,
So quick bright things come to confusion.

   Her. If then true lovers have been ever cross'd,
It stands as an edict in destiny:
Then let us teach our trial patience,
Because it is a customary cross;
As due to love, as thoughts, and dreams, and sighs,
Wishes, and tears, poor fancy's follower's.

   Lys. If thou lovest me then,
Steal forth thy father's house to-morrow night;
And in the wood, a league without the town,
Where I did meet thee once with Helena,
To do observance to a morn of May,
There will I stay for thee.

Her. My good Lysander!
I swear to thee by Cupid's strongest bow;
By his best arrow with the golden head;
By the simplicity of Venus' doves;
By that which knitteth souls, and prospers loves;
And by that fire which burn'd the Carthage queen,
When the false Trojan under sail was seen;
By all the vows that ever men have broke,
In number more than ever woman spoke;—
In that same place thou hast appointed me,
To-morrow truly will I meet with thee.

NOTICE OF LOVER'S MEETING.

Lys. Helen, to you our minds we will unfold:
To-morrow night, when Phœbe doth behold
Her silver visage in the wat'ry glass,
Decking with liquid pearl the bladed grass,
(A time that lovers' flights doth still conceal,)
Through Athens' gate have we devised to steal.

Her. And in the wood, where often you and I
Upon faint primrose-beds were wont to lie,
Emptying our bosoms of our counsel sweet,
There my Lysander and myself shall meet:
And thence, from Athens, turn away our eyes,
To seek new friends and stranger companies.
Farewell, sweet playfellow: pray thou for us,
And good luck grant thee thy Demetrius!—
Keep word, Lysander: we must starve our sight
From lovers' food, till morrow deep midnight.

SCENE II.

CONFERENCE OF AMATEUR ACTORS.

Snug. Have you the lion's part written? pray you, if it
be, give it me, for I am slow of study.

Quin. You may do it extempore, for it is nothing but roaring.

Bot. Let me play the lion too: I will roar, that I will do any man's heart good to hear me; I will roar, that I will make the duke say, *Let him roar again. Let him roar again.*

Quin. An you should do it too terribly, you would fright the duchess and the ladies, that they would shriek; and that were enough to hang us all.

All. That would hang us every mother's son.

Bot. I grant you, friends, if that you should fright the ladies out of their wits, they would have no more discretion but to hang us: but I will aggravate my voice so, that I will roar you as gently as any sucking dove; I will roar you an 'twere any nightingale.

LOVE'S POWERS.

Things base and vile, holding no quantity,
Love can transpose to form and dignity.

SCENE II.

LOVE.

Love looks not with the eyes, but with the mind;
And therefore is winged Cupid painted blind:
Nor hath Love's mind of any judgment taste;
Wings, and no eyes, figure unheedy haste:
And therefore is Love said to be a child,
Because in choice he is so oft beguiled.
As waggish boys in game themselves forswear,
So the boy Love is perjured everywhere:
For ere Demetrius look'd on Hermia's eyne,
He hail'd down oaths that he was only mine;
And when this hail some heat from Hermia felt,
So he dissolved, and showers of oaths did melt.

The flower with magic juice.

My gentle Puck, come hither: Thou remember'st
Since once I sat upon a promontory,
And heard a mermaid, on a dolphin's back,
Uttering such a dulcet and harmonious breath,
That the rude sea grew civil at her song;
And certain stars shot madly from their spheres,
To hear the sea-maid's music.

    Puck. I remember.

    Obe. That very time I saw (but thou couldst
        not,)
Flying between the cold moon and the earth,
Cupid all arm'd, a certain aim he took
At a fair vestal, throned by the west;
And loosed his love-shaft smartly from his bow,
As it should pierce a hundred thousand hearts;
But I might see young Cupid's fiery shaft
Quench'd in the chaste beams of the wat'ry moon;
And the imperial vot'ress passed on,
In maiden meditation, fancy free.
Yet mark'd I where the bolt of Cupid fell:
It fell upon a little western flower,—
Before, milk-white; now, purple with love's
        wound,—
And maidens call it, love-in-idleness.
Fetch me that flower; the herb I shew'd thee
        once;
The juice of it on sleeping eye-lids laid,
Will make a man or woman madly dote
Upon the next live creature that it sees.
Fetch me this herb; and be thou here again
Ere a leviathan can swim a league.

Puck. **I'**ll put a girdle round about the earth
In forty minutes.   [*Exit Puck.*

   Obe. Having once this juice,
I'll watch Titania when she is asleep,
And drop the liquor of it in her eyes:
The next thing when she waking looks upon,
(Be it on lion, bear, or wolf, or bull,
On meddling monkey, or on busy ape,)
She shall pursue it with the soul of love.
And ere I take this charm off from her sight,
(As I can take it, with another herb,)
I'll make her render up her page to me.—

Re-enter PUCK.

Hast thou the flower there? Welcome, wanderer.
   Puck. Ay, there it is.
   Obe. I pray thee give it me.
I know a bank whereon the wild thyme blows,
Where ox-lips and the nodding violet grows;
Quite over-canopied with lush woodbine,
With sweet musk-roses and with eglantine:
There sleeps Titania, some time of the night,
Lull'd in these flowers with dances and delight;
And there the snake throws her enamell'd skin,
Weed wide enough to wrap a fairy in:
And with the juice of this I'll streak her eyes:
And make her full of hateful fantasies.
Take thou some of it, and seek through this grove:
A sweet Athenian lady is in love
With a disdainful youth: anoint his eyes;
But do it, when the next thing he espies
May be the lady: Thou shalt know the man
By the Athenian garments he hath on.
Effect it with some care; that he may prove

More fond of her, than she upon her love:
And look thou meet me ere the first cock crow.

Scene III.

Love's caprice.

Lys. Content with Hermia? No: I do repent
The tedious minutes I with her have spent.
Not Hermia, but Helena I love:
Who will not change a raven for a dove?
The will of man is by his reason sway'd;
And reason says you are the worthier maid.
Things growing are not ripe till their season:
So I, being young, till now ripe not to reason;
And touching now the point of human skill,
Reason becomes the marshal to my will,
And leads me to your eyes; where I o'erlook
Love's stories, written in love's richest book.

Words of love.

Dem. (*Awaking.*) O Helen, goddess, nymph, per-
fect divine!
To what, my love, shall I compare thine eyne?
Crystal is muddy. O, how ripe in show
Thy lips, those kissing cherries tempting grow!
That pure congealed white, high Taurus snow,
Fand'd with the eastern wind, turns to a crow,
When thou hold'st up thy hand: O, let me kiss
This princess of pure white, this seal of bliss!

ACT III.

The fairies' duties.

Enter four Fairies.

1 *Fai.* Ready.
2 *Fai.* And I.

3 *Fai.* And I.

4 *Fai.* Where shall we go ?

Tita. Be kind and courteous to this **gentleman**;
Hop in his walks; and gambol in his eyes;
Feed him with apricots and dewberries,
With purple grapes, green figs, and mulberries;
The honey-bags steal from the humble-bees,
And, for night tapers, **crop** their waxen thighs,
And light them at the fiery glow-worm's eyes,
To have my love to bed, and **to arise**;
And **pluck** the wings from painted butterflies,
To fan the moonbeams from his sleeping eyes:
Nod to him, elves, and do him courtesies.

NECESSITY FOR HASTE IN LOVE MATTERS.

Puck. My fairy lord, **this must be done with haste**,
For night's swift dragons cut the clouds full fast,
And **yonder shines** Aurora's harbinger;
At whose approach ghosts, wandering **here and there**,
Troop home to church-yards: damned **spirits all**,
That in cross-ways and floods have burial,
Already to their wormy beds are gone;
For fear lest day should look their **shames upon**,
They **wilfully** themselves exile from light,
And must for aye consort with black-brow'd night.

Obe. But we are spirits of another sort:
I with **the morning's love** have oft made sport;
And, like a forester, the groves may tread,
Even till the eastern gate, all fiery red,
Opening on Neptune with fair blessed beams,
Turns into yellow gold his salt-green streams.
But, notwithstanding, haste; make no delay:
We may effect this business yet ere day.　　　[*Exit Ober.*

ACT IV.—Scene I.

Love bewitched.   .

Her dotage now I do begin to pity,
For meeting her of late, behind the wood,
Seeking sweet savours for this hateful fool,
I did upbraid her, and fall out with her:
For she his hairy temples then had rounded
With coronet of fresh and fragrant flowers,
And that same dew, which sometimes on the buds
Was wont to swell, like round and orient pearls,
Stood now within the pretty flowrets' eyes,
Like tears that did their own disgrace bewail.

ACT V.—Scene I.

Power of imagination in lover, lunatic and poet.

Lovers and madmen have such seething brains,
Such shaping fantasies, that apprehend
More than cool reason ever comprehends.
The lunatic, the lover, and the poet,
Are of imagination all compact:
One sees more devils than vast hell can hold—
That is, the madman; the lover, all as frantic,
Sees Helen's beauty in a brow of Egypt;
The poet's eye, in a fine frenzy rolling,
Doth glance from heaven to earth, from earth to heaven:
And, as imagination bodies forth
The forms of things unknown, the poet's pen
Turns them to shapes, and gives to airy nothing
A local habitation and a name.
Such tricks hath strong imagination;
That, if it would but apprehend some joy,
It comprehends some bringer of that joy;
Or, in the night, imagining some fear,
How easy is a bush supposed a bear.

The Merchant of Venice.

ACT I.—Scene I.

THE WORLD A STAGE.

Gra. You look not well, signior Antonio;
You have too much respect upon the world:
They lose it, they do buy it with much care,
Believe me, you are marvellously changed.

Ant. I hold the world but as the world, Gratiano;
A stage, where every man must play a part,
And mine a sad one.

CONTEMPTIBLE REASONS.

Bass. Gratiano speaks an infinite deal of nothing more
than any man in all Venice: His reasons are as two grains
of wheat hid in two bushels of chaff: you shall seek all day
ere you find them; and, when you have them, they are not
worth the search.

PORTIA'S VALUE.

Her name is Portia; nothing undervalued
To Cato's daughter, Brutus' Portia.
Nor is the wide world ignorant of her worth;
For the four winds blow in from every coast
Renowned suitors: and her sunny locks
Hang on her temples like a golden fleece.

ACT III.—SCENE I.

SHYLOCK'S DESCRIPTION OF A JEW.

Salar. Why, I am sure, if he forfeit, thou wilt not take his flesh: What's that good for?

Shy. To bait fish withal: if it will feed nothing else, it will feed my revenge. He hath disgraced me, and hindered me of half a million; laughed at my losses, mocked at my gains, scorned my nation, thwarted my bargains cooled my friends, heated mine enemies; and what's his reason? I am a Jew: Hath not a Jew eyes? hath not a Jew hands, organs, dimensions, senses, affections, passions? fed with the same food, hurt with the same weapons, subject to the same diseases, healed by the same means, warmed and cooled by the same winter and summer, as a Christian is? if you prick us, do we not bleed? if you tickle us, do we not laugh? if you poison us, do we not die? and if you wrong us, shall we not revenge? if we are like you in the rest, we will resemble you in that. If a Jew wrong a Christian, what is his humility? revenge; if a Christian wrong a Jew, what should his sufferance be by Christian example? why, revenge. The villainy you teach me, I will execute; and it shall go hard, but I will better the instruction.

PORTIA'S BEAUTIFUL PORTRAIT.

Bass. What find I here? (*Opening the leaden casket.*)
Fair Portia's counterfeit? What a demi-god
Hath come so near creation? Move these eyes?
Or whether, riding on the balls of mine,
Seem they in motion? Here are sever'd lips,
Parted with sugar breath; so sweet a bar
Should sunder such sweet friends: Here in her hairs
The painter plays the spider; and hath woven

A golden mesh **to entrap the** hearts of men,
Faster than gnats in cobwebs: But her eyes,—
How could he see to do them ?   Having made one,
Methinks, it should have power to steal both **his,**
And leave itself unfurnish'd.

ACT IV.—SCENE I.

HARDNESS OF SHYLOCK'S HEART.

Shy. What, wouldst thou have a serpent sting
thee twice ?
Ant. I pray you, think you question with the Jew:
You may as well go stand upon the beach,
And bid the main **flood bate** his usual height;
You **may as** well question with the wolf,
Why he hath made the ewe bleat, or the lamb;
You may as well forbid the mountain pines
To wag their high tops, and to make no **noise,**
When they are **fretted with the gusts of heaven:**
You may as **well do** any thing most hard
As seek to soften that (than which what 's **harder ?)**
His Jewish heart.

QUALITY OF MERCY.

Por. The **quality of** mercy is not strained;
It droppeth, as the gentle rain from heaven,
Upon the place beneath; it is twice bless'd,—
It blesseth him **that** gives, and him that takes,
'Tis mightiest in the mightiest: it becomes
The throned monarch better than his crown;
His sceptre shews the force of temporal power,
The attribute to awe and majesty,
Wherein doth sit the dread and fear of kings;
But mercy is above this sceptred sway,

It is enthroned in the hearts of kings,
It is an attribute to God himself;
And earthly power doth then shew likest God's
When mercy seasons justice.   Therefore, Jew,
Though justice be thy plea, consider this,—
That in the course of justice, none of us
Should see salvation: we do pray for mercy;
And that same prayer doth teach us all to render
The deeds of mercy.   I have spoke thus much
To mitigate the justice of thy plea;
Which if thou follow, this strict court of Venice
Must needs give sentence 'gainst the merchant
       there.

Shy. My deeds upon my head!   I crave the law,
The penalty and forfeit of my bond.

Por. Is he not able to discharge the money?

Bass. Yes, here I tender it for him in the court:
Yea, twice the sum: if that will not suffice,
I will be bound to pay it ten times o'er,
On forfeit of my hands, my head, my heart;
If this will not suffice, it must appear,
That malice bears down truth.   And I beseech you,
Wrest once the law to your authority:
To do a great right, do a little wrong,
And curb this cruel devil of his will.

Por. It must not be; there is no power in Venice
Can alter a decree established:
'Twill be recorded for a precedent;
And many an error, by the same example,
Will rush into the state.   It cannot be.

Shy. A Daniel come to judgment—yea, a Daniel!

ACT V—Scene I.

Moonlight and music.

How sweet the moonlight sleeps upon this bank!
Here will we sit, and let the sounds of music
Creep in our ears; soft stillness and the night,
Become the touches of sweet harmony.
Sit Jessica: Look how the floor of heaven
Is thick inlaid with patines of bright gold;
There's not the smallest orb, which thou behold'st,
But in his motion like an angel sings,
Still quiring to the young-eyed cherubims:
Such harmony is in immortal souls.

Power of music.

Therefore, the poet
Did feign, that Orpheus, drew trees, stones, and
        floods;
Since nought so stockish, hard, and full of rage,
But music for the time doth change his nature:
The man that hath no music in himself,
Nor is not moved with concord of sweet sounds,
Is fit for treasons, stratagems, and spoils;
The motions of his spirit are dull as night,
And his affections dark as Erebus,
Let no such man be trusted.

Great glory dims the less.

Enter Portia *and* Nerissa, *at a distance.*

Por. That light we see is burning in my hall.
How far that little candle throws his beams!
So shines a good deed in a naughty world.
    Ner. When the moon shone, we did not see the candle.

16

Por. So doth the greater glory dim the less:
A substitute shines brightly as a king,
Until a king be by; and then his state
Empties itself, as doth an inland brook
Into the main of waters.   Music! hark!
    Ner. It is your music, Madam, of the house.
    Por. Nothing is good, I see, without respect;
Methinks it sounds much sweeter than by day.
    Ner. Silence bestows that virtue on it, Madam.
    Por. The crow doth sing as sweetly as the lark,
When neither is attended; and I think
The nightingale, if she should sing by day,
When every goose is cackling, would be thought
No better musician than the wren.
How many things by season season'd are
To their right praise and true perfection!—
Peace, hoa! the moon sleeps with Endymion,
And would not be awaked!   [*Music ceases.*

All's Well That Ends Well.

Adoration of Love.

It were all one,
That I should love a bright particular star,
And think to wed it, is he so above me:
In his bright radiance and collateral light
Must I be comforted, not in his sphere.
The ambition in my love thus plagues itself:
The hind, that would be mated by the lion,
Must die for love. 'Twas pretty, though a plague,
To see him every hour; to sit and draw
His arched brows, his hawking eye, his curls, .
In our heart's table; heart, too capable
Of every line and trick of his sweet favour:
But now he's gone, and my idolatrous fancy
Must sanctify his relics.

Nothing impossible to Love.

Hel. Our remedies oft in ourselves do lie,
Which we ascribe to Heaven: the fated sky
Gives us free scope; only, doth backward pull
Our slow designs, when we ourselves are dull.
What power is it, which mounts my love so high,
That makes me see, and cannot feed mine eye?

The mightiest space in fortune nature brings
To join like likes and kiss like native things.
Impossible be strange attempts, to those
That weigh their pains in sense; and do suppose,
What hath been cannot be: Who ever strove
To show her merit, that did miss her love?

ACT II.—Scene III.

From lowest place where virtuous things proceed,
The place is dignified by the doer's deed:
Where great additions swell, and virtue none,
It is a dropsied honour: good alone
Is good, without a name: vileness is so:
The property by what it is should go,
Not by the title.
That is honour's scorn,
Which challenges itself as honour's born,
And is not like the sire: honours best thrive,
When rather from our acts we them derive
Than our fore-goers: the mere word's a slave,
Debauch'd on every tomb; on every grave,
A lying trophy; and as oft is dumb,
Where dust and damn'd oblivion is the tomb
Of honour'd bones indeed.   What should be said?

ACT IV.—Scene II.

Chasteness a jewel.

Dia. My chastity's the jewel of our house,
Bequeathed down from many ancestors;
Which were the greatest obloquy in the world
In me to lose.

Scene III.

The web of life.

1 *Lord.* The web of our life, is of a mingled yarn, good and ill together; our virtues would be proud, if our faults whipped them not; and our crimes would despair, if they were not cherished by our virtues.—

Corruption.

1 *Sold.* His qualities being at this poor price, I need not ask you if gold will corrupt him to revolt.

Par. Sir, for a *quart d'ecu* he will sell the fee-simple of his salvation, the inheritance of it; and cut the entail from all remainders, and a perpetual succession for it perpetually.

LOVE'S LABOR LOST.

ACT I.

SCENE I.—*Navarre. A Park with a Palace in it.*

FAME AND HONOR.

Enter the KING, BIRON, LONGAVILLE, *and* DUMAIN.

King. Let fame, that all hunt after in their lives,
Live register'd upon our brazen tombs,
And then grace us in the disgrace of death;
When, spite of cormorant devouring time,
The endeavor of this present breath may buy
That honour, which shall bathe his scythe's keen
   edge,
And make us heirs of all eternity.
Therefore, brave conquerors!—for so you are,
That war against your own affections,
And the huge army of the world's desires.—

STUDY'S REWARD.

Biron. Things hid and barr'd, you mean, from
   common sense?
King. Ay, that is study's god-like recompense.

STUDY.

Study is like the heaven's glorious sun,
 That will not be deep-search'd with saucy looks;
Small have continual plodders ever won,

Save base authority from others' books.
These earthly godfathers of heaven's lights,
That give a name to every fixed star,
Have no more profit of their shining nights,
Than those that walk, and wot not what they are.
Too much to know, is to know naught but fame,
And every godfather can give a name.

Scene II.

Soldiers' idea of love.

Arm. I do affect the very ground, which is base, where her shoe, which is baser, guided by her foot, which is basest, doth tread. I shall be forsworn, (which is a great argument of falsehood,) if I love: and how can that be true love, which is falsely attempted? Love is a familiar; love is a devil: there is no evil angel but love. Yet Samson was so tempted; and he had an excellent strength: yet was Solomon so seduced; and he had a very good wit. Cupid's butt-shaft is too hard for Hercules' club, and therefore too much odds for a Spaniard's rapier. The first and second cause will not serve my turn; the passado he respects not, the duello he regards not: his disgrace is to be called boy; but his glory is to subdue men. Adieu valour! rust, rapier! be still, drum! for your manager is in love; yea, he loveth. Assist me, some extemporal god of rhyme; for, I am sure, I shall turn sonneteer. Devise wit; write, pen; for I am for whole volumes in folio.

Beauty bought by the eye.

Prin. Good lord Boyet, my beauty, though but
    mean,
Needs not the painted flourish of your praise;
Beauty is bought by judgment of the eye,

Not utter'd by base sale of chapman's tongues:
I am less proud to hear you tell my worth,
Than you much willing to be counted wise
In spending your wit in the praise of mine.

ACT III.—Scene III.

Perjury for love.

Did not the heavenly rhetoric of thine eye
  ('Gainst whom the world cannot hold argument)
Persuade my heart to this false perjury ?
  Vows, for thee broke, deserve not punishment.
A woman I forswore ; but, I will prove,
  Thou being a goddess, I forswore not thee :
My vow was earthly; thou a heavenly love ;
  Thy grace, being gain'd, cures all disgrace in me.
Vows are but breath, and breath a vapour is :
  Then thou, fair sun. which on my earth dost shine,
Exhalest this vapour vow ; in thee it is ;
  If broken then, it is no fault of mine,
If by me broke.   What fool is not so wise,
To lose an oath to win a paradise ?

. ACT IV.—Scene III.

Rosaline's beauty.

Biron. Who sees the heavenly Rosaline,
That, like a rude and savage man of Inde,
  At the first opening of the gorgeous east,
Bows not his vassal head; and, strucken blind,
  Kisses the base ground with obedient breast ?
What peremptory eagle-sighted eye
Dares look upon the heaven of her brow,
That is not blinded by her majesty ?

King. **What zeal,** what fury hath inspired **thee**
    now ?
My love, **her mistress, is a gracious moon;**
She, an attending star, **scarce seen a** light.

POWER OF BEAUTY.

Beauty doth **varnish age, as if new-born,**
And gives the **crutch the cradle's infancy.**
O 'tis the sun that **maketh all things shine!**

POWER OF LOVE.

But love, **first learned in a lady's eyes,**
Lives not alone immured **in the brain;**
But with the motion **of all elements,**
Courses as swift **as thought in every** power,
And gives to **every power a double** power,
Above their functions and **their offices.**
It adds a precious **seeing to the eye,**
A lover's eyes will gaze an eagle blind;
A lover's ear will hear the lowest sound,
When the suspicious **head of theft is stopp'd;**
Love's **feeling is more soft and sensible**
Than are the tender **horns of cockled snails;**
Love's tongue proves dainty Bacchus gross in taste,
For valour, is not love a Hercules,
Still climbing trees in the Hesperides ?
Subtle as sphinx; as sweet and musical,
As bright Apollo's **lute, strung** with **his hair;**
And, when love **speaks, the voice of all the gods**
Makes heaven drowsy **with the harmony.**
Never durst poet touch **a pen to write,**
Until his ink were temper'd with **love's sighs:**
O, then his lines would **ravish savage ears,**

And plant in tyrants mild humility.
From woman's eyes this doctrine I derive:
They sparkle still the right Promethean fire;
They are the books, the arts, the academes,
That shew, contain, and nourish all the world;
Else, none at all in aught proves excellent.
Then fools you were these women to forswear;
Or, keeping what is sworn, you will prove fools.
For wisdom's sake, a word that all men love:
Or for love's sake, a word that loves all men;
Or for men's sake, the authors of these women;
Or women's sake, by whom we men are men;
Let us once lose our oaths to find ourselves,
Or else we lose ourselves to keep our oaths:
It is religion to be thus forsworn,
For charity itself fulfils the law;
And who can sever love from charity?

MUCH ADO ABOUT NOTHING.

ACT I—Scene I.

Love against friendship.

Friendship is constant in all other things,
Save in the office and affairs of love:
Therefore, all hearts in love use their own tongues;
Let every eye negotiate for itself,
And trust no agent: for beauty is a witch,
Against whose charms faith melteth into blood.

ACT III—Scene I.

Pleasant fishing.

Urs. The pleasant'st angling is to see the fish
Cut with her golden oars the silver stream,
And greedily devour the treacherous bait;
So angle we for Beatrice; who even now
Is couched in the woodbine coverture.

Disdain, scorn and hypocrisy.

Hero. O God of love! I know, he doth deserve
As much as may be yielded to a man;
But nature never framed a woman's heart
Of prouder stuff than that of Beatrice:
Disdain and scorn ride sparkling in her eyes,
Misprising what they look on; and her wit

Values itself so highly, that to her
All matter else seems weak: she cannot love.
Nor take no shape nor project of affection,
She is so self endeared.

Urs. Sure, I think so;
And therefore, certainly, it were not good,
She knew his love, lest she make sport at it.

Hero. Why, you speak truth; I never yet saw man,
How wise, how noble, young, how rarely featured,
But she would spell him backward; if fair-faced,
She'd swear, the gentleman should be her sister;
If black, why nature, drawing of an antic,
Made a foul blot; if tall, a lance ill-headed;
If low, an agate very vilely cut;
If speaking, why a vane blown with all winds;
If silent, why, a block moved with none.
So turns she every man the wrong side out;
And never gives to truth and virtue that
Which simpleness and merit purchaseth.

ACT IV—Scene I.

Clouded love.

Friar. Hear me a little;
For I have only been silent so long,
And given way unto this course of fortune,
By noting of the lady; I have mark'd
A thousand blushing apparitions start
Into her face; a thousand innocent shames
In angel whiteness bear away those blushes;
And in her eye there hath appear'd a fire,
To burn the errors that these princes hold
Against her maiden truth.

Possession lessens value.

For it so falls out,
That what we have we prize not to the worth
Whiles we enjoy it; but being lack'd and lost,
Why, then we rack the value, then we find
The virtue, that possession would not shew us
Whiles it was ours.

ACT V—Scene I.

To know a villain.

Leon. Which is the villian? Let me see his eyes,
That, when I note another man like him,
I may avoid him: Which of these is he?

Twelfth Night, or, What You Will.

ACT II.—Scene II.

Concealment of disappointed love.

She never told her love,
But let concealment, like a worm i' the bud,
Feed on her damask cheek: she pined in thought;
And, with a green and yellow melancholy,
She sat like Patience on a monument,
Smiling at grief.

ACT III.—Scene IV.

Hatred of ingratitude.

Ant. Will you deny me now?
Is 't possible, that my deserts to you
Can lack persuasion?   Do not tempt my misery,
Lest that it make me so unsound a man,
As to upbraid you with those kindnesses
That I have of you.
   Vio. I know of none;
Nor know I you by voice, or any feature:
I hate ingratitude more in a man,
Than lying, vainness, babbling, drunkenness,
Or any taint of vice, whose strong corruption
Inhabits our frail blood.

AS YOU LIKE IT.

ACT II.—Scene I.

Uses of adversity.

Sweet are the uses of adversity,
Which, like the toad, ugly and venomous,
Wears yet a precious jewel in his head;
And this our life exempt from public haunt,
Finds tongues in trees, books in the running brooks
Sermons in stones, and good in every thing.

Scene III.

Vigor of old age.

Though I look old, yet I am strong and lusty:
For in my youth I never did apply
Hot and rebellious liquors in my blood;
Nor did not with unbashful forehead woo
The means of weakness and debility;
Therefore my age is as a lusty winter,
Frosty, but kindly.

The seven ages of man.

Jaq. All the world's a stage,
And all the men and women merely players:
They have their exits, and their entrances;
And one man in his time plays many parts,

His acts being seven ages.   At first, the infant,
Mewling and puking in the nurse's arms:
And then, the whining school-boy, with his satchel,
And shining morning face, creeping like snail
Unwillingly to school: And then, the lover,
Sighing like furnace, with a woeful ballad
Made to his mistress' eye-brow: Then, a soldier
Full of strange oaths, and bearded like the pard,
Jealous in honour, sudden and quick in quarrel,
Seeking the bubble reputation
Even in the cannon's mouth: And then, the justice,
In fair round belly, with good capon lined,
With eyes severe, and beard of formal cut,
Full of wise saws and modern instances.
And so he plays his part: The sixth age shifts
Into the lean and slipper'd pantaloon;
With spectacles on nose, and pouch on side;
His youthful hose well saved, a world too wide
For his shrunk shank; and his big manly voice,
Turning again toward childish treble, pipes
And whistles in his sound: Last scene of all,
That ends this strange eventful history,
Is second childishness, and mere oblivion;
Sans teeth, sans eyes, sans taste, sans every thing.

THE TEMPEST.

ACT I.—SCENE II.

ARIEL, THE TEMPEST SPIRIT.

Enter ARIEL.

Ari. All hail, great master! grave sir, hail! I come
To answer thy best pleasure, be't to fly,
To swim, to dive into the fire, to ride
On the curl'd clouds; to thy strong bidding task
Ariel, and all his quality.

Pro. Hast thou, spirit,
Perform'd to point the tempest that I bade thee?

Ari. To every article.
I boarded the king's ship; now on the beak,
Now in the waist, the deck, in every cabin,
I flamed amazement. Sometimes I'd divide,
And burn in many places; on the top-mast,
The yards, and bowsprit, would I flame distinctly,
Then meet and join: Jove's lightnings, the
    precursors
O' the dreadful thunder-claps, more momentary
And sight-out-running were not the fire, and cracks
Of sulphurous roaring, the most mighty Neptune
Seem'd to besiege, and make his bold waves
    tremble;
Yes, his dread trident shake.

17

ACT II.—Scene I.

A bold swimmer.

Eran. Sir, he may live:
I saw him beat the surges under him,
And ride upon their backs; he trod the water,
Whose enmity he flung aside, and breasted
The surge most swoln that met him; his bold head
'Bove the contentious waves he kept, and oar'd
Himself with his good arms in lusty stroke
To the shore, that o'er his wave-born basis bow'd,
As stooping to relieve him.

ACT IV.—Scene I.

Enter Ceres.

Cer. Hail! many-colour'd messenger, that ne'r
Dost obey the wife of Jupiter;
Who, with thy saffron wings, upon my flowers
Diffusest honey-drops, refreshing showers;
And with each end of thy blue bow dost crown
My bosky acres, and my unshrubb'd down,
Rich scarf to my proud earth: why hath thy queen
Summon'd me hither, to this short grass'd green?

Unsubstantial character of the globe.

These our actors,
As I foretold you, were all spirits, and ·
Are melted into air, into thin air:
And, like the baseless fabric of this vision,
The cloud-capp'd towers, the gorgeous palaces,
The solemn temples, the great globe itself,
Yea, all which it inherit, shall dissolve;
And, like this insubstantial pageant faded,

Leave not a track behind.   We are such stuff
As dreams are made of, and our little life
Is rounded with a sleep.

ACT V—SCENE I.

ADDRESS TO THE TEMPESTS' SPIRITS.

Pro. Ye elves of hills, brooks, standing lakes, and groves
And ye, that on the sands with printless foot
Do chase the ebbing Neptune, and do fly him,
When he comes back: you demi-puppets, that
By moonshine do the green-sour ringlets make,
Whereof the ewe not bites; and you, whose pastime
Is to make midnight mushrooms; that rejoice
To hear the solemn curfew; by whose aid
(Weak masters though you be) I have bedimm'd
The noontide sun, call'd forth the mutinous winds,
And 'twixt the green sea and the azured vault
Set roaring war: to the dread rattling thunder
Have I given fire, and rifted Jove's stout oak
With his own bolt: the strong-based promontory
Have I made shake; and by the spurs pluck'd up
The pine and cedar: graves, at my command,
Have waked their sleepers; oped, and let them forth
By my so potent art.   But this rough magic
I here abjure: and, when I have required
Some heavenly music,,(which even now I do,)
To work mine end upon their senses, that
This airy charm is for, I'll break my staff,
Bury it certain fathoms in the earth,
And, deeper than did ever plummet sound,
I'll drown my book.

TAMING OF THE SHREW.

ACT I.—Scene I.

CONTEMPT FOR A SCOLDING WOMAN.

Pet. Think you a little din can daunt mine ears ?
Have I not in my time heard lions roar ?
Have I not heard the sea, puff'd up with winds,
Rage like an angry boar, chafed with sweat ?
Have I not heard great ordnance in the field,
And heaven's artillery thunder in the skies ?
Have I not in the pitched battle heard
Loud 'larums, neighingsteeds, and trumpets' clang ?
And do you tell me of a woman's tongue,
That gives not half so great a blow to the ear,
As will a chestnut in a farmer's fire ?

ACT IV.—Scene III.

HONOUR SUPERIOR TO POVERTY.

Pet. Well, come, my Kate; we will unto your father's,
Even in these honest mean habiliments;
Our purses shall be proud, our garments poor:
For 'tis the mind that makes the body rich;
And as the sun breaks through the darkest clouds,
So honour peereth in the meanest habit.
What, is the jay more precious than the lark,
Because his feathers are more beautiful ?
Or is the adder better than the eel,
Because his painted skin contents the eye ?

TWO GENTLEMEN OF VERONA.

———◆———

ACT II.—Scene IV.

The riches of a lover's mistress.

Val. Not for the world: why, man, she is mine own,
And I as rich in having such a jewel;
As twenty seas, if all their sands were pearl,
The water nectar, and the rocks pure gold.
Forgive me, that I do not dream on thee,
Because thou seest me dote upon my love,
My foolish rival, that her father likes,
Only for his possessions are so huge,
Is gone with her along; and I must after,
For love, thou know'st, is full of jealousy.

Scene VI.

A lover's changes.

Love bade me swear, and love bids me forswear:
O sweet suggesting love, if thou hast sinn'd,
Teach me, thy tempted subject, to excuse it.
At first I did adore a twinkling star,
But now I worship a celestial sun.
Unheedful vows may heedfully be broken,
And he wants wit, that wants resolved will
To learn his wit to change the bad for better.—
Fye, fye, unreverend tongue! to call her bad,
Whose sovereignty so oft thou hast preferr'd
With twenty thousand soul-confirming oaths.

Scene VII.

True love unquenchable.

Jul. A true-devoted pilgrim is not weary
To measure kingdoms with his feeble steps;
Much less shall she, that hath love's wings to fly;
And when the flight is made to one so dear,
Of such divine perfection, as Sir Proteus.

    Luc. Better forbear till Proteus make return.

    Jul. O, know'st thou not, his looks are my soul's food?
Pity the dearth that I have pined in,
By longing for that food so long a time.
Didst thou but know the inly touch of love,
Thou wouldst as soon go kindle fire with snow,
As seek to quench the fire of love with words.

    Luc. I do not seek to quench your love's hot fire,
But qualify the fire's extreme rage,
Lest it should burn above the bounds of reason.

    Jul. The more thou damn'st it up, the more it
        burns;
The current, that with gentle murmur glides,
Thou know'st, being stopp'd, impatiently doth rage;
But, when his fair course is not hindered,
He makes sweet music with the enamell'd stones,
Giving a gentle kiss to every sedge
He overtaketh in his pilgrimage.

Love's fidelity.

    Jul. That is the least, Lucetta, of my fear:
A thousand oaths, an ocean of his tears,
And instances as infinite of love,
Warrant me welcome to my Proteus.

Luc. All these are servants to deceitful men.

Jul. Base men, that use them to base effect!
But truer stars did govern Proteus' birth:
His words are bonds, his oaths are oracles;
His love sincere, his thoughts immaculate:
His tears, pure messengers sent from his heart:
His heart, as far from fraud as heaven from
   earth.

ACT III—Scene 1.

Love's daring.

Silvia, this night I will enfranchise thee:
'Tis so; and here's the ladder for the purpose.—
Why, Phaeton, (for thou art Merops' son,)
Wilt thou aspire to guide the heavenly car.
And with thy daring folly burn the world?
Wilt thou reach stars, because they shine on thee?

Scene II.

Advice to a lover.

Pro. Say, that upon the altar of her beauty
You sacrifice your tears, your sighs, you heart;
Write till your ink be dry; and with your tears
Moist it again; and frame some feeling line,
That may discover such integrity:
For Orpheus' lute was strung with poets' sinews,
Whose golden touch could soften steel and stones,
Make tigers tame, and huge leviathans
Forsake unsounded deeps to dance on sands.

ACT V—Scene IV.

Force of habit.

Vol. How use doth breed a habit in a man!
This shadowy desert, unfrequented woods,
I better brook than flourishing peopled towns
Here can I sit alone, unseen of any,
And, to the nightingales's complaining notes,
Tune my distresses, and record my woes,
O thou that dost inhabit in my breast,
Leave not the mansion so long tenantless;
Lest, growing ruinous, the building fall,
And leave no memory of what it was!

KING JOHN.

ACT II.—Scene I.
Devotion to loyalty.

Aust. Upon thy cheek lay I this zealous kiss,
As seal to this indenture of my love;
That to my home I will no more return,
Till Angiers, and the right thou hast in **France**,
Together with that pale, that white-faced shore,
Whose foot spurns back the ocean's roaring tides,
And coops from other lands her islanders,
Even till that **England**, hedged in with the main,
That water-walled bulwark, still secure
And confident from foreign purposes,
Even till that utmost corner of the west
Salute thee for her king.

False valor.

You are the hare of whom the proverb goes,
Whose valor plucks dead lions by the beard.

Scene II.
Death pleased at enraged royalty.

Ha, majesty! how high thy glory towers,
When the rich blood of kings is set on fire!
O, now doth death line his dead chaps with steel:
The swords of soldiers are his teeth, his fangs;

And now he feasts, mounting the flesh of men,
In undetermined differences of kings,—
Why stands these royal fronts amazed thus?
Cry havoc, kings! back to the stained field,
You equal potents, fiery-kindled spirits!
Then let confusion of one part confirm
The other's peace.

ACT III.—Scene I.

Great grief and sorrow.

Const. Thou may'st, thou shalt, I will not go with
　　　thee:
I will instruct my sorrows to be proud;
For grief is proud, and makes his owner stout.
To me, and to the state of my great grief,
Let kings assemble; for my grief's so great,
That no supporter but the huge firm earth
Can hold it up: here I and sorrow sit;
Here is my throne, bid kings come bow to it.

Day of triumph.

K. Phi. 'Tis true, fair daughter; and his blessed day
Ever in France shall be kept festival:
To solemnize this day, the glorious sun
Stays in his course, and plays the alchymist;
Turning, with splendour of his precious eye,
The meagre cloddy earth to glittering gold:
The yearly course, that brings this day about,
Shall never see it but a holiday.

Scene III.

Power of money.

Bast. Bell, book, and candle, shall not drive me
　　　back

When gold and silver becks me to come on,
I leave your highness.—

Scene IV.

Wish for power.

Const. No, no, I will not, having breath to cry:—
Oh, that my tongue were in the thunder's mouth!
Then with a passion would I shake the world,
And rouse from sleep that fell anatomy,
Which cannot hear a lady's feeble voice,
Which scorns a modern invocation.

Friendship in calamity.

K. Phi. Bind up those tresses: O, what love I
    note
In the fair multitude of those her hairs!
Where but by chance a silver drop hath fallen,
Even to that drop ten thousand wiry friends
Do glue themselves in social grief;
Like true, inseparable, faithful loves,
Sticking together in calamity.

Grief for loss of child.

Const. Grief fills the room up of my absent
    child,
Lies in his bed, walks up and down with me;
Puts on his pretty looks, repeats his words,
Remembers me of all his gracious parts,
Stuffs out his vacant garments with his form;
Then have I reason to be fond of grief.

Vanity of life.

Life is as tedious as a twice-told tale,
Vexing the dull ear of a drowsy man;

And bitter shame hath spoiled the sweet world's
        taste,
That it yields nought but shame and bitterness.

ACT IV.—Scene II.

Wasteful extravagance.

Sal. Therefore, to be possess'd with double
        pomp,
To guard a title that was rich before,
To gild refined gold, to paint the lily,
To throw a perfume on the violet,
To smooth the ice, or add another hue
Unto the rainbow, or with taper-light
To seek the beauteous eye of heaven to garnish,
Is wasteful, and ridiculous excess.

Scene III.

Extreme villainy.

              This is the very top,
The height, the crest, or crest unto the crest,
Of murder's arms: this is the bloodiest shame,
The wildest savagery, the vilest stroke,
That ever wall-eyed wrath, or staring rage
Presented to the tears of soft remorse.

ACT V.—Scene I.

How a king should act in war.

Bast. They found him dead, and cast into the
        streets;
An empty casket, where the jewel of life
By some damn'd hand was robb'd and ta'en away.

K. John. That villain Hubert told me he did
    live.

Bast. So, on my soul, he did, for aught he knew.
But wherefore do you droop? why look you sad?
Be great in act, as you have been in thought;
Let not the world see fear, and sad distrust,
Govern the motion of a kingly eye:
Be stirring as the time; be fire with fire:
Threaten the threatener, and outface the brow
Of bragging horror: so shall inferior eyes,
That borrow their behaviours from the great,
Grow great by your exomple, and put on
The dauntless spirit of resolution.
Away, and glister like the god of war,
When he intendeth to become the field:
Show boldness and aspiring confidence.
What, shall they seek the lion in his den,
And fright him there? and make him tremble
    there?
  O, let it not be said!—Forage, and run
To meet displeasure farther from the doors:
And grapple with him, ere he comes so nigh.

Scene II.

Advice to discord, tears, and weakness.

Lew. A noble temper dost thou shew in this;
And great affections, wrestling in thy bosom,
Do make an eartiquake of nobility.
O, what a noble combat thou hast fought,
Between compulsion and a brave respect!
Let me wipe off this honourable dew,
That silverly doth progress on they cheeks:

My heart hath melted at a lady's tears,
Being an ordinary inundation;
But this effusion of such manly drops,
This shower, blown up by the tempest of the soul,
Startles mine eyes, and makes me more amazed
Than had I seen the vaulty top of heaven
Figured quite o'er with burning meteors.

ACT V.—Scene VII.

England's defiance to the world.

Bast. O let us pay the time but needful woe,
Since it hath been beforehand with our griefs.—
This England never did (nor never shall)
Lie at the proud foot of a conqueror,
But when it first did help to wound itself.
Now these her princess are come home again,
Come the three corners of the world in arms,
And we shall shock them: Nought shall make us
      rue
If England to itself do rest but true.

KING HENRY VI.

PART I.

Bed. Hung be the heavens with black, yield day
    to night!
Comets, importing change of times and states,
Brandish your crystal tresses in the sky
And with them scourge the bad revolting stars,
That have consented unto Henry's death!
Henry the Fifth, too famous to live long!
England ne'er lost a king of so much worth.
  Glo. England ne'er had a king until his time,
Virtue he had, deserving to command:
His brandish'd sword d'd blind men with its
       beams;
His arms spread wider than a dragon's wings;
His sparkling eyes, replete with wrathful fire,
More dazzled and drove back his enemies,
Than mid-day sun, fierce bent against their faces.
What should I say? his deeds exceed all speech:
He ne'er lift up his hand, but conquered.
  Exe. We mourn in black: Why mourn we not
    in blood?

Henry is dead, and never shall revive:
Upon a wooden coffin we attend;
And death's dishonourable victory
We with our stately presence glorify,
Like captives bound to a triumphant car.
What? shall we curse the planets of mishap,
That plotted thus our glory's overthrow?
Or shall we think the subtle-witted French
Conjurors and sorcerers, that, afraid of him,
By magic verses have contrived his end?

Same.

Bed. Cease, cease these jars, and rest your minds
    in peace!
Let's to the altar:—Heralds, wait on us:—
Instead of gold we'll offer up our arms;
Since arms avail not now that Henry's dead.—
Posterity, await for wretched years,
When at their mothers' moist eyes babes shall
    suck;
Our isle be made a nourish of salt tears,
And none but women left to wail the dead.
Henry the Fifth! thy ghost I invocate:
Prosper this realm, keep it from civil broils!
Combat with adverse planets in the heavens;
A far more glorious star thy soul will make,
Than Julius Cæsar.

Scene II.

Woman's courage.

Puc. Dauphin, I am by birth a shepherd's
    daughter,
My wit untrain'd in any kind of art.
Heaven, and our Lady gracious, hath it pleased

To shine on my contemptible estate.
Lo, whilst I waited on my tender lambs,
And to sun's parching heat display'd my cheeks,
God's mother deigned to appear to me;
And, in a vision full of majesty,
Will'd me to leave my base vocation,
And free my country from calamity:
Her aid she promised, and assured success:
In complete glory she reveal'd herself;
And, whereas I was black and swart before,
With those clear rays which she infused on me,
That beauty am I bless'd with, which you see.
Ask me what question thou canst possible,
And I will answer unpremeditated:
My courage try by combat, if thou darest,
And thou shalt find that I exceed my sex.
Resolve on this: Thou shalt be fortunate,
If thou receive me for thy warlike mate.

GLORY.

Glory is like a circle in the water,
Which never ceaseth to enlarge itself,
Till, by broad spreading, it disperse to nought.
With Henry's death, the English circle ends;
Dispersed are the glories it included.
Now am I like that proud insulting ship,
Which Cæsar and his fortune bare at once.

Char. Was Mahomet inspired with a dove?
Thou with an eagle art inspired then.
Helen, the mother of great Constantine,
Nor yet Saint Phillip's daughters, were like thee.
Bright star of Venus, fall'n down on the earth,
How may I reverently worship thee enough?

18

ACT V.—Scene III.

Power of beauty.

As plays the sun upon the glassy streams,
Twinkling another counterfeited beam,
So seems this gorgeous beauty to mine eyes.
Fain would I woo her, yet I dare not speak:
Wilt thou be daunted at a woman's sight?
Ay; beauty's princely majesty is such,
Confounds the tongue, and makes the senses rough.

Attempt to crown a queen.

Suf. I'll undertake to make thee Henry's queen;
To put a golden sceptre in thy hand,
And set a precious crown upon thy head.

PART II.

ACT III.—Scene I.

Great and small men compared.

Small curs are not regarded when they grin;
But great men tremble when the lion roars;

Appearances deceitful.

K. Hen. My lords, at once: The care you have of
us,
To mow down thorns that would annoy our foot,
Is worthy praise: But shall I speak my conscience?
Our kinsman Gloster is as innocent

From meaning treason to our royal person,
As is the sucking lamb, or harmless dove:
The duke is virtuous, mild; and too well given,
To dream on evil, or to work my downfall.

   Q. Mar. Ah, what more dangerous than this
        fond affiance!
  Seems he a dove? his feathers are but borrow'd,
For he's disposed as the hateful raven.
Is he a lamb? his skin is surely lent him,
For he's inclined as are the ravenous wolves.
Who cannot steal a shape, that means deceit?
Take heed, my lord; the welfare of us all
Hangs on the cutting short that fraudful man.

Scene II.

Strength of circumstantial evidence.

  War. Who finds the heifer dead, and bleeding
       fresh,
And sees fast by a butcher with an axe,
But will suspect, 'twas he that made the slaughter?
Who finds the partridge in the puttock's nest,
But may imagine how the bird was dead,
Although the kite soar with unbloodied beak?
Even so suspicious is this tragedy.

Strength of a just cause.

  K. Hen. What stronger breast-plate than a heart
       untainted?
Thrice is he arm'd, that hath his quarrel just:
And he but naked, though lock'd up in steel,
Whose conscience with injustice is corrupted.

VARIETY OF CURSES.

Q. Mar. Fy, coward woman, and soft-hearted wretch!
Hast thou not spirit to curse thine enemies?

Suf. A plague upon them! wherefore should I
    curse them?

Would curses kill, as doth the mandrake's groan,
I would invent as bitter-searching terms,
[As curst, as harsh, and horrible to hear,]
Deliver'd strongly through my fixed teeth,
'With full as many signs of deadly hate,
As lean-faced envy in her loathsome cave:
My tongue should stumble in mine earnest words;
Mine eyes should sparkle like the beaten flint;
My hair be fix'd on end, as one distract;
Ay, every joint should seem to curse and ban:
And even now my burden'd heart would break,
Should I not curse them.   Poison be their drink!
Gall, worse than gall, the daintiest that they taste!
Their sweetest shade, a grove of cypress trees!
Their chiefest prospects, murdering basilisks!
Their softest touch, as smart as lizard's stings!
Their music, frightful as the serpent's hiss;
And boding screech-owls make the concert full!
All the foul-terrors in dark-seated hell—

Q. Mar. Enough, sweet Suffolk; thou torment'st
    thyself;
[And these dread curses—like the sun 'gainst glass,
Or like an over-charged gun,—recoil,
And turn the force of them upon thyself.]

STRONG ATTACHMENT.

Suff. If I depart from thee, I cannot live:
And in thy sight to die, what were it else

But like a pleasant slumber in thy lap ?
Here could I breath my soul into the air,
As mild and gentle as the cradle-babe.

ACT IV.—SCENE I.

HATE OF DISHONOR.

'Ne'er yet did base dishonor blur our name,
'But with our sword we wiped away the blot;
'Therefore, when merchant-like I sell revenge,
'Broke be my sword, my arms torn and defaced,
'And I proclaimed a coward through the world!

(Lays hold on Suffolk.)

CONTEMPT FOR SERVILE PERSONS.

Suf. O that I were a god, to shoot forth thunder
Upon these paltry, servile, abject drudges!
Small things that make base men proud: this villain
          here,
'Being captain of a pinnace, threatens more
'Than Bargulus, the strong Illyrian pirate.
'Drones suck not eagles' blood, but rob bee-
          hives.

PRIDE OF TRUE NOBILITY.

'*Suf.* Suffolk's imperial tongue is stern and rough,
'Used to command, untaught to plead for favour.
'For be it, we should honour such as these
'With humble suit: no, rather let my head
'Stoop to the block, than these knees bow to any,
'Save to the God of heaven, and to my king;
'And sooner dance upon a bloody pole,
'Than stand uncover'd to the vulgar groom.
[True nobility is exempt from fear:—]
'More can I bear, than you dare execute.

Scene II.

Dangers of lawyers and law.

'*Cade.* I thank you, good people; there shall be no
'money; all shall eat and drink on my score, and I will
'apparel them all in one livery, that they may agree like
'brothers, and worship me their lord.

'*Dick.* The first thing we do, let's kill all the lawyers.

Cade. Nay, that I mean to do. Is not this a lamentable
thing, that of the skin of an innocent lamb should be made
parchment? that parchment, being scribbled o'er should
undo a man? Some say, the bee stings: but I say, 'tis the
bee's wax, for I did but seal once to a thing, and I was
never mine own man since. How now? who's there?

Scene VII.

Justice and knowledge.

Justice with favour have I always done:
Prayers and tears have moved me, gifts could
       never.
When have I aught exacted at your hands,
But to maitain the king, the realm, and you?
Large gifts have I bestow'd on learn'd clerks,
Because my book preferr'd me to the king.
And—seeing ignorance is the curse of God,
Knowledge the wing wherewith we fly to
       heaven,—

Scene X.

'*Iden.* Nay, it shall ne'er be said, while England
       stands,
That Alexander iden, an esquire of Kent,
Took odds to combat a poor famish'd man.
'Oppose thy steadfast gazing eyes to mine,

'See if thou canst outface me with thy looks,
'Set limb to limb, and thou art far the lesser;
'Thy hand is but a finger to my fist;
'Thy leg a stick, compared with this truncheon;
'My foot shall fight with all the strength thou
      hast;
'And if my arm be heaved in the air,
'Thy grave is digg'd already in the earth.

REJOICING FOR KILLING A TRAITOR.

'*Iden.* Is't Cade that I have slain, that monstrous
    traitor?
'Sword, I will hallow thee for this thy deed,
'And hang thee o'er my tomb, when I am dead.
[Ne'er shall this blood be wiped from thy point;
But thou shalt wear it as a herald's coat,
To emblaze the honour that thy master got.]

ACT V.—SCENE II.

HATRED OF WAR.

Y. Clif. Shame and confusion! all is on the rout;
Fear frames disorder, and disorder wounds
Where it should guard. O war, thou son of hell,
When angry heavens do make their minister,
Throw in the frozen bosoms of our part
Hot coals of vengeance!—Let no soldier fly:
He that is truly dedicate to war
Hath no self-love; nor he, that loves himself,
Hath not essentially, but by circumstance,
The name of valour.- -O, let the vile world end,
               [*Seeing his dead father.*
And the premised flames of the last day
Knit earth and heaven together!

Now let the general trumpet blow his blast,
Particularities and petty sounds
To cease!—Wast thou ordain'd, dear father,
To lose thy youth in peace, and to achieve
The silver livery of advised age;
And, in thy reverence and thy chair-days, thus
To die in ruffian battle!

Scene III.

Ages' valor.

York. Of Salisbury, who can report of him;
That winter lion, who, in rage, forgets
Aged contusions, and all brush of time;
And, like a gallant in the brow of youth,
Repairs him with occasion?

PART III.

ACT I.—Scene I.

King Henry's refusal to leave his throne.

K. Hen. Think'st thou that I will leave my kingly
    throne,
Wherein my grandsire, and my father, sat?
No, first shall war unpeople this my realm;
'Ay, and their colours—often borne in France,
And now in England, to our heart's great sorrow,—
Shall be my winding-sheet.—Why faint you lords?
'May title's good, and better far than his.

THREATS OF WARWICK.

War. Do right unto this princely duke of York;
Or I will fill the house with armed men,
And o'er the chair of state, where now he sits,
Write up his title with usurping blood.

QUEEN MARGARET'S REPROACH TO THE KING FOR WEAKNESS.

Q. Mar. Enforced thee! art thou king, and wilt
    be forced?
I shame to hear thee speak. Ah, timorous wretch!
Thou hast undone thyself, thy son, and me;
'And given unto the house of Yorks such head,
[As thou shalt reign but by their sufferance.
To entail him and his heirs unto the crown,
What is it but to make the sepulchre,
And creep into it far before thy time?
Warwick is chancellor, and the lord of Calais;]
Stern Faulconbridge, commands the narrow seas;
The duke is made protector of the realm;
'And yet shalt thou be safe? [such safety finds
The trembling lamb, environed with wolves.]
'Had I been there, which am a silly woman,
'The soldiers should have toss'd me on their pikes,
'Before I would have granted to that act.
[But thou prefer'st thy life before thine honour.]

RESULT OF THE QUEEN'S AMBITION.

'*K. Hen.* Poor queen! how love to me and to her son,
'Hath made her break out into terms of rage!
'Revenged may she be on that hateful duke;
[Whose haughty spirit winged with desire,
Will cost my crown, and, like an empty eagle,
Tire on the flesh of me, and of my son!

Scene III.

Killing looks.

Rut. So looks the pent-up lion o'er the wretch
That trembles under his devouring paws:
And so he walks, insulting o'er his prey;
And so he comes to rend his limbs asunder,—
Ah, gentle Clifford, kill me with thy sword,
And not with such a cruel threat'ning look.

Scene IV.

Kingly Pride.

'*York.* The army of the queen hath got the field:
'My uncles both are slain in rescuing me;
'And all my followers to the eager foe
'Turn back and fly, like ships before the wind,
'Or lambs pursued by hunger-starved wolves.
'My sons—God knows what hath bechanced them:
But this I know,—they have demeaned themselves
Like men born to renown, by life or death.
'Three times did Richard made a lane to me;
And thrice cried,—*Courage, father! fight it out!*
'And full as oft came Edward to my side,
With purple faulchion, painted to the hilt
'In blood of those that had encounter'd him:
'And when the hardiest warriors did retire,
'Richard cried,—*Charge! and give no foot of ground!*
'And cried,—*A crown, or else a glorious tomb!*
'*A sceptre, or an earthly sepulchre!*
With this, we charged again: but, out, alas!
'We bodged again; as I have seen a swan
'With bootless labour swim against the tide,
And spend her strength with over-matching waves.

The phœnix and fight of cowards.

York. My ashes, as the phœnix, may bring
      forth
'A bird, that will revenge upon you all:
'And, in that hope, I throw mine eyes to heaven,
Scorning whate'er you can afflict me with.
'Why come you not? what? multitudes, and fear?
   Clif. So cowards fight, when they can fly no
      farther;
'So doves do peck the falcon's piercing talons;
So desperate thieves, all hopeless of their lives,
Breathe out invectives 'gainst the officers.

ACT II.—Scene II.

The wavering battle.

[*K. Hen.* This battle fares like to the morning
     war,
When dying clouds contend with growing light;
What time the shepherd, blowing of his nails,
Can neither call it perfect day nor night.]
'Now sways it this way, like a mighty sea,
'Forced by the tide to combat with the wind;
'Now sways it that way, like the self-same sea,
'Forced to retire by fury of the wind:
'Sometime, the flood prevails; and then,
     wind;
'Now, one the better; then, another best;
'Both tugging to be victors, breast to breast,
'Yet neither conqueror, nor conquered:
'So is the equal poise of this fell war.

Scene VI.

Attraction of Greatness for Small Things.

The common people swarm like summer-flies:
And whither fly the gnats, but to the sun?
And who shies now but Henry's enemies?
O Phœbus! hadst thou never given consent
That Phaeton should check thy fiery steeds,
Thy burning car never had scorch'd the earth.

ACT III.—Scene I.

Power of Women's Tears.

'By this account, then, Margaret may win him,
'For she's a woman to be pitied much:
Her sighs will make a battery in his breast;
Her tears will pierce into a marble heart;
The tiger will be mild, while she doth mourn;
And Nero will be tainted with remorse,
To hear, and see, her plaints, her brinish tears.

Content, a Crown.

K. *Hen.* My crown is in my heart, not on my
head;
[Not deck'd with diamonds and Indian stones,
Nor to be seen: my crown is call'd content:]
'A crown it is, that seldom kings enjoy.

ACT IV —Scene VI.

Government conceded to Warwick.

Clar. No, Warwick, thou art worthy of the sway,
To whom the heavens, in thy nativity,
Adjudged an olive branch and laurel crown,

As likely to be blest in peace and war;
And therefore I yield thee my free consent.

APPEARANCE OF PRINCE HENRY

K. Hen. Come, hither, England's hope. [*His hand on his
head.*] In secret powers
Suggest but truth to my divining thoughts,
This pretty lad will prove our country's bliss.
His looks are full of peaceful majesty;
His head by nature framed to wear a crown,
His hand to wield a sceptre; and himself
Likely in time to bless a regal throne.
Make much of him, my lords; for this is he
Must help you more than you are hurt by me.

ACT. V.—SCENE II.

WARWICK'S LAMENT FOR LOSS OF POWER.

War. Ah, who is nigh? come to me, friend or
foe,
And tell me, who is victor, York or Warwick?
Why ask I that? my mangled body shews,
[My blood, my want of strength, my sick heart
shews.]
That I must yield my body to the earth,
And, by my fall, the conquest of my foe.
Thus yields the cedar to the axe's edge,
Whose arms gave shelter to the princely eagle,
Under whose shade the ramping lion slept:
Whose top-branch overpeer'd Jove's spreading
tree,
And kept low shrubs from winter's powerful
wind.

These eyes, that now are dimm'd with death's black
      veil,
Have been as piercing as the mid-day sun,
To search the secret treasons of the world:|
The wrinkles in my brow, now fill'd with blood,
Were liken'd oft to kingly sepulchres;
For who lived king, but I could dig his grave ?
And who durst smile, when Warwick bent his
      brow ?
Lo, now my glory smear'd in dust and blood!
My parks, my walks, my manors that I had,
Even now forsake me; and of all my lands,
Is nothing left me, but my body's length!
Why, what is pomp, rule, reign, but earth and
      dust ?
And, live we how we can, yet die we must.

KING HENRY IV.

PART I.

ACT I.—Scene III.

HOTSPUR'S DESCRIPTION OF A COXCOMB IN WAR.

Hot. My liege, I did deny no prisoners.
But, I remember, when the fight is done,
When I was dry with rage and extreme toil,
Breathless and faint, leaning upon my sword,
Came there a certain lord, neat, trimly dress'd,
Fresh as a bridegroom; and his chin, new reap'd,
Shew'd like a stubble-land at harvest-home;
He was perfumed like a milliner;
And 'twixt his finger and his thumb he held
A pouncet-box, which ever and anon
He gave his nose, an took 't away again;—
Who, therewith angry, when it next came there,
Took it in snuff:—and still he smiled and talk'd;
And, as the soldiers bore dead bodies by,
He call'd them untaught knaves, unmannerly,
To bring a slovenly unhandsome corse
Betwixt the wind and his nobility.
With many holiday and lady terms
He question'd me; among the rest demanded
My prisoners, in your majesty's behalf.

I then, all smarting, with my wounds being cold,
To be so pester'd with a popinjay,
Out of my grief and my impatience,
Answer'd neglectingly, I know not what;
He should, or he should not;—for he made me mad
To see him shine so brisk, and smell so sweet,
And talk so like a waiting-gentlewoman,
Of guns, and drums, and wounds, (God save the mark!)
And telling me the sovereign'st thing on earth
Was spermaceti for an inward bruise;
And that it was great pity, so it was,
That villanous saltpetre should be digg'd
Out of the bowels of the harmless earth,
Which many a good tall fellow had destroy'd
So cowardly; and, but for these vile guns,
He would himself have been a soldier.
This bald unjointed chat of his, my lord,
I answer'd indirectly, as I said;
And, I beseech you, let not his report
Come current for an accusation,
Betwixt my love and your high majesty

HONOR.

Hot. If he fall in, good night:—or sink or swim:—
Send danger from the east unto the west,
So honour cross it from the north to south,
And let them grapple.—O! the blood more
        stirs,
To rouse a lion, than to start a hare.

HONOR FROM THE MOON.

Hot. By Heaven, methinks, it were an easy
        leap,

To pluck bright honour from the pale-faced
      moon:
Or dive into the bottom of the deep,
Where fathom-line could never touch the
      ground,
And pluck up drowned honour by the locks.

ACT III.—Scene I. .

Tediousness.

Mort. Fy, cousin, Percy! how you cross my
      father!
  Hot. I cannot choose: sometimes he angers
      me,
With telling me of the moldwarp and the ant,
Of the dreamer Merlin, and his prophecies;
And of a dragon and a finless fish, .
A clip-wing'd griffin, and a moulton raven,
A couching lion, and a ramping cat,
And such a deal of skimble-skamble stuff
As puts me from my faith. I tell you what,—
He held me but last night, at least nine hours,
In reckoning up the several devil's names,
That were his lackeys: I cried, humph,—and, well,
      —go to,—
But mark'd him not a word. O, he's as tedious
As is a tired horse, a railing wife;
Worse than a smoky house.

Disgust for mincing poetry.

  Hot. Marry, and I'm glad of it with all my heart;
I had rather be a kitten, and cry mew,
Then one of these same metre ballad-mongers:

19

I had rather hear a brazen canstick turn'd,
Or a dry wheel grate on an axle-tree;
And that would set my teeth nothing on edge,
Nothing so much as mincing poetry;
Tis like the forced gait of a shuffling nag.

LOVE'S CARESSES.

Glend. She bids you,
Upon the wanton rushes lay you down,
And rest your gentle head upon her lap,
And she will sing the song that pleaseth you,
And on your eye-lids crown the god of sleep,
Charming your blood with pleasing heaviness:
Making such difference 'twixt wake and sleep,
As the difference betwixt day and night,
The hour before the heavenly-harness'd team
Begins his golden progress in the east.

HARRY LIKE PEGASUS IN NOBLE HORSEMANSHIP.

Ver. All furnish'd, all in arms,
All plumed like estridges that wing the wind;
Bated like eagles having lately bathed;
Glittering in golden coats, like images;
As full of spirit as the month of May,
And gorgeous as the sun at midsummer;
I saw young Harry,—with his beaver on,
His cuisses on his thighs, gallantly arm'd,—
Rise from the ground like feather'd Mercury,
And vaulted with such ease into his seat,
As if an angel dropped down from the clouds,
To turn and wind a fiery Pegasus,
And witch the world with noble horsemanship.

PART II.

INDUCTION—RUMOUR.

Enter RUMOUR, painted full of tongues.

Rum. Open your ears; for which of you will stop
The vent of hearing, when loud Rumour speaks?
I, from the orient to the drooping west,
Making the wind my post-horse, still unfold
The acts commenced on this ball of earth:
Upon my tongues continual slanders ride;
The which in every language I pronounce,
Stuffing the ears of men with false reports.
I speak of peace, while covert enmity,
Under the smile of safety, wounds the world:
And who but Rumour, who but only I,
Make fearful musters, and prepared defence.

  * * * * * * *

Rumour is a pipe
Blown by surmises, jealousies, conjectures;
And of so easy and so plain a stop,
That the blunt monster with uncounted heads,
The still-discordant wavering multitude,
Can play upon it. But what need I thus
My well-known body to anatomize
Among my household?

ACT III.—SCENE I.

APOSTROPHE TO SLEEP.

Sleep, gentle sleep,
Nature's soft nurse, how have I frighted thee,

That thou no more wilt weigh my eyelids down,
And steep my senses in forgetfulness?
Why rather, sleep, liest thou in smoky cribs,
Upon uneasy pallets stretching thee,
And hush'd with buzzing night-flies to thy
      slumber;
Than in the perfumed chambers of the great,
Under the canopies of costly state,
And lull'd with sounds of sweetest melody?
O thou dull god, why liest thou with the vile
In loathsome beds; and leavest the kingly
      couch,
A watch-case, or a common 'larum bell?
Wilt thou upon the high and giddy mast
Seal up the ship-boy's eyes, and rock his brains
In cradle of the rude imperious surge:
And in the visitation of the winds,
Who take the ruffian billows by the top,
Curling their monstrous heads, and hanging
      them
With deaf'ning clamours in the slippery clouds, [shrouds]
That, with the hurly, death itself awakes?
Can'st thou, O partial sleep! give thy repose
To the wet sea-boy in an hour so rude:
And in the calmest and most stillest night;
With all appliances and means to boot,
Deny it to a king? Then, happy low, lie
      down;
Uneasy lies the head that wears a crown.

WONDERS OF CHANCES AND CHANGES.

K. Hen. O heaven! that one might read the book of
    fate,

And see the revolution of the times
Make mountains level, and the continent
(Weary of solid firmness) melt itself
Into the sea! and, other times, to see
The beachy girdle of the ocean
Too wide for Neptune's hips; how chances mock,
And changes fill the cup of alteration
With divers liquors!

ACT IV.—Scene IV.

Corrupting power of gold.

See, sons, what things you are!
How quickly nature falls into revolt,
When gold becomes her object!
For this, the foolish over-careful fathers
Have broke their sleep with thoughts, their brains
          with care,
Their bones with industry:
For this, they have engrossed and piled up
The canker'd heaps of strange-achieved gold;
For this, they have been thoughtful to invest
Their sons with arts, and martial exercises:
When, like the bee, culling from every flower
The virtuous sweets;
Our thighs pack'd with wax, our mouths with
          honey,
We bring it to the hive: and, like the bees,
Are murder'd for our pains.

KING HENRY V

O, for a muse of fire, that would ascend
The brightest heaven of invention!
A kingdom for a stage, princes to act,
And monarchs to behold the swelling scene.
Then should the warlike Harry, like Himself,
Assume the part of Mars; and, at his heels,
Leash'd in like hounds, should famine, sword, and
      fire,
Crouch for employment.

ACT I.—SCENE I.

COURAGE.

Ely. Awake remembrance of these valiant deeds,
And with your puissant arm renew their feats:
You are their heir, you sit upon their throne;
The blood and courage, that renowned them,
Runs in your veins; and my thrice-puissant liege
Is in the very May-morn of his youth,
Ripe for exploits and mighty enterprises.

   Exe. Your brother kings and monarchs of the
      earth
Do all expect that you should rouse yourself,
As did the former lions of your blood.

West. They know, your grace hath cause, and
      means, and might:
So hath your highness: **never** king of England
Had nobles richer, and **more** loyal subjects;
Whose hearts have left their bodies here in
      England,
And lie pavilion'd **in** the fields of France.

BEES' DIVISION OF LABOR.

Cant. True: therefore doth Heaven divide
The state of man in divers functions,
Setting endeavour in continual motion;
To which is fixed as an aim or butt,
Obedience: for so work the honey bees;
Creatures, that, by a rule in nature, teach
The act of order to a peopled kingdom.
They have a king, and officers of **sorts:**
Where some, like magistrates, correct at home;
Others, like merchants, venture trade abroad;
Others, like soldiers, armed in their stings,
Make boot upon the summer's velvet buds;
Which pillage they with merry march bring
      home
To the tent-royal of their emperor:
Who, busied in his majesty's surveys
The singing masons building roofs of gold;
The civil citizens kneading up the honey;
The poor mechanic porters crowding in
Their heavy burdens at his narrow gate;
The sad-ey'd justice, with his surly hum,
Delivering o'er to executors pale
The lazy yawning drone.

ACT. II.

MILITARY ENTHUSIASM.

Enter Chorus.

Chor. Now all the youth of England are on fire,
And silken dalliance in the wardrobe lies;
Now thrive the armourers, and honour's thought
Reigns solely in the breast of every man:
They sell the pasture now, to buy the horse;
Following the mirror of all Christian kings,
With winged heels, as English Mercuries.
For now sits expectation in the air;
And hides a sword, from hilts unto the point,
With crowns imperial, crowns, and coronets,
Promised to Harry, and his followers.

SCENE II.

MERCY.

K. Hen. We judge no less.—Uncle of Exeter,
Enlarge the man committed yesterday,
That rail'd against our person: we consider,
It was excess of wine that set him on;
And, on his more advice, we pardon him.

Scroop. That's mercy, but too much security.
Let him be punished, sovereign: lest example
Breed, by his sufferance, more of such a kind.

K. Hen. O, let us yet be merciful.

SCENE IV.

FEAR AND CAUTION.

Fr. King. Think we King Harry strong;
And princess, look, you strongly arm to meet him
The kindred of him hath been flesh'd upon us;

And he is bred out of that bloody strain,
That haunted us in our familiar paths:
Witness our too much memorable shame,
When Cressy battle fatally was struck,
And all our princes captivated, by the hand
Of that black name, Edward, black prince of
      Wales;
Whiles that his mountain sire,—on mountain
      standing.
Up in the air, crown'd with the golden sun,—
Saw his heroical seed, and smiled to see him
Mangle the work of nature, and deface
The patterns, that by God and by French fathers,
Had twenty years been made.

King Henry's rage and mercy.

Exe. Bloody constraint; for if you hide the crown
Even in your hearts, there will he rake for it:
And therefore in fierce tempests is he coming,
In thunder and in earthquake, like a Jove;
(That, if requiring fail, he will compel,)
And bids you, in the bowels of the Lord,
Deliver up the crown; and to take mercy
On the poor souls, for whom this hungry war
Opens his vasty jaws.

ACT III.—Scene I.

King Henry's speech to his soldiers on the eve of battle.

K. Hen. Once more unto the breach, dear friends,
      once more;
Or close the wall up with our English dead!
In peace, there's nothing so becomes a man,
As modest stillness and humility;

But when the blast of war blows in our ears,
Then imitate the action of the tiger;
Stiffen the sinews, summon up the blood,
Disguise fair nature with hard-favour'd rage,
Then lend the eye a terrible aspect;
Let it pry through the portage of the head,
Like the brass cannon; let the brow o'erwhelm it,
As fearfully as doth a galled rock
O'erhang and jutty his coufounded base
Swill'd with the wild and wasteful ocean.
Now set the teeth, and stretch the nostril wide;
Hold hard the breath, and bend up every spirit
To his full height!--On, on you noblest English,
Whose blood is fet from fathers of war-proof!
Fathers, that, like so many Alexanders,
Have, in these parts, from morn till even fought,
And sheathed their swords for lack of argument:
Be copy now to men of grosser blood,
And teach them how to war!--and you good yeo-
      men,
Whose limbs were made in England, shew us here
The mettle of your pasture; let us swear
That you are worth your breeding, which I doubt
      not;
For there is none of you so mean and base,
That hath not noble lustre in your eyes.
I see you stand like greyhounds in the slips,
Straining upon the start.   The game's afoot;
Follow your spirit: and, upon this charge,
Cry—God for Harry!   England! aud Saint
      George!

Scene VI.

Fortune's changes.

Flu. By your patience, ancient Pistol. Fortue is painted plind, with a muffler before her eyes, to signify to you, that fortune is plind: And she is painted also with a wheel; to signify to you, which is the moral of it, that she is turning, and inconstant, and variations, and mutabilities: and her foot, look you, is fixed upon a spherical stone, which rolls, and rolls, and rolls—In good truth, the poet is make a most excellent description of fortune: fortune, look you, is an excellent moral.

ACT IV.

Kingly character.

Enter Chorus.

K. Hen. No; nor it is not meet he should. For though I speak to you, I think, the king is but a man, as I am: the violet smells to him, as it doth to me; the element shews to him, as it doth to me; all his senses have but human conditions: his ceremonies laid by, in his nakedness he appears but a man; and though his affections are higher mounted than ours, yet, when they stoop, they stoop with the like wing; therefore when he sees reason of fears, as we do, his fears, out of doubt, be of the same relish as ours are.

Vanity and sleeplessness of royalty.

What drink'st thou oft, instead of homage sweet,
But poison'd flattery ? O, be sick, great greatness,
And bid thy ceremony give thee cure!
Think'st thou, the fiery fever will go out
With titles blown from adulation ?
Will it give place to flexure and low bending ?
Canst thou, when thou command'st the beggar's knee,

Command the health of it?   No, thou proud dream,
That play'st so subtly with a king's repose;
I am a king that find thee; and I know
'Tis not the balm, the sceptre, and the ball,
The sword, the mace, the crown imperial,
The inter-tissued robe of gold and pearl,
The farced title running 'fore the king,
The throne he sits on, nor the title of pomp
That beats upon the high shore of this world,—
No, not all these, thrice-gorgeous ceremony,
Not all these, laid in bed majestical,
Can sleep so soundly as the wretched slave,
Who, with a body fill'd, and vacant mind,
Gets him to rest, cramm'd with distressful bread;
Never sees horrid night, the child of hell:
But, like a lackey, from the rise to set,
Sweats in the eye of Phœbus, and all night
Sleeps in Elysium; next day, after dawn,
Doth rise, and help Hyperion to his horse;
And follows so the ever-running year,
With profitable labour, to his grave:
And, but for ceremony, such a wretch,
Winding up days with toil, and nights with sleep,
Had the fore-hand and vantage of a king.
The slave, a member of the country's peace,
Enjoys it; but in gross brain little wots
What watch the king keeps to maintain the peace,
Whose hours the peasant best advantages.

Scene III.

KINGLY DEFIANCE.

K. Hen. I pray thee, bear my former answer
  back;

Bid them achieve me, and then sell my bones.
Good God! why should they mock poor fellows
     thus ?
The man, that once did sell the lion's skin
While the beast lived, was killed with hunting
    him.

ACT V.—Scene II.

Good and bad lovers.

K. Hen. Marry, if you would put me to verses, or to dance for your sake, **Kate, why you** undid **me:** for the one, I have neither words nor **measure; and** for the other, **I have no** strength in measure, yet a reasonable measure in **strength.** If I could win a lady at leap-frog, or by vaulting into my saddle with my armour on my back, under the correction of bragging be it spoken, I should quickly leap into **a wife.** Or, if I might buffet for my love, or bound my horse for her favours, I could lay on like a butcher, and sit like a jacka-napes, never off; but, before God, I cannot look greenly, nor gasp out my **eloquence;** nor I have no cunning in pro-testation; only downright **oaths, which I never** use till urged, **nor** never break **for urging. If thou canst** love a fellow of this temper, **Kate, whose face is** not worth sun-burning, **that never** looks in his glass for love of anything he sees there, let thine eyes be thy cook I speak to thee, **plain** soldier: **If thou canst love me for this, take me;** if not, **to say to thee**—that I shall die, is true; but - for thy love, **by the lord, no:** yet I love thee, too. And while thou **livest, dear Kate, take a fellow of** plain and uncoined con-stancy: for he, perforce, **must** do the right, because he hath **not** the **gift** to **woo in** other places; for these fellows of **infinite tongue, that can** rhyme **themselves** into ladies' favours,—they do always reason themselves out again. What! a speaker is but a prater; a rhyme is but a ballad. A good leg will fall; a straight back will stoop; a black beard will turn white; a curled pate will grow bald; a fair face will wither; a full eye will wax hollow; but a good heart, Kate, is the sun and moon; rather, the sun, and not the moon; for it shines bright, and never changes, but keeps his course truly. If thou would have such a one, take me, take me; and take me, take a soldier; take a soldier, take a king: And what sayest thou then to my love? speak, my fair, and fairly, I pray thee.

K. Hen. O Kate, nice customs court'sy to great kings Dear Kate, you and I cannot be confined within the weak list of a country's fashion; we are the makers of manners, Kate; and the liberty that follows our places, stops the mouths of all find-faults; as I will do yours, for upholding the nice fashion of your country, in denying me a kiss; therefore, patiently and yielding. (*Kissing her.*) You have witchcraft in your lips, Kate: there is more eloquence in a sugar touch of them, than in the tongues of the French council; and they should sooner persuade Harry of England, than a general petition of monarchs. Here comes your father.

RICHARD II.

ACT I.—Scene I.

VALUE OF REPUTATION AND HONOUR.

The purest treasure mortal times afford,
Is—spotless reputation; that away,
Men are but gilded loam, or painted clay.
A jewel in a ten-times-barr'd-up chest
Is—a bold spirit in a loyal breast.
Mine honour is my life; both grow in one;
Take honour from me, and my life is done;
Then, dear my liege, mine honour let me try;
In that I live, and for that will I die.

JOY OF RECONCILIATION.

Never did captive with a freer heart
Cast off his chains of bondage, and embrace
His golden uncontroll'd enfranchisement,
More than my dancing soul doth celebrate
This feast of battle with mine adversary.—

ACT II.—Scene I.

ENGLAND'S GLORIES.

Gaunt. Methinks, I am a prophet new inspired;
And thus, expiring, do fortell of him:
His rash fierce blaze of riot cannot last;

For violent fires soon burn out themselves:
Small showers last long, but sudden storms are
      short;
He tires betimes, that spurs too fast betimes;
With eager feeding, food doth choke the feeder:
Light vanity, insatiate cormorant,
Consuming means, soon preys upon itself.
This royal throne of kings, this scepter'd isle,
This earth of majesty, this seat of Mars,
This other Eden, demi-paradise;
This fortress, built by nature for herself
Against infection, and the hand of war;
This happy breed of men, this little world;
This precious stone set in the silver sea,
Which serves it in the office of a wall,
Or as a mote defensive to a house,
Against the envy of less happier lands;
This blessed plot, this earth, this realm, this Eng-
      land,
This nurse, this teeming womb of royal kings,
Fear'd by their breed, and famous by their
      birth,
Renowned for their deeds as far from home,
(For Christian service, and true chivalry,)
As is the sepulchre in stubborn Jewry,
Of the world's ransom, blessed Mary's son:
This land of such dear souls, this dear dear
      land,
Dear for her reputation through the world,
Is now leased out, (I die pronouncing it,)
Like to a tenement, or pelting farm:
England, bound with the triumphant sea,
Whose rocky shore beats back the envious siege

Of watery Neptune, is now bound in with
      shame,
With inky blots, and rotten parchment bonds;
That England, that was wont to conquer others,
Hath made a shameful conquest of itself.

Scene II.

Grief's' illusions.

Bushy. Each substance of a grief hath twenty
      shadows,
Which shew like grief itself, but is not so:
For sorrow's eye, glazed with blinding tears,
Divines one thing entire to many objects;
Like perspectives, which, rightly gazed upon,
Show nothing but confusion.

Scene IV.

Omens of King Richard's death.

Cap. 'Tis thought the king is dead: we will not
      stay.
The bay-trees in our country are all wither'd,
And meteors fright the fix'd stars of heaven;
The pale-faced moon looks bloody on the earth.
And lean-look'd prophets whisper fearful change.
Rich men look sad, and ruffians dance and
      leap,—
The one, in fear to lose what they enjoy,
The other, to enjoy by rage and war:
These signs forerun the death or fall of kings.—
Farewell; our countrymen are gone and fled,
As well assured, Richard their king is dead.   [*Exit.*

    Sal. Ah, Richard! with the eyes of heavy mind,
  20

I see thy glory, like a shooting star,
Falls to the base earth from the firmament!
Thy sun sets weeping in the lowly west,
Witnessing storms to come, woe, and unrest:
Thy friends are fled, to wait upon thy foes;
And crossly to thy good all fortune goes.

ACT III.—Scene I.

CRIMES CANNOT ENDURE THE SUNLIGHT.

K. Rich. Discomfortable cousin! know'st thou
not,
That when the searching eye of Heaven is hid
Behind the globe that lights the lower world,
Then thieves and robbers range abroad unseen,
In murders, and in outrage, bloody here;
But when, from under this terrestrial ball,
He fires the proud tops of the eastern pines,
And darts his light through every guilty hole,
Then murders, treasons, and detested sins,
The cloak of night being pluck'd from off their
backs,
Stand bare and naked, trembling at themselves?
So when this thief, this traitor, Bolingbroke,—
Who all this while hath revell'd in the night,
Whilst we were wand'ring with the antipodes,—
Shall see us rising in our throne the east,
His treasons will sit blushing in his face,
Not able to endure the sight of day,
But, self-affrighted, tremble at his sin.
Not all the water in the rough rude sea
Can wash the balm from an anointed king:
The breath of wordly men cannot depose
The deputy elected by the Lord:

For every man, that Bolingbroke hath press'd
To lift shrewd steel against our golden crown,
God for his Richard hath in heavenly pay
A glorious angel: then. if angels fight,
Weak men must fall; for Heaven still guards the
    right.

Scene III.

King Richard's glory.

York. See, see, King Richard doth himself
    appear,
As doth the blushing discontented sun
From out the fiery portal of the east;
When he perceives the envious clouds are bent
To dim his glory, and to stain the track
Of his bright passage to the occident.
Yet looks he like a king; behold his eye,
As bright as is the eagle's, lightens forth
Controlling majesty.

King Richard's threats of vengeance.

For well we know, no hand of blood and bone
Can gripe the sacred handle of our sceptre,
Unless he do profane, steal, or usurp.
And though you think, that all, as you have done,
Have torn their souls, by turning them from us,
And we are barren, and bereft of friends;—
Yet know,—my master, God omnipotent,
Is mustering in his clouds, on our behalf,
Armies of pestilence; and they shall strike
Your children yet unborn,
That lift your vassal hands against my head,
And threat the glory of my precious crown.
Tell Bolingbroke, (for yond', methinks, he stands,)

That every stride he makes upon my land,
Is dangerous treason: He is come to ope
The purple testament of bleeding war;
But ere the crown he looks for live in peace,
Ten thousand bloody crowns of mother's sons
Shall ill become the flower of England's face;
Change the complexion of her maid-pale peace
To scarlet indignation, and bedew
Her pastures' grass with faithful English blood.

King Richard's abasement.

K. Rich. What must the king do now? Must he
    submit?
The king shall do it. Must he be deposed?
The king shall be contented. Must he lose
The name of king? o' God's name let it go:
I'll give my jewels, for a set of beads;
My gorgeous palace, for a hermitage;
My gay apparel, for an alms-man's gown;
My figured goblets, for a dish of wood;
My sceptre, for a palmer's walking staff;
My subjects, for a pair of carved saints;
And my large kingdom for a little grave,
A little little grave, an obscure grave:—
Or I'll be buried in the king's highway,
Some way of common trade, where subjects' feet
May hourly trample on their sovereign's head:
For on my heart they tread, now whilst I live;
And buried once, why not upon my head?—

ACT IV.—Scene I.
King Richard resigns his crown.

K. Rich. Your cares, set up, do not pluck my
    cares down.

My care is– loss of care, my old care done;
Your care is—gain of care, my new care won;
The cares I give, I have, though given away;
They tend the crown, yet still with me they stay.

   Boling. Are you contented to resign the crown ?

   K. Rich. Ay, no;—no, ay: for I must nothing
     be;
Therefore no no, for I resign to thee.
Now mark me how I will undo myself:—
I give this heavy weight from off my head,
And this unwieldy sceptre from my hand,
The pride of kingly sway from out my heart;
With mine own tears I wash away my balm,
With mine own hand I give away my crown,
With mine own tongue deny my sacred state,
With mine own breath release all duteous oaths :
All pomp and majesty I do forswear:
My manors, rents, and revenues, I forego;
My acts, decrees, and statutes, I deny;
God pardon all oaths, that are broke to me!
God keep all vows unbroke, are made to thee!

Rebuke of King Richard's weakness.

   Queen. What, is my Richard both in shape and in mind
Transform'd and weaken'd ? Hath Bolingbroke
Deposed thine intellect ? hath he been in thy heart ?
The lion, dying, thrusteth forth his paw,
And wounds the earth, if nothing else, with rage
To be o'erpower'd; and wilt thou, pupil-like,
Take thy correction mildly, kiss the rod,
And fawn on rage with base humility,
Which art a lion, and a king of beasts ?

KING RICHARD III.

ACT I.

Scene I.—*London. A Street.*

Enter Gloster.

Richard on peace.

Glo. Now is the winter of our discontent
Made glorious summer by this sun of York;
And all the clouds, that lower'd upon our house,
In the deep bosom of the ocean buried.
Now are our brows bound with victorious
        wreaths;
Our bruised arms hung up for monuments;
Our stern alarums changed to merry meetings,
Our dreadful marches to delightful measures.
Grim-visaged war hath smoothed his wrinkled
        front;
And now,—instead of mounting barbed steeds,
To fright the souls of fearful adversaries,—
He capers nimbly in a lady's chamber,
To the lascivious pleasing of a lute.
But I,—that am not shaped for sportive tricks,
Nor made to court an amorous looking-glass;
I, that am rudely stamped, and want love's ma-
        jesty,
To strut before a wanton ambling nymph;

I, that am curtail'd of this fair proportion,
Cheated of feature by dissembling nature,
Deform'd, unfinished, sent before my time
Into this breathing world, scarce half made up,
And that so lamely and unfashionable,
That dogs bark at me, as I halt by them;—
Why I, in this weak piping time of peace,
Have no delight to pass away the time;
Unless to spy my shadow in the sun,
And descant on mine own deformity:

SYMPATHY FOR TALENT.

Hast. More pity, that the eagle should be mew'd,
While kites and buzzards prey at liberty.

SCENE II.

POWER OF BEAUTY.

Glo. Your beauty was the cause of that effect;
Your beauty, which did haunt me in my sleep,
To undertake the death of all the world,
So I might live one hour in your sweet bosom.
   Anne. If I thought that, I tell thee, homicide,
These nails should rend that beauty from my cheeks.
   Glo These eyes could not endure that beauty's
      wreck,
You should not blemish it, if I stood by;
As all the world is cheer'd by the sun,
So I by that; it is my day, my life.

SCENE I.

PRESUMPTION.

Glo. I cannot tell:—the world is grown so bad,
That wrens make prey where eagles dare not perch:

Since every Jack became a gentleman,
There's many a gentle person made a Jack.

CONSCIENCE.

1 Murd. How dost thou feel thyself now?

2 Murd. Faith, some certain dregs of conscience are yet within me.

1 Murd. Remember our reward when the deed 's done.

2 Murd. Zounds, he dies: I had forgot the reward.

1 Murd. Where's thy conscience now?

2 Murd. In the duke of Gloster's purse.

1 Murd. So, when he opens his purse to give us our reward, thy conscience flies out.

2 Murd. 'Tis no matter; let it go; there's few or none will entertain it.

1 Murd. What, if it come to thee again?

2 Murd. I'll not meddle with it, it's a dangerous thing, it makes a man a coward; a man cannot steal, but it accuseth him; a man cannot swear, but it checks him.　　*　　*　　*
'Tis a blushing, shame-faced spirit, that mutinies in a man's bosom; it fills one full of obstacles; it made me once restore a purse of gold, that by chance I found; it beggars any man that keeps it: it is turned out of all towns and cities for a dangerous thing; and every man that means to live well, endeavours to trust to himself, and live without it.

ACT III.

SCENE I.—*The same.*　*A street.*

JULIUS CÆSAR'S CHARACTER.

Prince. That Julius Cæsar was a famous man;
With what his valour did enrich his wit,
His wit set down to make his valour live:

Death makes no conquest of this conqueror;
For now he lives in fame, though not in life.

ANGUISH.

Anne. And I with all unwillingness will go.
O, would to God, that the inclusive verge
Of golden metal, that must round my brow,
Were red-hot steel, to sear me to the brain!
Anointed let me be with deadly venom;
And die, ere man can say—God save the queen!
Q. Eliz. Go, go, poor soul, I envy not thy glory
To feed my humour, wish thyself no harm.

ACT IV.—SCENE II.

GOLD, ITS POWER.

K. Rich. Know'st thou not any, whom corrupting
gold
Would tempt unto a close exploit of death ?
Page. I know a discontented gentleman,
Whose humble means match not his haughty
mind:
Gold were as good as twenty orators,
And will, no doubt, tempt him to any thing.

SCENE III.

NECESSITY FOR PROMPT ACTION URGED.

K. Rich. Ely with Richmond troubles me more
near,
Than Buckingham and his rash-levied strength.
Come,—I have learn'd, that fearful commenting
Is leaden servitor to dull delay;
Delay leads impotent and snail-paced beggary:

Then fiery expedition be my wing,
Jove's Mercury, and herald for a king!
Go, muster men: My counsel is my shield;
We must be brief, when traitors brave the field.   [*Exeunt.*

ACT V.—SCENE III.

COURAGE.

K. Rich. A thousand hearts are great within my
          bosom:
Advance our standards, set upon our foes;
Our ancient world of courage, fair Saint George,
Inspire us with the spleen of fiery dragons!
Upon them! Victory sits on our helm.

SCENE IV.

A HORSE, A HORSE.

Alarum. Enter KING RICHARD.

K. Rich. A horse! a horse! my kingdom for a
          horse!
Cate. Withdraw, my lord, I'll help you to a horse.
K. Rich. Slave, I have set my life upon a cast,
And I will stand the hazard of the die:
I think, there be six Richmonds in the field;
Five have I slain to-day, instead of him:—
A horse! a horse! my kingdom for a horse!

KING HENRY VIII.

ACT II.—Scene II.

The queen's love for her husband.

And, out of all these to restore the king,
He counsels a divorce: a loss of her,
That, like a jewel, has hung twenty years
About his neck, yet never lost her lustre:
Of her, that loves him with that excellence,
That angels love good men with.

Scene III.

Advantages of low birth.

Anne. So much the more
Must pity drop upon her.   Verily,
I swear, 'tis better to be lowly born,
And range with humble livers in content,
Than to be perk'd up in a glistering grief,
And wear a golden sorrow.

Beauty and honor.

Beauty and honour in her are so mingled,
That they have caught the king: and who knows
                yet,
But from this lady may proceed a gem,.
To lighten all this isle ?

Scene IV.

The queen's true nobility.

K. Hen. Go thy ways, Kate!
That man i' th' world, who shall report he has
A better wife let him in naught be trusted,
For speaking false in that: Thou art, alone,
(If thy rare qualities, sweet gentleness,
Thy meekness saint-like, wife-like government,—
Obeying in commanding,—and thy parts
Sovereign and pious else, could speak thee out,)
The queen of earthly queens:—She is noble born:
And, like her true nobility, she has
Carried herself towards me.

ACT III.—Scene I.

Q. Kath. Speak it here;
There's nothing I have done yet, o' my conscience,
Deserves a corner: 'Would, all other women
Could speak this with as free a soul as I do!
My lords, I care not, (so much I am happy
Above a number,) if my actions
Were tried by every tongue, every eye saw them,
Envy and base opinion set against them,
I know my life so even: If your business
Seek me out, and that way I am wife in,
Out with it boldly; Truth loves open dealing.

The Queen's lament.

Q. Kath. 'Would I had never trod this English
   earth,
Or felt the flatteries that grow upon it!

Ye have angels' faces, but Heaven knows your
      hearts.
What will become of me now, wretched lady?
I am the most unhappy woman living.—
Alas! poor wenches, where are now your for-
      tunes?   (*To her woman.*)
Shipwreck'd upon a kingdom, where no pity,
No friends, no hope; no kindred weep for me,
Almost, no grave allow'd me: Like the Lily,
That once was mistress of the field, and flourish'd,
I'll hang my head and perish.

Scene II.

An angry husband's look.

Wol. What should this mean?
What sudden anger's this? how have I reap'd it?
He parted frowning from me, as if ruin
Leap'd from his eyes: So looks the chafed lion
Upon the daring huntsman, that has gall'd him;
Then makes him nothing.

Pity.

Cham. O my lord,
Press not a falling man too far; 'tis virtue:
His faults lie open to the laws; let them,
Not you correct him.   My heart weeps to see him
So little of his great self.

Caution against ambition.—Patriotism encouraged.

Wol. Cromwell, I did not think to shed a tear
In all my miseries; but thou hast forced me,
Out of thy honest truth, to play the woman.
Let's dry our eyes: and thus far hear me, Crom-
      well;

And,—when I am forgotten, as I shall be;
And sleep in dull cold marble, where no mention
Of me more must be heard of,—say, I taught thee,
Say, Wolsey,—that once trod the ways of glory,
And sounded all the depths and shoals of
       honour,—
Found thee a way, out of this wreck, to rise in;
A sure and safe one, though thy master miss'd it.
Mark but my fall, and that, that ruin'd me.
Cromwell, I charge thee, fling away ambition:
By that sin fell the angels, how can men then,
The image of his Maker, hope to win by't?
Love thyself last: cherish those hearts that hate
       thee;
Corruption wins not more than honesty.
Still in thy right hand carry gentle peace,
To silence envious tongues.   Be just, and fear not:
Let all the ends thou aim'st at, be thy country's,
Thy God's, and truth's.

ACT IV.—Scene II.

Hypocricy.

Kath   So may he rest; his faults lie gently on
      him!
Yet thus far, Griffith, give me leave to speak
      him,
And yet with charity,—He was a man
Of an unbounded stomach, ever ranking
Himself with princes; one, that by suggestion,
Tied all the kingdom: simony was fair play;
His own opinion was his law: I' the presence

He would say untruths; and be ever double,
Both in his words and meaning: He was never,
But where he meant to ruin, pitiful;
His promises were, as he was then, mighty;
But his performance, as he is now, nothing.
Of his own body he was ill, and gave
The clergy ill example.
   Grif. Noble madam,
Men's evil manners live in brass; their virtues
We write in water.

ACT V.—Scene IV.

Prophetic character of Queen Elizabeth.

  Cran. Let me speak, sir,
For heaven now bids me; and the words I utter
Let none think flattery, for they'll find them
     truth.
This royal infant, (Heaven still move about her!)
Though in her cradle, yet now promises
Upon this land a thousand thousand blessings,
Which time shall bring to ripeness: She shall be
(But few now living can behold that goodness)
A pattern to all princes living with her,
And all that shall succeed   Sheba was never
More covetous of wisdom and fair virtue,
Than this pure soul shall be: all princely graces,
That mould up such a mighty piece as this is,
With all the virtues that attend the good,
Shall still be doubled on her: truth shall nurse her,
Holy and heavenly thoughts still counsel her:
She shall be loved and fear'd: Her own shall bless
    her:

Her foes shake like a field of beaten corn,
And hang their heads with sorrow: Good grows
   with her;
In her days, every man shall eat in safety
Under his own vine, what he plants; and sing
The merry songs of peace to all his neighbors:
God shall be truly known; and those about her
From her shall read the perfect ways of honour.
And by those claims their greatness, not by blood.
Nor shall this peace sleep with her: But as when
The bird of wonder dies, the maiden phœnix,
Her ashes new create another heir,
As great in admiration as herself:
So shall she leave her blessedness to one,
(When heaven shall call her from this cloud of
   darkness,)
Who, from the sacred ashes of her honour,
Shall star-like rise, as great in fame as she was,
And so stand fix'd: Peace, plenty, love, truth,
   terror,
That were the servants to this chosen infant,
Shall then be his, and like a vine grow to him;
Wherever the bright sun of heaven shall shine,
His honour, and the greatness of his name
Shall be, and make new nations: He shall flourish,
And, like a mountain cedar, reach his branches
To all the plains about him.—Our children's chil-
   dren
Shall see this, and bless Heaven.

CONTENTS.

21

INDEX.